THE CROSSOVER

Seamus O Hoistin

Inquiries and Book Orders should be addressed to:

Great Writers Media
Email: info@greatwritersmedia.com
Phone: (302) 918-5570

ISBN: 978-1-956517-01-9 (sc)
ISBN: 978-1-956517-02-6 (ebk)

Rev 05/03/2021

CHAPTER 1

STANDING OVER THE GRAVE as the hurried "Holy Mary Mother of God" rosary was being piously muttered, he didn't feel grief, he didn't want to cry, he just felt numb, a kind of surreal feeling had enveloped him. The rest of the mourners just looked a bit pathetic from his viewpoint "blah blah blah" was what their prayers sounded like to him, maybe he thought he should take out a hanky and pretend to cry but then he thought Dualta would just piss himself and say "You pure bollix".

But then again Dualta wouldn't be saying anything, anytime soon as what remained of his lifeless body was currently being lowered into a 6 foot hole in the ground.

How could this be? His best friend of more than 25 years was going to some "eternal rest" according to a very young looking priest and would be earning his reward in heaven with Jesus and the angels. The only problem there "Father", he thought, was that Dualta didn't believe in Jesus and certainly didn't give a fuck about angels (unless it was the club in Leeson Street where they went to Paddy P's stag night). The thing was, it couldn't be real cause he'd known Dualta all his life and now just like that he was gone and Dominic was still there, standing shivering his balls off in a graveyard. A graveyard where they had both buried their grannies and played hide and seek among the headstones, till they'd got a slap from some aunty or other cause they should "show some respect".

But that was when they were 9 or 10 and now they were grownups, well at least Dom was, it was pretty obvious from the sound of the clay earth landing on the coffin that Dualta wasn't going to see his next birthday. Without even realising it he was now in a line of family members somberly shaking hands with everyone who had in fairness taken time out of their busy days to attend the funeral. "Sorry for your troubles", "Sorry for your troubles".

He made a mental note that he should probably invent something else for people to say at a funeral. Something along the lines that Dualta would have said like "Ah jeez, he was a pure bollix". He was smiling inwardly at that one when he realised aul Mrs McNabb was shaking his hand and grabbing it like a five pound note,

"Sorry for your troubles", Aye "yours too" he replied.

He said this to the old witch without really contemplating that she probably did have many many troubles that they had cared little about in their youthful arrogance. He had to stop himself giggling when he thought about himself and Dualta robbing her orchard and her coming out to give off to them when her whole front row of teeth fell out and landed on the ground. That was a good time, Dualta would still be laughing at that, except Dualta couldn't laugh anymore cause Dualta was now officially DEAD or else he'd be pretty pissed off about his burial. Dominic appreciated the finality in that world but it still didn't make any sense. How can someone you've spent your whole life with suddenly be gone? If only he'd left him alone, if only he hadn't got Dualta involved in his situation.

"Fuck sake" said Dominic, "I am the pure bollix here".

As they served the soup and sandwiches at the local Football Club he sat with some of their friends and he remembered the first time he'd met Dualta.

CHAPTER 2

BOOM BOOM, SHAKE THE ROOM

MOVING TO A NEW place wasn't really an issue for Dominic as he was only 4 and couldn't really have had any bonds to his current abode which as far as he knew was somewhere in Belfast. So the move to a new town was quite smooth without any traumas or issues.

The new town was small compared to the endless streets upon streets he'd known in Belfast. Down here on the "border "Dom couldn't believe how much greener it was and how you could see mountains from your own window. The town had a huge square right outside their flat and there was space everywhere and even the young Dom noticed that a lot of the houses in the new estates had gardens which you'd never see in Belfast.

And so he was enlisted into the local Primary School without any pomp or ceremony and he liked his new environment as it somehow seemed brighter and sunnier and warmer than the cold faceless place he had come from. The only thing that surprised him was the huge army look out post that dominated the Square but when he asked his Dad about it, it only seemed to make him angry so he soon stopped asking and the "security presence" became just another part of his new existence. The people of the town were really friendly and the family soon felt at home.

One beautiful sunny day he was out playing with his sisters and at least ten of their new and entertaining friends when a girl called Debbie suddenly announced

"I've a wee brother over in our house sitting on his own! I'll bring you over to meet him".

Now the last thing Dominic wanted to do was leave this perfectly good afternoon's craic to go and meet some random lad who couldn't even be bothered to come outside, but he went anyway because he felt obliged to do it. So two reluctant 4 year olds were thrust together and immediately hit it off big time, NOT! The conversation went something like:

"Alright?"

"Yeah"

"You alright?" "Yeah".

Despite the limited conversations, in the proceeding weeks Dualta stood religiously every morning and waited for Dom at the corner of the estate so they could walk into school together. Two big boys heading to Primary One, with the conversation continuing in the same vein,

"Alright?"

"Yeah"

"You alright?" "Yeah".

Weeks turned into months, and then out of the blue one day their highly stimulating usual conversation was interrupted by the sight of a huge dead horse lying on the school lawn. The boys joined the thronging mass around the horse which had obviously now been half eaten by some unknown rodents. The excitement was palpable as the Master ushered them away from the unexpected treasure into the assembly hall amid screams and whoops of both joy and fear in equal measures. Now this new turn of events was going to require a different type of conversation,

"Mmmmm…Alright?"Ah ah ah, yeah"

"Are you alright?", "Mmmmmm….Yeah

Boom, they'd nailed it! Proper heart felt conversation achieved at last and a lasting friendship now well and truly established.

Walking to school was now a ritual, as much a way of life as breakfast dinner and tea (nobody ever had lunch in those days). It wasn't so much as the boys bonded when left to their own devices it was more a series of events imposed on their friendship and pushed them closer and closer together.

The taller, more slender and blonde maned Dualta would wait patiently in all weathers every morning for his darker haired and stockier, swarthier skinned, best friend. By teatime those contrasting faces were usually covered in muck and dirt as the lads explored the fields, rivers and ditches that surrounded their home town. This was their world and it had endless possibilities which was more than fine by them.

One morning as the boys made their way to their P5 class with the conversation now having graduated to a lot more than just six syllables a day Dualta proudly announced the addition of a huge "Tri Colour" now flying above an electric pole outside the Primary School that he had just spotted. The boys and their other school friends watched on in awe as a group of British Soldiers with great pomp and ceremony scaled the pole and in some sort of display of triumph, proceeded to unceremoniously rip it down. This same ritual happened every day for over a week and if the boys were honest they'd long since stop caring, until one day when on their traditional route to St. Michael's PS they heard the loudest noise they'd ever experienced in their young lives, a massive bang reverberated across the area. The adult Dominic would tell you in no uncertain terms that what the young lads had actually heard for the first time on that fateful day was a massive bomb blast. As the British Soldiers shoveled the mutilated body of their colleague off the road, still clutching the Tri Colour, no one there could have realized that the lives of all of those innocent young children who had witnessed this would ever be the same again.

CHAPTER 3

I LIKE DRIVING "
IN MY..... TAXI

"THE TROUBLES" WAS A much understated word which described the extraordinary situation that the two best friends existed in as they reached the end of their Primary Schooling.

"Sorry for your troubles"

"Sorry for your troubles"

"Sorry for your troubles"

These were the words bouncing around Dominic's brain as he buried his best friend but in years gone by the "TROUBLES" was a very simplistic way to describe why their lives were so <u>not</u> normal and so (looking back on it) unreal and extraordinary.

When he was younger Dominic thought it was fantastic at first that from his vantage point in their flat where they lived looking across the village square, his dad and himself could watch the gun battles ensuing between the Brits and the IRA while the rest of the family cowered behind the dining room concrete wall for protection. Mum would scream at them to take cover away from the window but the lure of the bullets firing backwards and forwards was just too captivating to make him worry too much about any actual risk. Also Dad was equally as interested so was often heard saying:

"Don't worry mum we'll be fine".

Dominic recalled how those "real-life western nights" were brought to an end when the Brits opened fire on the flat and poor Granny's "decade" of the Rosary was rudely interrupted by a tracer bullet flying inches above her head.

It was a good job she was totally deaf Dominic remembered or she probably would have had her head blown off during the "joyful mysteries" which again might have been be an irony lost on the young Dominic.

***

The "troubles" became the way of life for the lads...bombs, bullets, checkpoints, harassment from the Brits, these were all just the norm, they didn't know any different so it was just their way of life. "It was what it was".

***

What was more pressing now in their young lives was the dreaded "11 plus" exam. It wasn't quite so pressing for their teacher who was a local farmer with an unusually red face who literally left the class via the window to tend to his cows, pigs or whatever, whenever he had to. To be honest, the lads didn't really know what farmers did as they'd rarely left the confines of the estate to investigate and couldn't care less anyway.

***

On the day of the results the lads were delighted to be told they had "passed" and could now go to the "Grammar School".

It seemed like something to celebrate but what it actually meant was a 32 mile round trip on an Ulsterbus to the nearest "big" town every day for at least the next 5 years. But the excitement of a new blazer and tie outweighed any doubts about the arduous trek to fulfil the local ambitions of so many educationally snobbish parents who agreed with the blatantly ridiculous 2 tiered education system that was employed in Northern Ireland (and nowhere else) that judged people (kids) at the age of 11 on one single criteria.

Anyway Dominic and Dualta were certainly not going to contemplate any of these issues as they ate an unusually large amount of ice cream and chocolate. And then the cherry on the cake was presented with a huge black taxi left abandoned in the middle of the estate. Like a pack of painted wolves the local kids surrounded the black machine, circled it and then as the first brick broke the front screen they all pounced and attacked with a ferocity hereto unseen. Windows, lights, the bonnet and the roof were all like a feast for the pack and the brick throwing, glass breaking and kicking action continued for a couple of days but the memory of the fun they had was to last a long time.

Dominic and Dualta lay in the back seat of the destroyed black taxi and knew they were now men of the world and in the vernacular of the area everything was "munya" (meaning perfect), well until Dualta's mum came out of their house and dragged them both into the house by the scruffs of their necks. The lads were wetting themselves right up until the kitchen drawer was opened and the dreaded "wooden spoon" came out.

C B S
"Christianity"?

CBS or "Christian Brothers School".

"Well that title has got to put anyone's worries at ease" Dominic naively thought.

They had done Religious instruction in Primary School and even though Canon Crilly had beaten them with a strap when they didn't recite their prayers perfectly, Dominic still had faith that the "Christian Brothers" would be a shining beacon of goodness. Well at the very least the Brothers were bound to be an improvement on their very peculiar Primary School Head Master, Mr Haley, who was a very violent man, more adept at showing a strap rather than compassion. But anyway Mr Haley and primary school would all be behind them soon as Dom and Dualta would be at the big school being looked after by the "Christian Brothers". The leading lights in Irish Education, sure what could go wrong?

Dominic had great plans for the future, great deeds to be done in the big town. Dualta (as usual) held his own counsel.

Dom "You alright?"

Dualta "Yeah

"You alright?" Dom "Yeah"

CHAPTER 4

HEY TEACHER! LEAVE THOSE KIDS ALONE

THE "CBS FRIARY" STOOD at the top of a very steep hill in the built up and drab industrial town. It seemed huge to the eyes of Dom and Dualta as the bus chugged up at what seemed to be an almost impossible angle. This was an all-boys school with a current population of 1000 adolescent males.

Dom and Dualta looked nervously at each other as the classes were called out and then the worst thing possible happened, the new classes were to be decided alphabetically. So for the first time in 7 years the best friends were going to be separated. Inside they screamed objections, inside they wanted to fight this injustice BUT being brought up in a good IRISH family they would actually just suck it up and say absolutely nothing.

The word "Christian" came in for a severe cross examination that year as the young lads settled into a world of brutality and probably the worst extremes of "Christianity" the lads had ever seen or could possibly have predicted. The "strap" was ok, Mr Haley at Primary had prepared them for that with his religious zeal and Old Testament temper but some of their new experiences were on a whole new level.

As the bell for break time rang young Dualta ran towards the door of the first year block carrying school bag, PE bag and a huge book for good measure which he was apparently supposed to guard on "pain of death" (a lot of responsibility for a first year, he mused).

Anyway Dualta was relieved to see Brother Mo at the door with the keys already jangling, that was until Bro Mo closed the door slowly locked it and reminded the youthful Dualta that the building should be vacated at precisely 1 minute after the bell. Within 30 seconds Dualta had been introduced to a "Tech drawing set square", an interesting implement which resembled an extremely large math's tool and although he wasn't exactly sure of its use, he was almost 100% sure it wasn't designed originally to "beat the shit" out of a young first years legs. Anyway despite the blood pouring down his leg, his first thought was "My trousers are cut, my ma is going to fucking kill me".

On the bus ride home the lads discussed the various punishments and beatings that appeared to be now an integral part of their education. Some teachers were actually really nice, interesting and good craic, but the brothers did seem to be a different breed. Both Dom and Dualta laughed on the way home that they weren't sure why men who had supposedly devoted their lives to the education and betterment of young Catholic boys, seemed to hate them so much. The beatings or strappings became a daily ritual and to be honest the boys quickly adapted and developed their own set of unspoken rules for dealing with it and ensuring that after "6 of the best" they would stop and move on to some other unfortunate bastard.

- Always keep eye contact.
- Never pull away.
- DO NOT cry.

Life in the "Friary" was okay if you negotiated all the main rules of the "classroom" and of course "the yard". 1,000 boys taking a break together when 750 of them smoke was fraught with its own dangers. The sixth years were beyond this particular "pale" but from Years 1 to 5 it was open season on bullying, treachery, violence and general skullduggery.

As first year pupils the lads were careful enough to stand back and observe, watch, look, listen, learn, not unlike a prison yard. Survival of the fittest, like in a David Attenborough documentary.

***

On one particular break Dualta found himself in the middle of an altercation with one of his classmates. Dutifully the antagonists threw blows at each other with a fervour and enthusiasm that would have been roundly appreciated by all the older watchers in the "playground". No harm done, a couple of scrapes and perhaps a bloody nose but what happened next shocked and surprised the lads.

Brother Mo "Can you two report to me in the Gym at lunch" Boys in unison "Yes Brother"

When lunch did arrive the boys responded to their request and turned up on time at the gym. When Brother Mo (Maurice) sat down at a small desk and pulled out his tomato soup and cheese sandwiches and commanded the boys to resume their boxing match, it became clear to both pugilists that this was a new direction in their education and to be honest it was just "fucking weird".

"It's over Brother, we don't want to fight anymore"

"FIGHT" screamed the Brother

The boys fought to an honourable draw but the Brother was not satisfied and wanted a winner, someone to admit defeat or draw first blood.

"Holy fuck" thought Dualta, "We're only first years"

***

The daily grind became a ritual.

"Get your hands well roasted on the radiators so they're numb when you get the strap"

So then more fights would take place between the lads as to who could get the best position on the radiators to "numb" their wrists before the Brother's daily registration massacre would happen.

Brother Baxter, "Homework?" "No Brother", "left it on the bus"

Beating commenced with the other classmates recoiling in horror when the Brother actually beat him round the face and neck with his strap. Davey Mac was like a "H block prisoner", denying any wrong-doing..

Brother Baxter "Stop lying, you haven't done it have you? You're a liar?

Davy, "No Brother, not me Brother"

Davy's stoicism would have made him an ideal candidate for the "Long Kesh dirty protest" which was brewing at the time.

***

Life in the "Friary" continued relentlessly and the daily "slaps" and "thumps" were something that the boys quickly accepted as normal.

The lads were growing up and enjoying life as puberty hit but one thing that happened struck Dualta as being totally weird and really out of order.

During the customary PE swimming lesson, the boys in "BF1" (The class name) had brilliant craic in their first experience of a huge "swimming pool". The boy's only previous swimming experience had been in the unforgiving confines of the local "Lough Moss".

Anyway the lads in Dualta's class were enjoying the fact that Brother Baxter was allowing them to jump into the deep end, with what probably was at best only a rudimentary knowledge of water survival (let alone swimming skills). They were loving the craic, somersaults, dives, "dive bombs", were all the order of the day and what a relief to be out of school. Being an all-boys school they laughed at the poster that screamed "No Petting".

Everything was going super fine until Dualta and the boys came back to get changed and get ready to go back to school.

It was at this point Dualta was given the most peculiar instruction he had ever received in his young life (if only Dom had been with him, he would have told him what to do). But Dominic was in History or Geography with his own class and couldn't help him here.

Straight out of the blue Brother Baxter insisted the boys did not use their towels to dry themselves but instead ran around the communal changing room naked to dry. The boys nervously acquiesced to this request. While Brother Baxter sat in their midst in his huge black cassock he made the boys run round the changing rooms naked, jumping up and down as they ran round and round.

On the bus home Dualta never mentioned it to Dominic nor did he mention it to his mum or dad, who were always keen to hear news of his successes and achievements. This episode did not seem like either to Dominic. It was a very uncomfortable situation, he wanted so much to talk to Dominic about it but how could he? Boys didn't have feelings? Boys didn't talk about things like that.

When he did broach it. Dom did listen, Dom did know what he meant, because lads in his class had been through the same shit, maybe not as overt or as embarrassing but yeah, he knew what was going on. Micky, Tommy, Joe, Frank, the list was endless but the one thing the best friends knew without discussing it was that the "Christian Brothers" had a great knack of making lads feel very uncomfortable. A hand on the knee, a slap on the bum, a moment too long on the arm, yeah most of the Brothers could make you feel very uncomfortable indeed.

As the boys moved from second year into third year, they became harder, tougher, took the beatings in their stride and even some events became so crazy that they were actually funny. Like the time when Dom had lost his math's book and was about to be beaten by Brother Bob, until he let off the smelliest fart ever and Brother Bob couldn't even get near him.

Or the time when Micky Woods jumped onto a table and told Brother Baxter to "Fuck off".

Woodsy, "Fuck off. I'll get my Da for you"

Brother Baxter, "Bring him up! I hope he has a few brothers, oh and bring your Grandad and uncles too"

Woodsy, "Why?"

Brother Baxter, "Cause you are a total waste of space the whole lot of you, not one of your family ever did a day's work in your lives, so I doubt they'll be bothered to get out of bed for this."

Woodsy, "Fuck you!" And then he threw the duster at Brother Baxter. He made his way towards the door and as his hand rested securely on the door knob he fired a few more expletives towards the Brother. Little did he know the door was locked, "Oh shit" he thought.

Woodsy had no option as Brother Baxter descended on him (strap in hand) but to jump out the window. Luckily the window led to a balcony roof from which Woodsy could climb right to the top floor of the school and proceed to throw stones down at the unrepentant Brother Baxter.

Dom didn't witness it but he had it on reliable truth from the town lads that Woodsy did not come down from the roof until 9pm, when the Brothers, Police, Fire Brigade, School authorities, parents, grandparents and local assembled groups were all there. When he eventually did come down the first thing that happened was he got six of the best from the delighted and definitely resilient Brother Bob. It was totally ironic that Brother Bobs strap sported a "save the children" charity sticker on one end.

Then there was that other time that Dualta often recounted when during a history lesson Brother Baxter gave them a map drawing exercise for homework. The next day as Brother Baxter decided to correct the homework on the spot, Dualta watched in amazement as Brendy B presented the most fabulously coloured map of post war Europe he or any other Year 10 pupil had ever seen before, with each country coloured in different shades of pastel, it was amazing, until Brother Baxter started beating him round the neck with a leather strap for using felt tip pens which were not allowed, as apparently they tainted the next page (who knew?)

Anyway while watching the massacre of Brendy B, Dualta had a hushed conversation with his classmate immediately in front called Smelly Happy Paddy who was very aptly named!

Smelly Paddy "Holy fuck, I haven't even mine done"

Dualta "Fuck up, I'm trying to finish mine"

Smelly Paddy "Gimme your compass" Dualta "What, fuck off"

Smelly Paddy "Seriously give me your compass"

18

Reluctantly Dualta handed forward his compass and got back to some scattered scribbling and shading on his distinctly less than average map of post was Europe, when Smelly Happy Paddy shoved the aforementioned compass straight up his nose in order to make it bleed on purpose so that he could escape.

Smelly Happy Paddy "Excuse me Brother, may I be excused?"

Brother Baxter "Of course son, just leave your homework on my desk before you go".

Smelly Happy Paddy "Oh fuck".

CHAPTER 5

LIFE IN A NORTHERN TOWN

IF LIFE AT SCHOOL was a daily grind then like a good tonic, home and weekends came to the rescue. There was nothing better than taking in the Friday night air that signaled "freedom", "Embassy Regal" and maybe a sneaky wee vodka. Of course girls were the main objective on these weekends and the local disco provided an excellent opportunity for a "liaison dangereuse" with some neighbourhood beauty. The gang of lads would immerse themselves in the music, drink a few stiffeners, dance with each other and then carefully choreograph who would actually be snogging who outside at the end of the evening.

By now Dom and Dualta were delighted to be moved on from the church disco where the local parish priest would actually patrol the outside of the Hall and bring a very abrupt end to any kissing with his meter stick. For the boys it was a "paradise" the music was Ska and represented a whole new way of life. They were young and immortal enjoying concerts, discos, clothes and girls. Taking up residence in the local chippy or amusement arcade, dressed in their drainpipe trousers and Fred Perry tops, where the music was pumping, it felt that like life just couldn't be better. But life in this town could never be NORMAL, not when a fifth of the population of the village belonged to the occupying forces of the British Army.

At first the harassment was minimal and inconvenient. On the way to matches with the local club the lads would be stopped, searched and held up which was something they expected and accepted without much fuss. Indeed, the spectacle of a helicopter sweeping across their football pitch to land in the "stolen ground" the British now called home was a much bigger problem for the visiting teams than it was for the local lads. However, as the time progressed the stop became longer and the search became more aggressive and the lads became bitter and a little more aggrieved as to why this was happening to them in their hometown by strangers who obviously did not belong there.

A lot of local older lads were being imprisoned in Long Kesh and the lads knew this place had changed since they'd visited their own fathers their during internment where they seemed to spend most of their time off learning Irish, studying history and becoming very proficient in woodwork making an excellent array of "Celtic crosses" and "fiddles". But now Long Kesh was a sinister and foreboding place with rumours of "dirty protestors" and a potential hunger strike. This was some serious shit for the boys to digest or think about so they did the noblest thing possible and didn't think about it or talk about it at all.

Dom "You alright?"

Dualta "Yeah"

"You alright?"

Dom "Yeah"

However things in general were not ok and that summer would set into motion a series of events that were to change their lives forever.

If the boys were honest it all started off as a bit of fun and excitement like the day they were on their way to school and some of the older lads hi-jacked the huge Ulster bus and set it on fire much to the delight of the younger pupils who eagerly joined in the ensuing riot against the RUC.

Throwing petrol bombs was an acquired skill and unfortunately many of the young "would be" freedom fighters held the milk bottles the wrong way up and only succeeded in drenching themselves in petrol, and in a few isolated but hilarious incidents they also managed to set themselves on fire. It became a competition between the friends to see who could collect the most "plastic bullets" that had been fired during the riot. Oblivious to the danger, the boys embraced this new way of life and if truth be told they couldn't wait for the next incident. One of the next incidents was however not fun or exciting and scarred the boys for life.

***

During another one of the daily rituals of stop and search the lads were gathered against the wall of the local library with their faces to the wall and their hands on their heads (as per usual) when without warning the most almighty bomb blast shook the very earth and brought a momentary, incomprehensive, surreal silence as if time had stood still. Amid the rubble and ruin, the dust and the fog the boys couldn't hear anything as their ears had momentarily been made redundant due to the blast. The first thing Dominic heard was the painful cry (scream) of a Paratrooper Private who appeared to have been actually split in two by the explosion. How he was still alive was incomprehensible but as he was pleading for his mother a grizzled looking Sergeant who the boys "affectionately" referred to as "2 heads" knelt down beside the stricken soldier and cradled what was left of his head in his arms. (It wasn't actually until many years later that Dominic realised that "2 heads" had actually covered his mouth thereby ending both his suffering and also his life).

The incidents of war came thick and fast after that and daily loss of local life became a natural and normal occurrence except of course when it was a Brit because they weren't people, they were soldiers and got what they deserved.

The boys couldn't have described it but they know this was a different kind of war, like the one they'd learnt about in History in Vietnam where the mightiest military power in the world couldn't defeat the local Vietcong because they COULDN'T FIND THEM.

In this scenario the lads were quick to realise that if the Brits couldn't see the enemy ANYWHERE then they saw the enemy

EVERYWHERE and that now included THEM. Which means they were a TARGET.

On a bright and cheery May Day a tractor and silage trailer pulled into the square of their local village as the lads hung about on the corner smoking a few cigarettes and having a laugh. Nothing extraordinary in that scene until the farmer reversed his "silage" tank right smack in the middle of the village and proceeded to set alight to its cargo of oil. As it spat out its dragon like cargo all over the unwitting occupants of the army lookout post, who had no choice but to abandon their station and run back to the safety of their barracks.

On another Saturday morning during an episode of one of their favourites "The multi coloured swap shop" a single white van was being subjected to a normal checkpoint when the backdoor of the van was kicked open to reveal both a masked man and a machine gun pointed directly at (and soon to be shooting towards) the forces of occupation that walked the streets and subsequently brought each and every one of them to the ground.

The shockwaves that these attacks caused around the world were totally lost on the lads who just accepted it was another part of life. But even at that what they witnessed next was definitely peculiar by anyone's standards.

A local "character" or perhaps more accurately "drunk" by the name of "Jimmy Custard" took great pride in his republican heritage and often on his visits into collect his brew cheque would park his bike underneath the now burnt out "look out post" and invite the Brits out with a chorus of republican invites and songs. Being in his late 60's he didn't seem to pose much of a threat to the paratroopers in their post but they took great pleasure in coming out from their relative security to engage with Jimmy on the ground and almost inevitably take his bike for a wee spin as he threw futile punches in their direction.

This pattern would be repeated almost on a weekly basis where "Jimmy" would park his bike at the gates of a local pub and begin the ritual of the mock fight and the bike steal. The local community were bored of it but the soldiers seemed to find it funny and a release from their mundane rituals. That was until the day one unfortunate Private (possibly on his first tour of duty) was cajoled to take Jimmy's bike to wind him up. Again the soldiers found this hilarious until they realised someone had switched Jimmy's bike at the gate with an altogether different machine. The story, as heard locally, was that the soldiers were laughing loudly right up until private "newbie" was blown into bits on the bike that had been somehow changed at the pub gates.

Ironically poor "Custard" did not meet his maker at the hands of the vengeful British Army but rather at the back of the local fire brigades fence as he had chosen that particular place to make a bed for the night just when the local volunteers had burst through on a mission of mercy.

Amidst all these incidents a young man called Bobby Sands became the MP for Fermanagh and South Tyrone. Nothing unusual there at first. However this young man was a hunger striker serving time in the Maze H Blocks and only days from a very untimely death. The summer after Bobby Sands death and the ensuing events would change life in Ireland forever and ultimately lead to a peace process. But for Dominic and Dualta it marked the beginning of the end.

CHAPTER 6

THE SUMMER OF '81

THE PREVIOUS SUMMER DOMINIC'S sister had been on an exchange visit to Paris where she had met an extremely charismatic German student and as Irish people tend to do, she'd invited him to come and visit "anytime" you wish.

In Ireland this is a traditional "lie" that Dominic and everyone understood you don't really mean or ever expect to happen. However, "Gunther" had more persistence than most and took his sister literally and straight out of the blue arrived on the doorstep of the household one day and announced he was here to visit Andrea. The fact Andrea was midway through a 3 week stay at the Gaeltacht in Donegal did seem to be a major spanner in his "romantic works".

So without much deliberation or discussion it was decided that the 15 year old Dominic would escort Gunther to Donegal to visit Andrea and make good use of the very sturdy tent he was carrying. (Dominic often looked back on these particular set of circumstances and wondered how the snowflake generation would have coped but they were different times and different people in those days).

Back at the time he just needed to do one thing.

Phone rings Dualta, "Hello"

Dominic, "You wanna go to Donegal?"

Dualta, "Yeah, ok"

Dominic, "Maybe for a week"

Dualta, "Yeah, ok"

Dominic, "We've no lift, we will have to thumb it"

Dualta, "Yeah, ok"

Dominic, "Oh, I also have to bring a German"

Dualta, "Ok. Where we staying?"

Dominic, "German lad has a big tent" Dualta, "Yeah, ok. See you in the morning"

***

Thumbing a lift to Donegal? What could go wrong?

"Thumbing a lift" is what most young people did in those days to get from point A to B, literally stand on the side of the road stick out your thumb. For the lads and their German cargo this was to be a much longer journey than normal, how the fuck do you even get to Donegal thought Dominic.

Dualta reassured him that it was somewhere near Derry. "Where the fuck is Derry?"

So the lads were ready for a big adventure and despite the fact they couldn't understand the German lad, he seemed ok. Even despite his leopard print drainpipe trousers.

So according to several farmers, lorry drivers and kind citizens, Derry apparently was right up at the coast near Donegal. So the lads were rightly proud at making it so far before dark with their German cargo. So here the lads stood in the lovely Derry (Waterside) dressed in their Fred Perry jackets, DM boots, drainpipes and "hunger striker" badges looking for somewhere to pitch a tent, what could possibly go WRONG.

***

So Protestants exist after all.

Having been brought up in a rural community where every-one was catholic except for the Brits, the lads knew very little about the rest of "Norn Iron" let alone the world.

Yes, they had cheered for "Norn Iron" when Pat Jennings and Martin O'Neill, the only obvious fenians in the team had led them to the World Cup in 1982 with victory over Spain but other than that they had little or no interaction with the "other sort". In their community the only antagonist or enemy was the Brits/Police and the boys genuinely thought they would know a Protestant if they ever met one (probably by the horns that would be protruding slightly from their skulls).

They were not however expecting their introduction to a "PROTESTANT HOOD" to be quite so soon or so violent. Through the chasing, name calling, bricks, stones, boots, thumps and general vitriol they were experiencing they were trying to explain to a "crying" German that the WATERSIDE residents were not particularly anti German but rather anti Irish.

In fairness the abundance of "Union jacks" and "UVF" flags should have been a huge warning to the lads but they were "immortal" and didn't really see risks. Although "Gunther" was nearly 18 his counsel could hardly have stretched to the loyalist clad confines of the Waterside of Derry. He probably just thought people in this particular city had taken greater exception to the Germans than other places he'd been.

Anyway a welcome bus to the city centre brought relief from the situation and a chance to catch their breath and re-evaluate the "hunger strike" badges and general republican vibe.

"I thought Derry was full of fenians" said Dualta

"So did I" said Dominic.

"That bloody Sunday must have wrecked the whole show" said Dualta as he watched Gunther crying into his chips in a city centre café. "Bet you wish you stayed at home now you bollix" laughed Dualta as Gunther spilled half a bottle of vinegar onto his food.

Surprisingly Derry was literally a mile from the border and once they had gathered their belongings and Gunther's dignity off the café floor they were soon walking across the border to the Republic of Ireland.

"How the fuck can this be by Inishowen the most northernly point in Ireland" said Dualta.

"I dunno" said Dominic.

"Well if we are now in the South how can it be North?" asked Dualta. "It's not the South it's the Republic of Ireland, it's in the North of the country" said Dominic.

"How the fuck is it in the North when my cousins always go down South for their holidays in Donegal" raged Dualta.

"It's not the South, they just call it the South cause the rest of the Republic is in the South" insisted Dominic.

"Ah fuck up you bollix" said Daulta.

They both looked towards Gunther for a little support but he was still crying quietly to himself.

CHAPTER 7

THE HILLS OF DONEGAL

DONEGAL SEEMED TO BE brighter and sunnier than Derry. Walking along the road the lads felt a certain freedom, no Brits, no cops, no checkpoints, no stop and no search (imagine 3 lads walking down the road with backpacks where they came from and you knew exactly where they would be after half an hour, in the local RUC station).

The lads liked this new atmosphere and even Gunther stopped sobbing and started to appreciate the beauty of the Republic of Ireland. As they decided to stop for the night and Gunther, in better spirits, now began to set up his tent the lads did begin to wonder about the history of the island and why the most northernly part of Ireland was "not" in Norn Iron.

Gunther was nearly 18 but had "ID" so he had no problem getting a few beers for the lads at a local off licence. Sitting outside that tent somewhere between Letterkenny and Ranafast the lads tried to explain the politics of Norn Iron to Gunther. And that was not as easy as it seemed.

Gunther's thoughts

"Is Ireland not an Island?"

Lads, "Yes, but the Brits own a bit of it"

Gunther, "Why?"

Lads, "Cause there was 800 years of occupation and troubles and the Brits took over the whole of Ireland cause they thought someone would use it (i.e. Spain) as a backdoor to attack England"
Gunther, "Ok, so what happened?"
Lads, "Well they fought for 800 years and then the Brits gave 26 Counties back but kept 6"
Gunther, "Why?"
Lads, "Because I think that's where all the prods lived"
Gunther, "Why were they there?"
Lads, "Cause the Birts sent them there it was called plantation"
Gunther, "Why? What does that mean?"
Lads, "They basically sent prods over to live as English and take over the Country"
Gunther, "So why did they not become Irish like most people would?"
Dualta, "I dunno, fuck up you bollix, give me another can of Harp"
The next day the lads (due to a lift from a very accommodating trucker) arrived in the Gaeltacht area of Ranafast.

***

And the lads arrived

In what could only be described as the craziest thing or the most remarkable coincidence in history, as the lads arrived into Anagry Co Donegal a contingent of Dundalk/Monaghan lads were literally marching into town at the exact same time.

Now these were not "Irish language" enthusiasts or Irish Republicans but just a gang of free state lads who heard there was a lot of single ladies up in the North. The lads weren't exactly friends but they immediately bonded on neutral territory, the objective being GIRLS, GIRLS, GIRLS.

That summer in Donegal was heavenly, sun, blue skies and wall to wall girls.

The now swollen ranks of eight lads were of course not welcomed by the Gaeltacht authorities so they set up camp a little way out of town near an abandoned old cottage and set to work on being a very bad influence on anyone that they could persuade to tread the path to their camp. This caused no end of trouble with not only the authorities but also the Gaeltacht lads and the local lads but these altercations only served to make the experience much more fun and exciting, as several bouts of fisticuffs ended up in them making more and more new friends as boys tend to do once the macho gesticulating is out of the way.

Of course Gunther was a different story, Dominic's sister took one look at her long distance suitor and recoiled so far away from him that the attack in the Waterside paled into insignificance compared to the brutality of affairs of the heart. However he eventually joined in the party and was quite pleased to learn that some of the less discerning Irish girls were intrigued by his leopard print trousers and his strange accent. Within a week he'd forgotten all about the original mission and was enjoying his life on the sheep shit covered scrap of derelict land along with all the other lads and their now increasing band of followers.

The weeks on that Donegal coast were magical but for very different reasons. For Dom it was all about the craic, the cider and the notches on the "figurative bedpost". But for Dualta something different was happening. Yes of course he enjoyed the craic and the girls but he was also blown away by the culture of Irishness and he would often enjoy long and probing political discussions with the new friends from far off destinations of Derry, Galway, Dundalk and Sligo. He didn't admit it but Dominic became jealous of Dualta's new relationships. It had always just been them but now Dualta's attentions were elsewhere.

Dom, "Come on the fuck, stop talking shite and let's go get some women"

Dualta, "Fuck off you bollix"

CHAPTER 8

BACK HOME FROM DERRY

SO AFTER EVENTUALLY DUMPING the German, the lads returned home, their one week mercy mission had turned into a three week life changing event. For Dominic he realised he loved the craic, the life and the girls, oh and football and "soccer" as well. The Derry lads hated when they called it soccer, it really annoyed them, and so the lads did it every time.

Back at home life took on its normal monotony but both lads had been changed inside.

Dualta now examined every nuance in detail. The troubles, the conflict, the occupation, the solution. He began to think that realistically there was only one solution, violence, but he wasn't exactly sure where he would fit into the situation. He missed Donegal, he missed talking to likeminded people. Of course he had his blood brother Dominic, they were soulmates but he just didn't get it, Dom just cared about the craic he didn't think deep, didn't care deep. He didn't blame him he just couldn't relate to him anymore. Dualta was naturally a much quieter and modest lad than his best friend and if truth were told, he was sometimes embarrassed by how loud Dom could be and how he could dominate conversations without letting other people have their say but he didn't bring it up cause he wouldn't knowingly hurt anyone's feelings. However, they did get on really well together and were a great team. They spent time listening to popular bands like Madness, The Specials and UB40 and hitting on the girls which was as natural to the gang of lads as breathing. But while their bond could never be broken it was starting to be obvious that their future paths would be in different directions.

CHAPTER 9

BACK AT SCHOOL

IT WASN'T HUGELY OVERT but over the next year the lads just weren't as close as they had been, fate had chosen different paths for them and they were just getting on with it. They were still inseparable most days, but the days that they weren't together began to become more and more frequent and obvious.

School was still the normal chore but funnily enough now they were bigger the "Brothers" didn't beat them as much or try to embarrass or ridicule them. Life now revolved around exams, football and of course girls. Sure they would be fine they'd pass the aul "O" Levels and be grand thought Dominic.

"I'm going back to Donegal" said Dualta

"What?" Dominic wasn't really listening

"I'm going back to the Gaeltacht, but I'm going as a student this year" said Dualta

"Wise up you dick, why would you do that?" said Dominic

"I've just been writing to some of the Gaeltacht lads and I just wanna go back and, well you know, just do it again" said Dualta

"Don't be a dick, you can't go back. We weren't students, we lived in a fucking tent, we drank cider and fucked girls" said Dominic. "You can't go back and be a student. It doesn't make any sense"

"Well I'm going to and that's that" said Dualta, conversation over.

Life had a very boring rhythm that winter as they settled down to study for their "O" Levels.

Football took over as both lads were selected for the club Senior Team and the County Minor Squad. So they had more than enough to occupy their time. But Dualta still burned with a desire to return to Donegal. He knew Dominic had forgotten about it but he was still determined to go, even though he knew he couldn't actually afford to go as a student. But as he was walking down the school corridor one morning he noticed a very pointed message on the bulletin board.

"Mentors needed to instruct Year 8 pupils on the Gaeltacht bursary."

"Excuse me Brother" said Dualta to a passing teacher. "What does the mentor get?"

"A free holiday I'd imagine" laughed Brother Baxter.

So Dualta applied and duly was appointed mentor of the Year 8 pupils who were going to apply for the Gaeltacht Scholarship Award. It was a "piece of piss" all he had to do was teach the first years a few words and phrases of Irish, get them through the exam and HE WOULD GET A COMPLETELY FREE bursary to go back to Donegal and re unite with his friends who really understood him in what had become his spiritual home. It wasn't that Dominic didn't understand him but Dom was becoming shallow, football, girls and party was his agenda, but Dualta knew there was MORE.

It was perfect for Dualta and to be honest it was easy, teach a few stock phrases to the first years and he was home and dry, full scholarship back to Donegal. Only one thing bothered Dualta and nagged at the back of his mind.

Brother Baxter was always around, yeah he was the supervisor and had to be there but Dualta couldn't help remember the stories about him from school and it made him shudder. He was just TOO friendly, just TOO touchy, it just wasn't RIGHT. One minute he would be slapping the boys and a minute later he would be hugging them. Dualta never felt comfortable in his company but for the time being he had to get that scholarship, get back to his spiritual home and address the greater issues of his Country's "freedom" which he could only discuss with his Republican colleagues, Yes Dominic was still his "brother" but he didn't have the same passion or understanding of what it meant to be a deep thinking Republican and finding a way to free Ireland.

Dominic thought Dualta had forgotten all about going back to Donegal as they hadn't really been talking that much recently, they had got through their exams but they weren't in the same class so they'd really only talked on the bus to and from school.

Actually Dominic wasn't even thinking about Dualta's issues. He was doing well at "soccer" and had actually been picked for the team to go over to a tournament in England that summer. Soccer wasn't viewed very well in the town but sure this was going to be such a great opportunity, he'd go over there, be discovered and become the next Gary Lineker or Paul Gascoigne, happy days, easy street.

Dominic missed Dualta, yeah they were still together but they didn't talk the way they used to, they were more just part of the same crowd of friends now. A group of close friends who would have each other's back and would fight for each other, who played together on the pitch and could be considered as a tight unit. But he and Dualta had been more than that, they were the lads who had blood in each other's veins, but recently it didn't seem like it anymore. Dualta was too political now, too intelligent.

"Jeez, just chill out" said Dominic

"Fuck up, ye bollix" replied Dualta

So as Dominic headed off to London for the chance of a life time, Dualta headed off to Donegal as a mentor to the younger kids. If truth be told on that fateful day Dualta was the much happier of the two.

With butterflies in his stomach Dominic boarded the plane to London roughly at the same time Dualta was boarding the coach to Donegal.

***

Heading to Donegal on a bright and sunny morning filled Dualta with absolute joy. He was excited and delighted to be going, it was "bliss", not a word he would normally use but it did seem to capture the mood quite well so he laughed to himself as he allowed his mood to be "blissful".

His mood was now onto ecstatic when the coach pulled into Ranafast and he was reunited with his political family as they all stood joyfully on the steps of the old square outside the Gaeltacht's main centre. Any apprehension or nervousness disappeared as he took in all the faces, embraces and kisses of the friends he'd missed so much. This was perfect, this was where he was meant to be, miles from where he lived but home. Immediately they took up where they'd left off, like they'd never stopped and were soon back into the comfortable yet dynamic relationship he had found so fulfilling.

***

If "bliss" was the happy word Dualta had settled on to describe his experience then Dominic would have had to find the exact "opposite" word to describe what he was feeling, he didn't know the exact opposite word but he was pretty sure "shit" wasn't even strong enough to describe it, it was like, worse than shit.

Dom had arrived in London expecting to be met by the manager of QPR but what he was met by was an old minibus that took him to an old council pitch with 80 (yes 80) other trialists who were all seeking to live the dream.

After a lifetime of filling in forms and standing in lines, he realised he was the only one who didn't have a dad or a significant adult with him, which was shit cause most adults just brushed him aside and he ended up 4 places back in the queue, AGAIN.

"Jeez" he thought "Why don't you let your pathetic wee dick of a son speak for himself"

Pushy parents seemed to dominate the waiting lines of players but since he didn't have one he didn't know how to push. Eventually he was processed, not last but third from last with two other innocuous looking lads who also had no adult supervision.

They were shuffled off on another bus that took them to a dark and dingy hostel that contained a dormitory of bunkbeds and one shower room/toilet that was supposed to service sixteen adolescents all of whom were thinking of auditioning for the role of ALPHA MALE. Dominic was a little more at ease in here because he'd lived his whole life without any luxury or finesse and without their daddies or pushy mums, these lads weren't so tough or scary at all.

In fact Dom pretty soon felt better. They went to the pitches and did drills and played football and the coaches at QPR were very professional and understanding but they had very few resources and certainly were in no position to train and talent spot eighty of the cockiest wee shits you ever saw.

Anyway the hostel became a more neutral ground now that they were there on their own and soon they sort of bonded. In fact so much so that at training and trials they linked together and following their regular night time discussions they decided on a strategy of kicking the shit out of all the other teams and out on the pitches they became a unit, an immoveable force, unbeatable and full of confidence. When Adrian from Newcastle suggested they should go out for a few pints, Dom thought that was the best idea ever and all the dorm agreed. They were the top men, they were kicking ass, they were indestructible.

That night as they put on their best trousers and shirts they felt invincible and as they were allowed entry to the Soho nightclub they knew they were invincible. They "strode the world like a colossus".

The next morning, things were not quite as they should have been for potential premiership footballers. Lads from all over the UK were fighting to be sick in the same toilet, a few to be honest were now vehemently heaving in the communal shower.

Dominic could vaguely remember snogging some girl from Fulham but couldn't quite remember if it had led to more than that and as he pondered on that sweet issue, the tannoy requested all the QPR trailists to make their way to the common room ASAP. So Dom's dreams of his future "Miss World" would have to wait until after they were assigned to the clubs that were going to secure their footballing futures.

The screaming of the coach did not help what Dom now real-ised to be a huge hangover but really there was no need to slap the young Watford player who had just vomited on the floor of the common area. Suddenly shit got real and as his heart began to race, Dom realized through the various English accents that the invincibles, the hard lads, the buddies, the bonded lads were all being told to fuck off home, cause they would never make it as pro footballers, that they had let everyone down, their families, friends, mentors, coaches, EVERYONE.

Now fuck off and don't expect to come back.

Oh shit shit shit shit.

What that fuck was he going to do now?

Dominic didn't have any money or the means to even fuck off. Luckily what he did have was a sister, Andrea. She lived in London and he could contact her.

Over the next few days Andrea was brilliant, she lifted him from the hostel and took him to her house where she fed and looked after him until she was able to find and pay for a suitable flight to get him home. Coming home with your tail between your legs is not such a great experience. Those that knew him and gen-uinely cared for him were very sympathetic, but there was also a huge number of individuals who were not short of advice for the returning defeated and subdued warrior,

"Ye bollix".

The next few weeks were hell but there was also plenty of sup-port, the local GAA Club rallied round and became a focal point of Dom's existence. When everyone else wanted to see him down and took some pleasure in his failure, it was the local GAA Club who stood up and got him through his predicament.

Meanwhile he needed to sort out his future, since he wasn't going to be a footballer he better get himself a trade, join the masses of the workers.

***

By contrast Dualta was enjoying the Gaeltacht life to the full. He met up with his original friends from last year, the people from the Bogside, the Falls and those who knew the story, those who lived through the troubles. But where his real enlightenment came from was from others who he met, kids like himself who didn't live in a war zone. Young people who actually lived normal lives in nice places and didn't think it was an average day when you saw a burnt out bus and a bomb scene or a riot or had graffiti all over your house, and that intrigued him, because he'd been so caught up in his own existence he barely knew there were other existences possible.

Here he met other Catholic/Republican people who had no idea of the suffering and pain that his community experienced on a daily basis and he wanted to know why? It made him think it was also maybe time he did something about it.

He was very at peace with himself at that moment and it was only the continual presence of Brother Baxter that was a fly in the ointment.

***

Dominic had decisions to make as the day of the GCSE results loomed large, he wished he could take his mother's advice and leave it in the hands of GOD but deep down he suspected even baby Jesus would have done a lot more revision than he had.

He decided to wait until Dualta got home and then sure they could decide together what they were going to do. No point in panicking about it now.

For the rest of the summer his dad had got him a job out labouring on a building site. It was ok, the lads were good craic and the pay was pretty great considering he did as little as possible. Yeah he had to put up with the banter of the lads wondering why he wasn't away with "Lineker or Gascoigne" but it was all good hearted and enjoyable to be honest.

Of course the TROUBLES continued and by now there was a morbid tit for tat element to the killings. So on a Monday a UDR soldier gets shot and by Wednesday some innocent Catholic taxi driver gets shot while just doing his job. But life went on, life always has that habit of going on and on and Dominic soon realised that tears and crying soon disappeared for most people, probably with the exception of the families themselves. But for everyone else, life goes continued as before.

Dominic made a very astute observation during this summer. He was by no means a philosopher but one thing really came home, to him if had to sum it all up in one sentence he would have said,

"Unless it's at your door, then no one really, truly, honestly or deeply gives a fuck, cause they've all got their own problems"

Actually he thought "Maybe I am a philosopher" only he couldn't spell it so he thought "fuck it!"

Life resumed its normal routine that summer and in the eyes of the locals it was just as it was, normal. And that was until it just became really abnormal.

***

On a Friday evening the lads had a football fixture against a team from Co Louth, which was across the border and a great opportunity to play a meaningless match, have a bit of fun and then obviously get drunk as fuck. Unfortunately the lads got evicted from their nightclub of choice but as luck would have it they spent the remaining hours of the evening enjoying the delights of a "free state" curry.

Not bad, not bad at all thought Dominic before he had a chance to lick the inside of the carton. By now his mate Jerry had grabbed him by the arm and told him if he didn't mind being a "wee bit" of a Judas then the two of them had a lift in a car to the next town, where they would still be 15 minutes to go in the disco so they could definitely pull some talent.

Anyway, as it stood there were eight lads going home and just Dom and Jerry looking to go on to the other town so a division in the camp naturally occurred. Boldly the lads ventured forth only to be told, sorry that lift has gone and there's no taxis.

"Never worry" said jerry, "We'll thumb it"

Three hours later they were definitely sure their choice was the wrong one. After three long hours with no success and no further forward it was time for action so Jerry lay down in the middle of the road and acted like he'd just been run over. A very dangerous thing to do in the midst of a County used to daily violence and massacres, however on this occasion he was lucky as a good Samaritan stopped and whilst a little taken aback about Jerry's state of health he did offer the lads a lift down home or at least to the border.

His name was Tim and he seemed like an absolutely genuine lad, he said he would leave the lads home but he just needed to call home for a minute to get a shower and a bite to eat as he'd been working the night shift.

So the two boys found themselves in Tim's kitchen eating a surprisingly delicious egg and onion sandwich as they waited for his reappearance. To be honest at this point, not that they would admit it, both lads were shitting themselves thinking at any moment Tim was going to reappear and go all "chainsaw massacre" on them. But he didn't and it turned out Tim was just about as nice a fellow as you would ever meet.

He fed them, offered them a drink and once he was ready he went way out of his way to give them a lift home the lads had never really witnessed kindness like this before.

Tim left them off in the centre of their village at approximately 6.30 am and the lads wandered home vacantly and slept for a few hours. The next day or morning to be exact, Dominic heard a battering at his door, it was Jerry.

"Come on and we'll get a wee swally (cure), a few of the lads are up in FARMERS and we are on the session"

Dom thought Jerry had never been "off" the session but he gathered himself together and lumbered up to the pub just cause he was nosey as fuck and didn't want to miss anything.

Jeez what a day's craic they had. At first Dom was not in the mood to drink but Georgy Mac said

"If you have a couple of pints you'll be fine"

Well as it turned out Georgy was absolutely spot on, a few pints and the Jazz band kicking in with a few classics such as "Bad bad Leeroy Brown" and a Disney classic "I'm the king of the swingers" (from Jungle Book apparently) and as the morning progressed the lads knew exactly what the term "cure" meant. They were buzzing, dancing, feeling good!

It was then Jerry said "We should go visit Tim"

Dominic, "Yeah, Tim is the best lad ever! We should go see him and maybe bring him a bottle of whiskey, to say thanks"

The drunken lads thought this was the greatest idea ever.

"So let's just find someone sober enough to drive and we can go across the border and find the lad"

In the pub nobody was willing to drive but they decided to ring Kembo who they knew would be at home. Reluctantly Kembo said he would drive them for £5 each, sound!

When they arrived in the general vicinity of the house as far as they could remember from the night before there was a huge amount of cars outside, inside and around the property which were definitely not there the night before.

As the drunk duo approached the door of the house there were loads of somber looking men surrounding the house, to be honest it was a little intimidating. The boys worried that they were walking into trouble.

But suddenly a very comforting and matronly woman greeted them at the door.

"Thank fuck" said Dom

"Hello Mrs, is Tim here?"

"Yes, he's just home about half an hour"

"Oh ok, sorry to interrupt your party but can we see him for a minute? We've something for him" said Dominic

"Oh that's very kind of you boys, go on down to
that back room and that's where he is"

Although freaked out now, the lads went down the corridor
until they turned into the last room on the left where Tim was.
Unfortunately Tim was lying in the finest pine coffin the boys had
ever seen and was definitely in no mood to accept the lads paltry
offering of a half bottle of whiskey by the way of thanks.

As they staggered towards the front door they picked up bits
and pieces of the general conversation that told them poor Tim
had been killed in a car accident on his way home from a town
across the border at 7am in the morning, no one knew what on
earth he had been doing there at all.

CHAPTER 10

THE INCIDENT

DETAILS WERE SKETCHY AT first, the radio said there had been a major incident at the port of Gweedore but didn't give names or details, just that there had been a tragic accident.

The rumours spread around the town like wildfire that someone had died, drowned, a Christian Brother from the local High School. There were also children involved but as yet there was no confirmation of any other fatalities.

On and on it went until Dominic's head was going to burst. "Dualta was up there"

He knew in his guts something was wrong.

"Should he go up there?" He thought to himself. Dualta's mum still hadn't had a phone call to say he was ok.

As the day went on details began to emerge, it turned out there had been a huge incident on the pier in Gweedore where in saving the life of a young student who had fallen into the water, Brother Baxter had tragically been drowned and was undoubtedly a hero. Another, older boy had also been in the water but unfortunately his whereabouts were still unaccounted for.

Dominic's guts just twisted and turned he knew it was Dualta, just knew it, he felt it in his bones, please, no, please, no, don't let it be him. When the details did emerge of the heroic rescue in which Brother Baxter tragically died it rocked the whole greater community.

BBC News reported "Brother Baxter had come upon the two boys in obvious difficulty off the pier, at this point and with no regard for his own safety, he hurled himself into the perilous waters and emerged with the young boy but as he went back to save the older boy, both were swept beneath the swell and it was a couple of hours before the body of Brother Baxter was recovered, at this point the body of the other boy has not, as yet, been recovered."

Dominic felt sick, and with good reason. Within hours it was common knowledge that Dualta was missing. No one had seen him for hours and it soon transpired that he hadn't returned to his house the previous night and he hadn't been seen him since 6pm the day before.

The minutes turned into hours, hours into days and all his worst nightmares were realised.

Dualta was gone, just gone!

Apparently Brother Baxter had come across Dualta and another boy who had been pier jumping and got into difficulty and with no regard for his own safety he had sacrificed his own life in a heroic attempt to save the boys.

"What a hero" screamed the TV and Newspaper headlines. He was posthumously awarded medals of valour and the mother of the pupil who had been saved posed for photographs with Brother Baxter's photo. He brought honour and courage back into vogue and hundreds upon hundreds of people attended his funeral which was a fitting homage to a fallen hero. A courageous man who had given his life to the education of young boys and ultimately given his life, no one would ever forget this honourable man.

Dominic had been at the "show piece" funeral and had seen the actual Irish President carry a wreath, but he still didn't know where his friend was. Dualta was still MISSING (obviously presumed dead) despite the best efforts of the heroic brother.

The currents and rip tides of the Atlantic Ocean were brutal and unforgiving and the search for the body might take weeks or months. Well weeks and months did go by and the body was never found, the family were distraught as was Dominic who spent as much time as he could with them, but it was soul destroying, he couldn't go on like this. He needed to do something.

So he started to trace the path Dualta had followed, looking at history, origin and roots, where he had come from. He was amazed at what he found, for someone living through the troubles and studying history in school he knew fuck all about it.

Yes, he had enjoyed the riots cause they were exciting and an adventure but why were they doing it? He needed to dig deeper. He remembered history class in the CBS, it was about the Vikings, the Normans, the Scottish/English plantation, Holy Fuck, he never really learned anything about the Irish, only how we affected the huge line of colonialists who wanted our Island.

He read and read, and then read deeper but it all came back to the same outcome, we Irish had been colonised, destroyed, raped and pillaged by an abundance of foreign powers for hundreds of years, but mainly the English.

Dominic spent months upon months reading and researching through the annals of historical journals, history books and diaries and then he slowly began to realise, "I think I understand"

He finally came to the same conclusion Dualta had come to, "It's not about the riots or the shootings, it's about the fact we have been colonised and controlled by a foreign government who have bled us dry and only used us for their own ends" He remembered Dualta lectured him.

So Dominic looked closely at his options, and there were clearly two, the bullet or the ballot box?

In fairness the vast majority of the Republicans at the time were doing both, "Vote early and vote often" was a local slogan that resonated. But Dominic thought he might be able to make "a difference". So he joined Sinn Fein and he put himself forward to represent the locals. His family joked at the thoughts of him being a "Politician" but it really wasn't like that, he wanted to carry on the work of his fallen friend, he felt it was his duty rather than a calling, but the more he got involved the more shocked and disgusted he became.

He hated violence and would never have willingly seen anyone die or be injured in the name of religion or politics. But he couldn't move away from the injustices that had been done to his people and what they had suffered. The civil rights movement which was battered into submission by the crown forces and willing UDR/RUC collaborators, innocent people being beaten and bloodied just because they wanted equality.

Dominic was voracious in his appetite for reading now and he read extensively of the work of the civil rights movement in the USA and South Africa. It occurred to him that if you swapped a skin colour for a religion, then the people of Northern Ireland were going through exactly the same thing, although the skin colour made it more difficult for the bigots to find identify their targets.

When Dominic socialized , he couldn't quite tell straight away who was a Prod or a Taig without asking the usual three questions,

What's your name? (If it was Siobhan or Mary, then you knew)

What school did you go to? (Sacred Heart no, Royal Academy), then you knew straight away.

Who do you vote for? (SDLP- bad, Sinn Fein - bingo, DUP/UUP- fuck off)

Dominic started off campaigning for Sinn Fein and was happy to do his bit, knock the doors and explain the situation to a community of people who had largely become immune to the horror and inhumanity of their everyday lives. Dominic continued his working week on the building site but every spare hour he had was divided equally between football and campaigning. As a teenager he'd lived through the hunger strikes and now he felt that it was time for peace, if he could help out in any way, then for fucks sake he owed it to everyone to try.

Times were changing, there were whispers of "talks" with the Brits and "talks" with the UVF. Dom didn't know much about that but he did know if he campaigned in a certain estate he would be fed a nice fry in one particular house and possibly given a very warm welcome in another house (if the hubby was still in jail) and be driven off by a shot gun in another house, so he generally let his campaign partner do those ones.

Did he think about his friend, his brother Dualta? Every day, and he knew this is what drove him on.

Eventually it looked like the Brits might be open to talks and negotiations to end the troubles. Dom was excited by this but didn't by any means think it was a forgone conclusion but he was hopeful and positive at the same time.

The IRA cease fire was a huge move towards that longed for PEACE. Dom joined the thronging crowds who celebrated the momentous occasion and he'd be lying if he said he didn't have a lot of beer and possibly a wee visit down to number 33 "Crescent Road". It was "euphoric" there was genuine hope that peace was on the horizon and the pain, violence, torture, killings and murders that he had known all his life would finally be over. Dom was elated and in that movement he thought

"Fuck it! I'm going to stand for election"

He could understand now what had motivated Martin Luther King, Malcolm X and Nelson Mandela to give their lives to a cause, to do something that mattered.

To do the right thing. So many brave and courageous people had done the right thing in his mind and peacefully protested but it had only brought it so far but not far enough. But he watched in hope as the landscape unfolded. He stood for election and was defeated because their constituency was configured against him -60% Unionist, 40% Nationalist, so realistically he was never going to win. But the peace process still offered hope and he would be happy to continue on and do his part.

The world was now involved in Ireland's political situation. With Clinton and all the movers and shakers taking part it seemed inevitable that peace would follow.

And then, for probably the first time in his entire life, Dom became aware of the "Marching season". An ancient and tribal

activity whereby the Protestants of Northern Ireland chose to celebrate their stranglehold over the Nationalist community by marching through their homesteads and playing provocative songs to celebrate their ascendency. Dom had never witnessed this before as his
village was 100% Nationalist and he'd never really ever knowingly
met Protestants, let alone ORANGE MEN and WOMEN.

CHAPTER 11

THE MARCHING SEASON

AND THEN IT HAPPENED! The PEACE PROCESS as it was, was going well until a determined cohort of ORANGEMEN insisted they needed to walk through their "traditional route" in Portadown. In layman's terms, this meant they had to walk to their place of worship (fine) but then walk home through what now was a totally Nationalist area.

Anyone with an ounce of sense would say just go another way, but they insisted on making this march, regardless of the consequences, "and the consequences were going to be catastrophic" thought Dominic. This led to a "standoff" watched by the whole world. Dom thought that the world were bound to be embarrassed by the pettiness of the Orange Order's insistence on causing millions of pounds worth of human and collateral danger just to walk and march over the remains of your once adversaries.

The fact that these adversaries just wanted "parity of esteem" was lost as the leaders of UNIONISM claimed they were the ones who were being hard done by. Dom couldn't help but think "why are these politicians who had ALL donned the garb of Unionist terrorism groups dare to call him a "Terrorist". As far as he could see from his studies the British Empire had "plundered countless nations", "Divided many lands". They had "Terrorised many, many indigenous populations" and massacred so many native people in the name of King and Country. The fact that it was now being done in the name of a Queen did not make it any less brutal or make it right.

Whilst sitting in his living room, Dom pondered why all his many cousins who had by now spread across the globe in search of a better life, still spoke English.

The USA, Canada, South Africa, New Zealand and Australia, were all places that his cousins had ventured to and ALL spoke with the ENGLISH tongue. His further research led him to conclude the English had colonised or more accurately "invaded" the whole world. His studies enlightened him, making him excited and angry in equal measures.

Why had he not learned this in school, instead of learning about Henry "the fucking 8th and all his wives". Through his research Dom soon discerned that the education policy was a form of indoctrination. All about stopping them speaking Irish, stopping them being self-sufficient. A flawless plan, "except it hadn't factored in how hard and resilient the Irish are" thought Dom, "You won't defeat the Irish".

His optimism and positivity were buoyed by the fact the British Government refused to allow this Orange Order march down through the completely Nationalist aea of Mid Northern Ireland, just because they said it was a "Traditional route".

The protestant people demanded this should happen and Dom thought that they should probably have more to worry about in their lives but as it turned out, they didn't. In fact they were happy to stay there for a week insisting they could march back to a CHURCH? Now this really fucked up Dom's thinking. These people are willing to destroy and kill in the name of their religion? He himself would be the first to admit he wasn't religious in the slightest but if he was, it would never be based on hating someone. As himself and Dualta had grown up they had never hated anyone, fought, yes, punched, yes, kicked, yes, called names, yes, hated, never.

Dom honestly couldn't understand how people could insist on this level of aggression and hatred in the name of their LORD and it never failed to baffle him that literally ALL their leaders appeared to be "men of cloth" or "religious leaders". It did remind him of a debate he had had with Dualta in the gallery of the church at home.

Dom, "Jeez, that's a good service! Kinda had a warm feeling to it?"

Dualta, "Fuck up, you bollix, it was a load of shit. I wouldn't be here only I don't want to annoy me ma"

And there thought Dom was genuine "sacrifice", doing it for the love of others not the hatred. Anyway it looked like sense would prevail as the Brits seemed determined to prevent the "bullies" from breaking through the barricades of decency and normality and equality. That was until they did, suddenly the threat of violence won the day and the ORANGE ORDER were allowed to walk through the Nationalist community and stick their jack boots right through the peace process. The fact that the RUC "beat" the determined group of nationalist protestors off the road shocked the WORLD and brought the gob smacked Dominic to a steely resolve.

"For fucks sake! This can't be right? I need to do something!"

CHAPTER 12

DUALTA'S ODYSSEY

WHEN HE CAME ROUND, he was cold, confused and totally disorientated. It was very disconcerting that everything was swaying and moving, like that time himself and Dom had got drunk at a local disco and he couldn't get to sleep cause his head was spinning so much and then he was violently sick. He didn't remember drinking anything at all but he sure as hell was violently as sick as he had.

The next voice he heard above his own violent "chuggs" was not one he recognised, come to think of it he didn't know if they were speaking English or Irish, it sounded more like French, yeah French, but he didn't understand it at all. He gave up trying and lay down on the floor beside the toilet, but the room wouldn't stop moving and if anything it was moving even more side to side. He was dazed and sore but he knew he needed to focus and try and remember what was going on,

"Oh fuck" he thought, "I killed him"

"Oh fuck, oh fuck, oh fuck, I killed him!"

The door opened and a portly man with an unmistakable air of kindness and friendliness greeted him. Despite not recognising the accent (still possibly French) he understood the words he was saying and soon realised he was on a fishing trawler in the middle of the Atlantic Ocean. He was immediately sick again. Soon after a few questions emerged in his head:

Was he under arrest and in some sort of prison or hell?

If so how could he possibly get off this fucking boat?

And most important of all How the fuck did he get here?

Hours turned into days and although he was feeling better and not quite so sick anymore any questions he asked the fishermen were met with huge belly laughs and over enthusiastic slaps on the back. The fisherman and his comrades were huge, rugged and aggressive but showed nothing but kindness to him.

He couldn't fully comprehend what had happened. His last recollection was being on the pier in Donegal but he couldn't quite remember exactly what had happened that night. He vaguely remembered having words with Brother Baxter, a scuffle, a limp body floating in the water but nothing after that.

"Oh Jesus, I must've killed him and now I'm in hell" he thought, "doomed to feel as sick as he did now for all eternity"

It was then he remembered his dad telling him stories of his uncle Eamon being imprisoned on a prison ship called the "Maidstone" in Belfast Lough for five years. He himself was old enough to remember that great uncle Eamon was never the "full shilling" ever again and walked with a sway for the rest of his days.

It was such a surreal existence on this boat but as the days passed by and the sickness became less he worked out from the language being spoken and the red maple leaf insignia on the bow that he was on a "French/Canadian" fishing trawler. He asked if he could be dropped back to Donegal but from his very limited understanding of the language he gathered that these lads would not be very welcome on Irish shores and given the distinct lack of fish on this boat, Dualta guessed their cargo was less Captain

Birdseye and more Captain Hook. They assured him he would be ok and they would look after him, which to be honest was more reassuring then returning to the scene of the crime, where he was almost sure he'd murdered a Christian Brother.

When the boat finally reached dry land Dualta crawled on his hands and knees and actually kissed "terra firma" in gratitude. He was totally confused as to his new surroundings but being on hard ground did represent an upturn in his fortunes, and things looked decidedly better when the sailors pointed him in the direction of an adjacent compound. He soon found himself in a canteen with a huge man with a checked shirt, blue jeans and an impressive white goatee beard, a bit like Kenny Rodgers, who spoke English. By his side was an absolutely stunning looking girl, with long red shoulder length hair, shouldering eyes and a figure that wouldn't have looked out of place on the pages of Vogue magazine. Thankfully she looked way too young to be his wife, so hopefully she was his daughter and unattached.

Soon over the worst cup of coffee he'd ever tasted (Dualta never liked coffee anyway but this one was really bad) Dualta learned the reality of his current situation.

The trawler crew had found him floating semi-conscious on a buoy off the coast of Donegal. They hadn't taken him back as he had no ID and they knew they would not have been welcomed back by the Irish authorities due to their questionable fishing methods, quotas and perhaps due to some other considerations that even in his weakened state, he knew not to ask about or question. (One of the inherent skills of being from Ireland)

As the weeks passed, his new benefactor gained a name, "Big Hank" and he welcomed Dualta into his world of "Trawler men" and the brutally hard business of trying to make a living fishing off the beautiful but dangerous Canadian coast. Hank, unlike his rescuers was strictly legit but that didn't stop him from being very intimidating.

Dualta didn't speak much or say too much in case anyone would find out about his murderous past, but he found his new surroundings strangely enjoyable and if truth be told this was mainly because of the few glimpses and very short interactions with "Big Hank's" daughter Sofia.

She was the most beautiful girl Dualta had ever seen and he was totally smitten. His new home was a bunk house on a large industrial fishing site but he could see the homestead where "Big Hank" and "Sofia" lived on the hill above the piers, trawlers, nets, cranes and lobster pots, which actually reminded him of his beloved Donegal and made him feel calm and secure. But this place was a million miles from where he'd come from and here he was invisible.

Of course he was sad for the people who might be worrying about him, even mourning him like Dominic and his mum but he also wasn't ready to go to Long Kesh for a life sentence for literally a crime he "did not commit". He didn't think anyone would listen to his version of events so he reckoned he'd be better just staying here and forgetting about his old life.

As the weeks passed into months Dualta made himself busy working on the yard and was recognised by "Big Hank" as a grafter, a worker and not one to shirk any duty, except for going on that fecking trawler, no way was Dualta going to work on that horror show again.

Thankfully "Big Hank" had numerous business interests and Dualta was both a good worker and a willing learner and one morning his Christian Brother education brought him to the notice of the "Big Boss". The crew were measuring a length of fencing around a particular site and the sums were not adding up, when all of a sudden "Big Hank" shouts

"Hey Irish, can you add up" laughing loudly.

Despite thinking this was hugely patronising, Dualta gulped deeply and replied, "Actually boss, I sure can" (totally and utterly putting his faith in the very education system that had completely ruined his life). It turned out he actually could add up and the Math's work he'd done under a very eccentric but mild-mannered Brother Bob had paid dividends and he knew his equations.

Anyway, the result of his surprising ability to do some Math's was an invitation to "Big Hanks" large house and a very big Canadian breakfast served by Mrs "Big Hank" and eaten in the presence of Hanks children Fred, Chad and of course the beautiful Sofia.

It didn't take a psychologist to work out that Fred was an arsehole. Studying "Law" in the nearby city, he was the epitome of a lad that had forgotten all the values his dad's hard work had been based on and had an air of entitlement and condescension all around him that really made him impossible to like.

Chad however was a genuinely good guy, probably hadn't succeeded too much at school but worked tirelessly round the yard and was well liked by all the other lads as they knew he wasn't above getting involved and getting his hands dirty even though he didn't have to as his dad was the owner.

And then there was Sofia, she was beautiful, stunning and friendly. She was studying Business at the local University, but came home most weekends and was fond of having a bit of craic and banter with the workers.

During this impromptu invitation to breakfast, Dualta couldn't help but feel a very improbable connection to Sofia. She seemed genuinely interested in him and asked a lot of questions. Whilst he was delighted about her interest in him, there was very little he could tell her or very few answers he could provide ("What's your story Dualta", "can you tell me", "Yeah Sofia, I'm here because I killed a man")

There was no disputing however that they did have a real connection and Dualta began to look forward to the weekends and hope that Sofia would be home and they could have a chat. He often fantasised about being with her but he knew their situation was impossible, the Irishman with the shady past and the daughter of the boss, it was a no brainer.

Due to his lack of willingness to go back out on the sea Dualta increasingly found himself working on more engineering projects and one in particular caught his imagination. A particular group of lads worked on constructing "dredges" for gold mining projects in the Canadian outback. Dualta was immediately interested and found this part of the work captivating, so much so that he was offered the chance to go out and experience a season of gold mining at first hand with the added perks of receiving a percentage of any fortune mined in real GOLD. He had never seen such breathtaking scenery before. The environment was absolutely amazing, high sheer rock faces, with water literally hurtling down at breakneck pace, he finally understood how the water looked like "white horses "when it rides in crests. His home seemed so small compared to the sheer magnitude of this beautiful, stunning and slightly scary place.

The work on the gold mine was dangerous, thrilling and horrendous all at the same time. Camping conditions were poor and they risked their lives on a daily basis in white water rivers and treacherous waterfalls searching for tiny nuggets of gold that were the size of half a fingernail. But Dualta had nowhere else to be so this seemed as good an option as any, the only downside was he had no chance of seeing the beautiful Sofia or having a little chat with her. But there was going to be a weekend off in 6 weeks' time and the whole crew would be taken to the big city for a well-deserved rest and recuperation OR alternatively for a drunken, debauched session. Normally, he would have been happy to be given the opportunity to meet some attractive girls and chance his luck with them but it just didn't seem the same now as all he could think about was the beautiful, auburn flame haired Sofia,

"Oh my God", he thought to himself,

"Am I in love?" "Oh jeez, I'm a bollix",

CHAPTER 13

DOMINIC'S DECISION

"I NEED TO DO something", "I need to do something"

Playing guitar in the pub and singing Irish rebel songs was great craic but it wasn't going to free Ireland. He had also recently experienced how the uneven and prejudiced voting system made it impossible to get a fair hearing in political terms in this place. Dom was angry, Dom was frustrated, Dom was alone.

The only person who could understand him was gone, disappeared, lost, probably dead so what could he do, there was no talking to anyone now, there was no point talking anymore, he was sick of talking, sick of listening. He was shocked how the political leaders had listened to the threats, the vitriol and the lies from the Orangemen and of the injustice but without his best friend and only ally in the world he found himself completely lost.

His own life was in a rut, he'd been through lots of different jobs from labouring to bookkeeping, but nothing really satisfied him or made him happy. His personal life was equally as diverse as he'd met a few girls he really liked but none had really been a true love. Even though he was now the proud dad of a little lad called "Jude" to be honest he barely knew his mum. They'd been together for 10 months before she announced she was pregnant, but Dominic still hadn't experienced that once in a lifetime connection. They tried to be a couple for the sake of the baby but neither of them felt their heart was in it.

However, here was a beautiful bouncing baby boy and therein lay Dominic's heart. He was smitten, totally in love and never had expected to feel such unbridled joy in his heart. He wanted to call the baby "Dualta", but his ex-lovers dad was much too big to have a fight with on that issue, so Dom was happy enough to have equal custody. The fact his parents were very supportive meant he could be the best dad possible, well apart from the fact he hadn't a clue what to do.

Little Jude made him analyse his existence and his function in life. Everything in his life now centred around Jude but at the same time it all seemed perfectly natural and normal. His life revolved around his baby boy and everything else became secondary but he became increasingly aware of what the future might hold for his son, and that worried and concerned Dominic greatly.

Only a parent can realise how all-consuming the love for a child can be but Dom relished it and was proud to be a dad. The best thing he had ever achieved he regularly mused. But he had to provide for this child and that became his main function in life.

Earn a living, provide for Jude. Earn a living, provide for Jude. Earn a living, provide for Jude.

Providing for Jude was easier said than done. Work was scarce and not exactly well paid, but he'd do his best. He'd work wherever and whenever he could which consisted of working all day and then doing a shift in his dad's taxi at night time.

Life settled into a routine and little by little he thought less about Dualta and more of his own life and that of Jude's until two events happened which shattered the very fabric of life as he knew it and from that time on he knew it would never be the same again.

CHAPTER 14

WHITE WATER CANADA

DUALTA WAS GETTING HARDENED to the difficult existence of a "White Water gold miner". Daily dicing with death was exhilarating but also exhausting. So the 6 weekly R and R in the city was a welcome target and a well needed distraction. Also walking into the city on these occasions with a shit load of cash gave the lads a nice air of importance.

On the occasion of this particular trip Big Hank had organised a helicopter to fly the lads in style and despite his last experience of being in a helicopter was being flown to "Gough Barracks, Armagh" under the boots and fists of the Brits, Dualta decided to relax and enjoy it and his well-deserved bit of luxury.

So they started with an early morning spa and champagne breakfast courtesy of "Big Hank" and then a few free chips in the casino. Everything was going great until Fred arrived at the bar with free beer tokens for all the workers. While on the surface of this, the concept of buying the lads some free beers seemed perfectly nice but the fact that Fred was delivering this "gift horse" really "demeaned it" thought Dualta. No one liked him, he was patronising, antagonising and the exact opposite of his dad "Big Hank" who all the workers revered, but the lads accepted his tokens in good humour and smiled pretending it was Big Hank offering them. Eventually Fred became more of a peripheral figure and was sitting almost on his own as the lads enjoyed and relished their time off and the boss' kindness.

Unfortunately, the night's "free gifts" came at a price, feeling shunned, Fred became more paranoid and increasingly agitated demanding lap dances off the local girls, where he assumed he was entitled to much more than the paltry fee they had charged offered.

And as with so many bar room brawls and nightclub fights, Fred was very soon being forcibly led to the door and the night-club exit. In truth none of the workers would have turned a head except they were all thrown out on his account.

"Guilt by association" thought Dualta, just the same as in Ireland, he laughed as the bouncer more cajoled then threw him out. And at that exact point (not for the first time) Dualta's life would be defined by one moment of impulse.

While in general the sight of Fred being thrown out of the nightclub was greeted with a sense of satisfaction by most of the lads, it was the unnecessary and forceful abuse that Fred was now receiving at the hands of the door staff that began to annoy Dualta. They were totally over aggressive, reminding him of how the police had dealt with Nationalist protests back home, and he felt he had no option but to remonstrate with them only to be met by a swift uppercut to the face.

In his pursuit of justice for what he saw as an injustice even for someone he quite frankly didn't really care for, Dualta started fighting like he'd never fought before. He threw jabs, uppercuts, straight rights, body shots and crosses like they were second nature. Every detail he'd learned from coach "Marty B" when he was a youngster flowed forth that night and when the dust had set-tled Fred was rescued as 3 bouncers lay prostrate and his co-work-ers stood open jawed and stunned on the pavement.

But after a pizza and a good night's sleep the lads forgot about the nights excitement and headed back to the "goldmine" gener-ally refreshed and entertained, even enjoying a few last beers on the train home as "Big Hank's" helicopter seemed to be engaged elsewhere.

What amused the lads most on their return was the amazing tales of how Fred had heroically beaten off 3 out of control bouncers who had unjustly pushed a vulnerable girl before he had seen red and got involved in the cause of justice.

Fred was now viewed in a new light across the Yukon and all those who has considered him an entitled little bollix were now eating their words.

Dualta said nothing, no point really. He and his colleagues knew the truth so it didn't matter until Sofia came down to the yard one spring day and began to ask some pointed questions about the night in "Provincetown". Dualta laughed it off but could see in her eyes that she knew the truth and when she touched his cheek he thought his heart might burst. They went for a long walk and talked the entire night away until they found themselves back near the main house as the sun was rising.

Dualta, "mmm, well goodnight then"

Sofia, "Yeah, night, oh for flip sake aren't you ever going to kiss me?"

Dualta, "Oh yeah, sorry, come here" he laughed nervously.

From that point onwards they became an item, inseparable. Dualta was happy but scared of what "Hank" would think and he never felt he was good enough for Sofia.

CHAPTER 15

2 FOLD TRAGEDY

DOM CONTINUED TO WORK during the day and then pick up Jude whenever he could then do a few shifts in his dad's taxi at night. Not a fantastic existence but every moment with his son made it worthwhile.

It was his mum who first told him of the story that was beginning to unfold on the UTV news.

A young lad who had been involved in the "Donegal Drowning" (as the press were now calling it) had come forward and made a statement about the incident from years ago. Now an adult he wanted to come forward and tell the truth about the events that happened on the "pier" at the Gaeltacht in Gweedore years before.

In a nutshell, the young man wanted to state that after many years of drink induced depression he had realised that now as an adult he must take responsibility and come clean about the events of that fateful night and tell everyone what actually happened.

Live from his institution where he was being treated for his alcohol and drug addiction he came forward and told that it wasn't Brother Baxter who had saved him but it was an older school boy called "Dualta" who had actually intervened and prevented the Brother (who had been grooming him) from actually molesting and assaulting him that night.

The community was stunned and shocked. The hero Brother Baxter was being exposed for what he actually was and it made Dom's blood run cold. Of course it all made sense now.

As the story unfolded it was reported that Dualta had followed the pair who were in the Brothers car on the pier when the altercation ensued. The young man reported he was in grave danger until Dualta appeared and wrestled with the Brother when they both disappeared over the walls of the pier into the dark abyss and that was the last time he saw either of them alive.

He reported that he really wanted to say something but everyone thought the Brother was a hero and he was scared to say anything without Dualta being there. He added that Dualta had been really kind to him and in his eyes he was the real HERO as he saved him from a terrible fate.

The community was rocked, there had been many whispers about Brother Baxter but no one had ever had the guts to come forward and tell the truth before. It was shocking but it was also a breakthrough.

"Oh Dualta" he screamed. "Where are you? If only you were here today"

"Where the fuck are you mate?"

The Pier (Ryan's Story)

Ryan sat petrified in the car as Brother Baxter turned off the engine. It was a windy night which had caused most other traffic off the pier but here he was with Bro Baxter, who he had never felt completely comfortable with. He knew Brother Baxter liked him but he didn't really understand why?

Sitting in the car (a Vauxhall Astra he thought) he was literally terrified as the rain beat down, the wind actually shook the small car and at one point he thought the whole car might end up over the pier and in the water, which was a scary enough thought until Brother Baxter moved closer to him and so far into his personal space he could smell his rancid breath and then he wished the car would just fall into the water, and end this nightmare.

Suddenly he heard a loud bang, thud and scream and although his eyes were closed, he realised someone was wrestling Brother Baxter out of the car and onto the pier. The two figures continued to wrestle across the pier and blows were being exchanged but it was hard for Ryan to tell as he was still terrified and could only see vague figures through the darkness and rain until all of a sudden they were both gone, and now he was ALONE.

He sat frozen until some indefinite period of time later he was lifted out of the (Astra) and carefully led into an ambulance.

CHAPTER 16

DOM CONTINUES

THIS REVELATION HAD SHAKEN him to the core but Dom couldn't have been prouder of his best friend, he actually felt guilty that he hadn't actually worked it out himself but he was still happy. He just knew Dualta was out there somewhere, it was like a sixth sense, a gut instinct that he was still alive and now he could come home as he was innocent and in fact he was the hero.

Dom was bouncing and proud, life was good, hard as always but good and Jude was growing and the biggest source of joy ever.

Dom was now working in the local Youth Support Council and putting his athletic experience to good use. Life was good and although the political climate was very volatile as the political parties tried to broker a peace deal, on the ground where existence moved on in their village things were ok. Most people hoped for peace but as long as there was no violence in their own back door for a while life was enjoyable, the sun seemed to shine more frequently and the air seemed a little bit warmer.

CHAPTER 17

SUMMER SUN

DURING THAT SUMMER HE would go to work early and get home early so he could take Jude out for the afternoon. Their favourite place was the local Lough where the local council had built a paddling pool and the kids enjoyed endless fun in the water.

He had brought a picnic and as the sun shone and he laughed between eating chicken and cheese sandwiches and of course copious amounts of crisps and chocolates, he was blissfully unaware of the time.

Dom had promised his dad he'd do the evening taxi shift but everything was just too good, too perfect between him and his son that he didn't so much forget as maybe just NOT remember.

It didn't help too much when a girl he'd been seeing for a while called "Simone" joined him and Jude. She was looking fine and her body language was giving very positive signals and what a body, she was absolutely stunning and even he thought he was "punching above his weight" just being in her company. That day on the side of the Lough could be categorised as "just perfect".

To top it all Simone invited him home to her house where Jude could play with her daughter Brenda and the perfect day continued. Well ok he still had his dad moaning about having to do the extra shift but Dom promised him he would do his next three night shifts in return. Jamesy (dad) reluctantly agreed and

Dom returned to the company of "Simone" where both the kids magically fell asleep on the living room floor and were very easily lifted up to bed and oblivion. Dom didn't waste the opportunity to take Simone in his arms and like some character out of a book, for that moment everything was as he'd always dreamed it could and should be, he didn't say it out loud but at that precise minute he thought to himself "holy feck, I think I'm in love, finally things are going well for me"

Before Dom fell asleep he felt a huge sense of contentment, maybe life was just now heading in the direction it should be, maybe his life was at a turning point, maybe, just maybe, he was going to be happy as he fell asleep with Simone in his arms.

Bang, Boom, Crash, Thud "What the fuck?" Dom startled "Bang! Bang! Bang!" on the door.

Confusion reigned as Simone hastily dressed and went to investigate the commotion.

"Excuse me miss, this is the RUC!"

"Is Dominic O'Donnell here?"

Simone, "I don't understand! What do you want with him, he's been here all night! He hasn't done anything"

RUC, "We need to speak to him urgently miss! Can you get him please"?

For fuck sake, it was one thing getting this hassle at his own house but to bring it to Simone's door was really annoying. He thought his charm offensive had been going really well and quite frankly he really liked her and the impression of a man being hunted by the Brits was certainly not the image he wanted to por-tray or indeed, he felt sure, the kind of activity Simone would want around her daughter.

He pulled on his jeans and screamed.

"I'm coming, I'm coming, for fucks sake could you not have waited until after breakfast before you start inventing charges against me?"

"Mr O'Donnell, It's your father" Dominic, "What my father? Where is he? What's wrong? Is he ok?" "Mr O'Donnell, I'm sorry to inform you but your father Mr Jamesy O'Donnell was shot last night! He's currently in ICU in Hill Hospital"

The rest of the cops words were lost on him as his mind spun and his stomach summersaulted as he thought out loud, "No, no, no, there must be a mistake, you stupid bastard! It can't be my dad, he's the most mild mannered man you could ever meet, he's from Limerick for fucks sake, why would anyone want to hurt him? He never said a cross word to anyone in his life, you're wrong, there must be a mistake"

"You're probably right, Mr O'Donnell" said the cop.

"We believe the attack was carried out by the UVF, who believed YOU were driving the taxi"

Dom felt his feet give way and he just about made it to the sofa before he collapsed. He needed to get to the hospital and oh my god, what about mum, he needed to get home.

Simone said she'd take care of Jude as he raced to the car and headed home to the flat where he was surprised to see so many people already gathered there. His mum was crying uncontrollably and he hugged her tightly but he was also impatient to get to the hospital to see his dad, hopefully speak to him, tell him how sorry he was that he hadn't worked last night, that he'd put him in the firing line (literally).

"Don't worry dad I'll do all the nightshifts from now on" "Everything will be fine dad, no worries, you'll be back out doing what you love, fishing on the river, in no time"

He practised this speech over and over as his sister drove them all to the hospital. There was a huge police presence at reception but he ran through the cordon and all but carried his mum into the lift.

"It'll be fine mum, he's ok, he's going to be fine"

BUT HE WASN'T FINE! In fact he was the opposite of fine, he was awful, he was unconscious, he had apparently a very small chance of survival but the next 48 hours would be crucial. He didn't want to leave the hospital but couldn't put Jude through this. Simone agreed to keep him for another sleepover, which

Jude was delighted about and this made him feel another bit closer to Simone.

He wandered through the hospital corridors while on a break from sitting by his dad's bed and all those horrible leads, tubes and machines, bleeping and flashing, heart rate monitor going up and down. He tried not to look but couldn't seem to look away. During this break he found the hospital oratory (which is a multi-faith kinda church place) for people to go and communicate with their God.

Dom hadn't been to Mass for years nor did he actually believe in God but he was still a devout Political Catholic so he immediately got down to some serious negotiations with the God character (as only true Catholics can).

"Now here God, wait 'til I tell you. "If you let him survive, I will go back to mass every week, I promise" "I'll be charitable and give loads of money away, I'll stop smoking or maybe drinking, just let him live and I'll do anything you want. PLEASE JUST LET HIM LIVE"

Dom told his sister to take his mum home and make her get some rest and he'd go home later and get a shower and maybe something to eat. Things seemed peaceful in the room as he watched his dad sleep and he realised the 48 critical hours were soon coming to an end, which provided some hope.

He could also have sworn his dad opened his eyes and faintly said "What the feck are you doing here?"

But maybe he imagined it. Things were really positive now so he thought he could maybe renegotiate that deal with God. Maybe do the MASS thing but not give away ALL his money? Anyway himself and God could thrash out all the "back to religion details" when dad was home, safe and sound. Yeah, maybe mass once a month, definitely once a month and he'd surely be a nicer person all round.

He was still mulling these things around when his mum and sister arrived back to the hospital and as dad was "stable" he allowed himself to be sent home for a shower and maybe a bite to eat.

He called at Simone's house but he didn't speak to Jude as it was too late but when he held Simone tightly he knew that he had a future with this girl, "note to self" he thought "she was definitely a keeper"

Was he falling in love? As he drifted into an uneasy sleep he thought he'd get more serious about Simone once dad was home and on the mend. This thought was still in his almost unconscious mind until the shrill of phone scared the shit out of his senses.

"Dom" said his sister "Dad just died. Massive heart attack, he's gone Dom"

CHAPTER 18

A WAKE

AN OUT OF BODY experience for Dom.

Only a Catholic and probably only an Irish Catholic could understand the concept of the WAKE. So in the middle of your most heart wrenching and most broken moments of your life, you don't lie down! Oh no, you hold a party.

The guest of honour arrives in a beautifully ornate wooden overcoat and we place them strategically so everyone can have a good look and say what a fantastic person they were (now they're dead)! Something they almost certainly never said to the actual person when they were ALIVE. "Doesn't he look great" and "doesn't he look like himself" are other frequently heard phrases, all complete nonsense but part of the charade.

And we don't just invite friends and family round, oh no!

We open the house to everyone, in fact we have to go to the local GAA club to borrow chairs cause we've invited so many people round we need extra seats for them to sit on, and drink tea and eat sandwiches, and there needs to be a team of relatives on shift work to supply those never ending sandwiches and treats that you never would have in your house when the "guest of honour" would have maybe fancied a wee treat during their actual "life".

But you willingly engage and talk shit to strangers, and you wonder what the fuck it's all about! Until that 3am moment when you find yourself alone in the room with the "dead body" of your loved one and you touch a frozen cold hand or an "ice like brow" and you talk to them like they're still there BUT they're not and a little bit of you now realises that come tomorrow when they close this lid they will never see or speak to you again.

CHAPTER 19

A FUNERAL

ANOTHER CATHOLIC TRADITION, THE funeral is a community event. Everyone gets a chance to carry the coffin and feel that they are a part of the grieving process and to be honest that is well welcomed. And then after we've buried our loved one in the cold dark earth we have a quick visit to the local Parish centre for soup and sandwiches (again).

Then we can relax and adjourn to the local pub where at first we will be very sad but after a few pints the atmosphere will turn into a session of crying, music, more crying and finish with the inevitable singing of IRISH rebel songs, which most in attendance won't know the words of but will energetically join in with the chorus and rest peacefully knowing Ireland has been freed once again.

CHAPTER 20

THE AFTERMATH

THE WAKE AND FUNERAL went along the predictable line of an "Irish event" and then suddenly, boom, it's over and you're expected to just go back to life, continue "as you were". But you're not the same.

Dom had gone through the "bubble" of the "wake/funeral" in a daze. If truth be told, he wasn't feeling much except numbness, yeah, that described it, NUMB. And then comes the ANGER, and in his case the GUILT.

His poor innocent dad was slaughtered by those bastards because he was a Catholic, but also because they thought he was Dominic. Why? Because he'd stood for Sinn Fein in an election, cause he was a Catholic. Because he was finally happy? Why? Why? Why?

CHAPTER 21

THE INVESTIGATION

FIRST FACT OF THE investigation was the fact the RUC knew exactly who did it! Second fact was they were never going to be found guilty or sentenced for this, the Northern Irish system of justice made it very unlikely any UVF/UDA murderer was going to stand trial as their defence bench would always contain certain church members, political representatives and last but not least, members of the good aul security forces!

His mum and sister would fight for justice but Dom knew in his heart that it would never ever come, but one alternative that had a relatively high chance of success was REVENGE. Now that didn't require the authority of the British regime, that could be served cold and served often, and that's the path he was almost blindly led down.

Over the grieving period he became so much closer to Simone, she became such a rock for him and soon they'd moved in together and he felt very at ease with her. He still couldn't talk about his feelings or any shit like that but she made it very easy to be in her company and to be honest she helped his grief more than she could ever know just by being there.

Part of him thought that Dualta would have appeared over the period of the funeral cause he would have felt and sensed his grief but he didn't, Dom often thought of his best friend and how hurt he'd be at Jamesy's death but the truth was he was gone and probably just as DEAD and soon to be forgotten by everyone else as Jamesy.

Although he knew it made sense he couldn't allow himself to believe it. He'd just lost his dad and his best friend wasn't there to help him. He was gone too but in his mind's eye he thought he'd be back. Even though realistically he knew it wouldn't happen.

Dualta, "For fuck sake ya bollix, I'm gone!"
"Move on"

CHAPTER 22

THE UNKNOWN ZONE

AUNTY META ONCE TOLD Dualta
"What you don't know doesn't hurt you"
Mmmm, "Ok old woman" thought the very young Dualta as he loudly asked his dad why Aunty Meta had a moustache. After receiving a swift slap to the back of the head, the young Dualta never thought of revisiting this scenario again.

But Aunty Meta was right, and oblivious to the pain and heartache going on at home, Dualta was beginning to find his feet and possibly a future in his NEW FOUND LAND.

Despite his fear of "Big Hank" he was continuing to see Sofia and she didn't seem any less enthused by their friendship now he was home working on the yard and not seeking his fortune on the "White Water" goldmines.

They stole whatever moments they could together but the fact he shared a bunk house with 6 transient drunkards didn't increase their chances of intimacy. Sofia lived for the most part in the city so Dualta thought after so many years it was maybe time to break the apron strings and move away from the security of "Big Hank's" yard. A great idea, only Dualta had no ID, no passport, medical records, insurance number, nothing, all was left behind in Ireland where he was a statistic, a missing person, a nothing, a phantom.

But here in Canada, he felt quite the opposite, he felt very much alive and probably for the first time, "important", well maybe not important in general but important to someone. In his case Sofia, and he also began to realise that in his years on the yard he'd made a sufficient impression on "Big Hank" that he maybe, just maybe thought he had a chance to make something with the beautiful SOFIA. So much so that they were now openly going out as a couple in the town and everyone seemed ok with that, the fact he always had his guitar and was ready to sing a few Irish rebel tunes always meant it was easier for Dualta to be more relaxed in the city.

CHAPTER 23

FLY IN THE OINTMENT

WHEN HIS GRANNY SUSAN had told him that expression, he generally thought that there was literally a little insect crawling through the medicine making it useless.

But as he had grown and developed he recognised the "metaphor" the fly is the person or thing that spoils it for everyone, the pest that wrecks good/happy times for everyone, the insects that are always there! Never important but important enough to destroy everything.

The most literal thing he now understood due to Granny Susan was that these parasites were not of the insect variety but were very much human form.

The Brother, the bullies, the British Army, the teachers, the cheaters, the liars, the wasters, all walks of society, all "flies" in Grannies ointment.

And right on cue as if Granny Susan had forebode it, here came his latest "fly in the ointment"

Fred was back from university and qualified in the "law". He'd now be taking over some of the running of the business. "Happy days" NOT!

CHAPTER 24

MYTHOLOGY

SINCE THE FIGHT IN "Provincetown" some years earlier, Fred had developed an aura and a mystique to match in the city, somewhat of a legal eagle but also someone who could fight crime if needed, a bit like a mythical character like "batman".

Mythology, "usually someone being the hero of an event, without a determinable basis of fact or explanation.

Dualta and his mates knew the facts but doubted if they would make any difference to the legend of Fred the Corporate slayer and street fighter for justice.

The myth of Fred hadn't gone unnoticed in the city and he was heralded in most quarters of the town and not least the Irish community who always love and respect a hero. The fact this particular hero had no substance became irrelevant when he proved to be a reasonably good singer and obviously a master of mimicry as he remembered a couple of Dualta's Irish songs and passed them off quite ably (it must be said) as his own.

"Oh Grace just hold me in your arms and let this moment linger, They'll take me out at dawn and I will die", Fred's singing of the classic song didn't leave a dry eye in the Irish bars around "Provincetown" and everyone knew who he was and he liked and enjoyed an notoriety that was not normally afforded to non-Irish lads who had never experienced the conflict, never been in Ireland or indeed if truth be told "didn't give one fuck about Ireland".

Anyway, Fred took advantage of his unique situation and it was working a treat in the Canadian/Irish community where "Fighting Fred" was becoming nothing less than a living legend. The girls loved him, the publicans loved him, the casinos loved him, the bookies loved him!

Credit was unlimited, "Another drink?" no problem Fred! "Another girl?" no problem Fred! "Another bet?" no problem Fred! "No problem Fred, whatever you need Fred!" "You're a hero Fred, a legend Fred!"

"More credit Fred? No problem Fred, how much?"

So when does credit run out? Probably when Fred went on the biggest bender of his life. "Do you know who I am?"

To most people it's an awkward and cringey thing to say, for some Z list celebrities it's the fuel of life for them, for those who everyone knows, there is never a need to say it, but for Fred it was just stupid, just really stupid. As he was welcomed into the back room of the casino, he was offered free drinks and hospitality that a Hollywood star would have been pleased with, but things took a turn for the worse when the door closed and Fred was led into a somewhat corporate office.

Mr X "Sit down Fred, do you wanna drink?"

Fred, "No, I'm ok, what's going on?"

Mr X, "Fred, it's just that we thought you might wanna sit down and take a breath before you do any bets tonight? You know you have credit here Fred cause you're a local celebrity and also cause we know your daddy is "Big Hank"

Fred, "Yeah, so what?"

Mr X, "Do you know what your debt is now Fred?"

Fred, "No, I'll sort it tomorrow no problem"

Mr X, "Will you Fred? Really? Cause all we see is a losing streak here Fred, can you guess how much you owe me?"

Fred, "Are you joking? We are friends. You and me are friends, you know who I am?"

Mr X, "Yeah but now we gotta get real and see we have a problem here Fred as your credit is over £25,000 so we have a major problem, unless of course you can pay this off?"

It was at that moment that Fred realised he had royally fucked up! "Oh yeah, no problem! I'll sort it next week. I just need to go home and talk to my daddy, and we'll sort it out"

Mr X, "No Freddie boy, we don't want you talking to daddy, we want you to talk to Irish and tell him we need him on board"

Fred, "Who the fuck is Irish? On board with what? What the fuck are you talking about?"

Mr X, "Go home Fred! Relax, chill, its ok! You owe us £25,000 and we need a payment like in the next two weeks or else someone is going to pay, Fred and that someone might just be you Fred or maybe your pretty sister SOFIA? It's up to you Fred, let us know"

Fred, "Oh fuck sake what is going on?"

Mr X, "We will be in touch, just make sure Irish is on board"

Fred was appalled! He was terrified he was going to be beaten up or maybe even his sister was going to be involved but to be honest he was more annoyed that he kept talking about Irish.

Fred, "Who the fuck is Irish?"

Mr X, "You know who he is, arrange a meeting ASAP or we might have to call on "Big Hank" or SOFIA".

Of course Fred knew who Irish was! That Irish dick who was always around and was a "pet" to his dad and even more to his sister! How could he be important? He hated him, also deep down he knew, he knew that it was Irish (or whatever his name was) who had done all the work on his night of infamy, and he didn't want to ever admit that.

CHAPTER 25

ONE NIGHT IN "PROVINCETOWN"

WHEN FRED ASKED DUALTA to come on a wee jolly to "Provincetown" he immediately smelt a rat. He knew no good was going to come of this.

He spoke to Sofia but she was excited that maybe they were going to bond and Fred was finally going to accept him but Dualta knew different, he knew this would never be the case.

So what did Fred want?

The evening started very awkwardly, because they definitely were not friends, so Dualta was totally on his guard.

"No shots, no drugs, keep your senses about you" he told himself.

Just a couple of beers in when the real agenda for the evening began. By this stage Fred was already off his head on whatever concoction of drink/drugs he'd been on and was totally wasted. So Dualta was pretty intrigued as to what was going to happen next. He didn't have to wait long for the answer. He was almost immediately brought through to a dull and cramped office with a bespeckled man smoking on a huge cigar and holding court in the middle.

"Nice to meet you Irish" seemed a genuine enough greeting.

"I'm sure your wondering why you're here. No worries, we just want a little chat"

"We know certain things about you and need to know if we can maybe come to an understanding?"

"You have a certain relationship with Fred here? Do you not Irish?"

Dualta, "Not really"

Mr X, "Well you may have certain attachments to other members of his family who have become, let's say precious to you, such as "Big Hank" and "Sofia". Let's just say this useless piece of shit has overstayed his welcome in our hospitality zone and we now need to call in his markers! But we would really rather not upset his lovely family so we can see a way where you might be able to help Irish, is that something you'd like to do or should we ring Sofia?"

Dualta still hadn't a clue what was going on and he just felt sick and weak kneed but he also knew enough to not give anything away, so he stood stony faced and non-committal just as he had during many interrogations at the local RUC station back home.

CHAPTER 26

THE PROPOSAL

AFTER LISTENING TO MR X for a good half hour without a break, Dualta still didn't understand what was happening. Just like back in the good old CBS days he could pretend to listen very intently and not actually take one thing in. So when a kindly soul called Rico sat down beside him and offered him a JD and coke he readily accepted and whispered,

"Rico, what the fuck is going on?"

Rico happened to be a very handsome articulate Latin guy who actually looked, dressed and spoke just like a gangster from the Godfather. So Dualta was well impressed.

"To cut a long story short" as his mum used to always say, the boss man was pissed off cause Fred owed him a lot of money and he knew he couldn't pay it back. No he didn't want to hurt Fred's family (unless he had to) but he had a plan that might solve everyone's issues. In a nutshell it went like this, "Hey Irish, do you have a passport?"

Dualta, "mmm, I dunno"

"No you don't Irish, cause you washed up on these shores outta nowhere didn't you? What you running away from Irish?"

Dualta, "I dunno what you're on about?"

"You killed that PRIEST Irish didn't you? They're going to lock you up! Throw away the key, Irish!"

Dualta, "Fuck off, you don't know what you're talking about!"

"Relax, Irish I'm on your side, I know he was a paedo, but I still need you to do me a favour"

So what was the favour?

CHAPTER 27

TREASURE ISLAND, NOT

SO THE PLAN WAS the Canadian gang were going to use their new found Irish friend to take a shipment of "weapons" to Ireland on behalf of NORAID, and smuggle those guns/weapons into the North of Ireland where they would be used to wage the war against the Brits.

While in principal Dualta had no real objections to the concept of this operation, his problem was that he didn't want to hurt "Big Hank" or "Sofia". But as was pointed out to him if he didn't do it that is exactly what would happen. As Granny Susan also said, "You're between a rock and a hard place"

"Fuck sake", he wanted to punch Fred's lights out, but of course true to character Fred had disappeared off the radar. Gun running, that's what it was called. He'd heard about it but he didn't know how it was supposed to work.

"Relax" said Rico, "You're just gonna take the ship into Irish waters, talk to anyone who asks and bluff your way through, then we're gonna get the guns to South Armagh, Belfast and Derry and then we're good and "big Hank" and "Sofia" will be fine. Look Irish, you are the only one who knows these roads and routes so that's gonna be your job" said Rico

"Holy fuck" thought Dualta, "I can't go back, I'm gonna die in prison regardless of the gun running. But if I don't go back they might hurt "Big Hank" and "Sofia" "FUCK SAKE"

After Rico left him off at his hotel room he cursed Fred and the night in Provincetown and opened a bottle of JD, it only helped so much in that it knocked him out.

"We'll be in touch soon" were the last words he'd remembered before Rico left him to his JD induced coma. So what next? He was actually not surprised when the phone rang the next morning and despite wanting to hurl he clearly heard the words from Rico "You ready for a voyage to treasure island Irish?"

The sound of laughter didn't help the sick feeling in the pit of his stomach.

"Ah bollix"

CHAPTER 28

BACK IN IRELAND

COMING INTO DUN LAOGHAIRE Pier was an awesome sight for Dualta, he had been there once before to catch a ferry on a family holiday to visit his uncle and family in London and the whole adventure was absolutely amazing. He had heard about Disneyland but to him the Port with all its lights and a hive of activity at night time was amazing.

It was all about the pride he felt in being Irish and the wonder of the land he came from. In truth he hadn't wanted to come home and although he desperately missed his family and his soulmate Dom, he had found peace and happiness in Canada with Sofia. Being so close to his home town now made him ache to see his family and friend again but he was scared of what might happen to him if he was found.

The Landing

But obviously they weren't going to land on Dun Laoghaire Pier and be embraced by family and friends. They would be sailing far down the coast to dump off their cargo of death on to the soil of a beautiful troubled nation that needed anything but their delivery of destruction. Despite not having smoked in months Dualta lit up a cigarette and with his head in his hands he thought "Why does it have to be so hard?"

Just as he heard the yell, "Here Irish, you're home now, we going for a drink?"

Although anger was normally his first response with these morons, right now in his own environment, he felt sorry for these stupid mercenaries. They had no home, no loyalty, no heritage, no identity. They were in his homeland now but they were ambivalent to it all, their strength available to anyone for the price of an extra Zero in their bank account.

"Surely there has to be more to life than that" thought Dualta. But soon the trawler was well past the bright lights of Dun Laoghaire and being beckoned onto the much more diminutive and much less grand surrounding of Dunleer, County Louth. Dualta doubted if the ship would actually be able to dock such was the size of the Pier but after several heavy thuds he realised they had come to a very welcome STOP. He was still thinking of his love for Sofia and his anguish at not being able to see his family and the quandary it left him in, when the boat bounced recklessly off the harbour wall and he was left spread-eagled across the deck.

CHAPTER 29

DOM "ASU"

AS DOMINIC LAY IN the ditch holding his breath, he wondered if he would ever be able to exhale again or would he just pass out. His ASU (Active Service Unit) were in position to ambush a patrol near the border close to an old farm that had long since ceased to be productive.

Although it was May, he was freezing. The lazy sunrise had given way to a heavy dew on the grass and he felt the damp chill go through him but the nerves and the tight grip on the Armalite rifle he was cradling kept him from focusing on the cold.

Since he had volunteered he had mostly been doing reconnaissance and intelligence missions but now was his chance to prove he could handle the actual field engagement part of the struggle.

There was no turning back now, when the target came into sight he would pull the trigger, or would he? He hoped he would. Sure it was only a Brit soldier and he had long since de-humanised them as foreign pawns unjustly occupying his land.

In his own mind he had tried the peaceful approach but it had led him down the wrong path and ultimately got his father killed, so what other option or choice did he have? He knew the only way this could end now was through military action and if that meant him shooting his target then so be it, a nameless, faceless target would not weigh heavy on his conscience. After 800 years of tyranny, anyone who dons the uniform of the British army can expect the full wrath of the Republican forces.

CHAPTER 30

BOOM BOOM CRASH

WHAT HE WASN'T EXPECTING was the noise and confusion, panic and fear of an actual war situation. Practice manoeuvres in the local mountains were very taxing and strenuous but now this was real, "Holy fuck", "I'm an inch from being shot here"

His first reaction was to run, to hide, to crawl away and survive but he had to focus, breath, survey and assess his situation, remember the training.

With his heart pounding he returned to the lip of the ditch to see if he could get a visual on what was happening.

In the downlight he could see, actually fucking see bullets being fired in each direction. A further recon revealed a few lifeless bodies on the lush green meadows. In the scene of devastation unfolding before him, it was very difficult to tell who they were, He sat back on the mound of earth beneath him and breathed deep, nothing had prepared him for this action but he knew in this moment it was all or nothing he had to do what he had to do, he slowly turned and moved up the bank, coiling like a snake with the Armalite his potent and poisonous fangs. Now in position he actually had a clear view of the situation, to his surprise he seemed to be on the periphery of the main battle due in more part to luck rather than any sense of actual battle tactics, and his surprise turned to astonishment when he saw a British soldier walking at a 90 degree angle away from him but large as life and an absolutely huge target. He raised the Armalite and took aim, he fleetingly thought the young soldier resembled a young black midfielder he'd met and bonded with in London when he'd gone for the football trials but that was irrelevant now as he took aim and pulled the trigger. He was actually blown back into the ditch from the power of the shots but when he summed up the strength and courage to get back up to the lip of the ditch he clearly saw the young Brit was down on the ground and wasn't moving.

He must have sat down and waited for (what seemed like an eternity) but probably 10 minutes before cramp and a complete inward panic caused him to stir and survey the devastation before him.

ASU's comprised of four active volunteers so his first objective were to account for their whereabouts. First he crawled and hunched towards the epicentre of the conflict and counted 1, 2, 3 lifeless bodies before he witnessed his own handy work in the form of the dead body of his young target, bingo, result! Now to find his comrades? Unfortunately, two of them were also lifeless but he did find another comrade and together they made the decision to get the "fuck out of here" as there could be another patrol of Brits in the area.

Time now to get rid of the evidence. When he got home he scrubbed the stink and stench of the ditch away with a long hot shower and he contemplated his first active duty, and to his surprise he felt, nothing! He'd just shot another human being but he was a British soldier, so he felt nothing. "How many people have been killed by them" he thought. Now Dom had been a Catholic, an altar boy and a pupil of the Christian Brothers, guilt was his best qualification, every Catholic child in Ireland has a degree in GUILT. Dom felt guilty about everything he'd ever done from drinking and smoking at 13 to taking a young girl out the back of the parish centre after the local disco, to not doing his homework and cheating on exams and mitching school and lying to his mum about where he was staying at night while pretending to go to the cinema, the list goes on and on. But now, after breaking the biggest of all the Catholic commandments, he didn't feel guilt or remorse, he felt NOTHING. Now he was a soldier and it was "them or us".

The deaths of the two active volunteers had decimated the unit but Dom has been informed there were more volunteers ready to take their place and they were expecting a large shipment of weapons from North America that would get them back on the offensive as soon as possible. Also with the two fatalities Dom would now have to lead his ASU, a promotion that was totally unwarranted but necessary in the situation and this new direction filled Dom with a sense of purpose. The fact he'd seen active duty was really irrelevant as he also knew the panic and fear that accompanied such incidents but being a keen student of history he also thought it might be time to think differently.

He loved the stories of Vietnam that he'd learned and how the biggest army in the world had been brought to their knees by a well organised and determined guerrilla army, in the form of the VIETCONG. He didn't know all the details as Dualta would but he thought his best friend would be proud of him now if only he was around to see what he was achieving. But Dualta wasn't here so he'd have to do it without him. He missed Dualta and to be honest he was a different person now Dualta was gone, but he had learned enough to know that his path was laid out in front of him. It wasn't a step taken lightly and he knew the consequences of his commitment to the cause would mean less time spent with Jude and virtually no time spent with Simone, which would be a huge pity as he really liked her and could definitely see a future with her but he was in too deep now and it wouldn't be fair to drag her in with him. Perhaps if they could escalate the war against the occupier then they would bring them to their knees and broker a peace deal and he would reignite his passion with Simone but these fanciful thoughts were soon put out of his head by the stark and terrifying reality that he was now a soldier and a leader.

At the local meeting of the organisation he was introduced to his two new ASU members and admired their determination. They were totally ready to engage the enemy again, and plus there was the new shipment of weapons coming in from North America. Once they had those they would strike a real blow at the heart of British power and shock them to their roots. At that moment he remembered when himself and his best friend had taken on the local school bullies in a stand up fight in the local town and won, their destiny was sealed that day, just tragic that Dualta wasn't here to join him in this campaign.

CHAPTER 31

RETURN OF THE NATIVE

LIKE A PAGE FROM a novel, Dualta landed on the coast of Ireland in the early hours of a May morning, he couldn't help but notice the stunning and beautiful coast and on a sunny morning like this there wasn't anywhere better to be (and that included his adopted country of choice Canada).

One thing he had learned was that both countries had merits. He'd never ever questioned the love he had for his native land before but now he felt a strange attraction and pull towards his homeland and to his eternal shock that wasn't Ireland, it was Canada. He'd seen the beauty of both countries and that was fine but what made the heart pull to one or the other? He'd questioned that for a long time now, if truth be told he would never have chosen to come back here but now although he recognized his homeland something was missing, it was Sofia and at that moment he realised he loved her and it didn't matter where he was, Ireland, Canada, the North Pole or 10,000 meters under the sea it was all irrelevant if you weren't with the person you loved. Love was what gave meaning to your life.

Yes Dualta had Dominic and a few mates but he'd never had much of a home life and now for once he had everything he'd ever wanted in Canada. He felt a bit disloyal to the essence of Irishness, on which he'd built the foundations of his whole life but here he was being confronted with a whole new reality. That he wanted to go back to Sofia and not exactly forget about Ireland but deal with the fact his future now lay elsewhere. His only regret would be never seeing Dom and his family again but he was sure Dom had moved on and his family would survive without him.

These thoughts were all still swirling round his head when the boat docked and the crew started to unload the lethal cargo of bombs, guns and bullets into waiting trucks. The operation seemed to be going very smoothly and on time to the extent that Dualta began to relax and chill for the first time in months.

"Soon this will be over and I'll be back home with Sofia".

The fact he'd even said "back home" shocked him but in truth that is what his heart felt. But his comfort and peace was shattered by the screams of fear, gunshots and sirens as he realised they were caught, the police were all over the pier, the beach, the landing, it didn't take a genius to work out they were sailing into a trap, a set up.

"Oh fuck, you bollix"

He knew immediately who the mole was!

When they'd suggested bringing Fred on this journey he had his doubts but he did it because he was Sofia's brother and he felt obliged to try and keep him alive. Big Hank had saved his life so he felt he owed him some pay back, but right now in the heat of this battle he saw Fred with his hands up running towards the Garda siochana and trying to save his own miserable life, his miserable pathetic existence at the expense of everyone on the trawler. With those thoughts pushed to the back of his mind, he focused on his current predicament and how he was going to get out of it!

Although he hated water, he soon realised his only option was to jump over the side and swim like fuck, thankfully he was still alive when he finally breathlessly reached the surface and desperately swam towards the nearest rock he could just vaguely see. Although he was exhausted he reached the shore quickly enough and hid behind the biggest outcrop of rock he could see. Shivering and confused he just lay there and drifted in and out of a sort of semi dream state.

"That rat Fred" had betrayed the mission, the evidence was clear from his own visual memory! Was he surprised or disappointed, no! He was totally in possession of all the facts, the betrayal wasn't a surprise, what shocked Dualta was that Fred had betrayed the Canadian crime gang. He didn't imagine that they would take too kindly to that and Fred was probably a dead man walking, if he ever made his way back to Canada, But he couldn't worry about that now, he needed to get out of here and he needed to do it quickly. He moved South along the shore as far as he safely could until he saw a caravan park on the beach in the distance. His mind began to race, "It's May, so the season hasn't really started" he thought, so there are bound to be empty caravans where he could hold up and rest, possibly even think of a plan.

As he went from caravan to caravan he noticed how desolate the place was! Beautiful, fantastic, but desolate!

Finally, he found a window he could open and climbed through it, slumping on the master bedroom floor and crawling on to the double bed where he closed his eyes and let himself drift off for a moment. When he startled to life again it was only due to fact he was frozen and soaked through. He quickly undressed and began to search the caravan for resources. Other than a couple of blankets, it was empty, which was obviously expected during the off season but the heat was working and there was an electric shower which he availed of gratefully. Wrapped in a woolly blanket he scrutinised his view out the living room window and noticed a lot of sole, elderly dog walkers on the beach. Maybe he could just about get out of here unnoticed. He thought of Sofia and how all this would affect their relationship and it scared him how angry she might be but at least he knew her and Hank would be safe now as Fred's betrayal had surely signed his death warrant and his death would be the end of his debt.

CHAPTER 32

BORDER PATROL

DOM AND HIS ASU had been on high alert all week. They knew the shipment was due to arrive but due to communication difficulties they didn't know what time or the exact place so the coast between Gyles' Quay and Dunleer was their hunting ground until further notice.

After completing six missions without loss of any volunteers and with a few successful targets taken out Dom was now a unit leader with responsibility for four ASU's. His new found responsibility didn't weigh heavily on his shoulders but rather gave him a sense of purpose and direction in his life. His relationship with his girlfriend and son had suffered greatly as he had suspected they would when he chose this path but he didn't really have a choice, he was a freedom fighter now and that would require all of his attention. He could no longer suffer fools gladly and his temper was quick to rise in normal circumstances but in the field of action he was calm, intelligent and focused. He was also now cold and emotionless, a persona he needed to survive in his new environment and he had decided that walking away from his potential soulmate Simone was the best course of action for all concerned.

He told himself "Gladiators have no friends"

Operations became routine and he became an expert at pulling a trigger or exploding a device without thinking and being totally emotionally remote.

This latest mission to bring the lorry up to Clogherhead in Co Louth and pick up a shipment of arms would actually be a very easy day at the office and would furnish him and his ASU with the capability of waging war on the British with an increased intensity.

It was only on the carriageway outside of the town that he remembered going to this seaside paradise as a young lad with Dualta and all the lads and spending the best four days of their lives in a huge tent, drinking beer and chasing girls and generally having the best time of their youth.

CHAPTER 33

DUALTA REMEMBERS

AFTER BREAKING INTO AN old lads caravan and stealing his "Sunday best outfit" Dualta walked carefully into the town and the shock was as real as a slap in the face when he realised courtesy of a street sign that he was entering "Clogherhead"

He knew he was in the vicinity but being here brought very real emotions and memories up of Dominic and all the lads having such good times here, spending four blissful days in a huge tent drinking and laughing the days away.

As he walked through the deserted town he searched for the "Ripe chestnut" pub, where himself and the lads had celebrated a big football championship win of their youth but his inward smile was soon halted by the scream of a patrol car siren just a few streets away. Quickly he flung himself into the nearest alleyway and brought himself back to reality with a thud.

"You bollix" he thought.

He'd been so in love with his Irish nationalism that he had convinced himself that that was all that mattered but if he had only followed Dom's thinking on life he'd have enjoyed it much more and been so much more relaxed, like Dom was. He wondered what Dom was doing this fine morning and hoped he was enjoying life but reality brought him back to earth yet again when another siren bombed past the building next to him. As luck would have it the one shop that was open was the local charity shop "Aid for Romania" and within its confines he managed to kit himself out for the reasonably priced swap of a garden hose which he had requisitioned from an empty caravan on the way up the town. Stopping off to borrow a few pints of milk he was back in the caravan, but what now? He quickly evaluated his situation and the prospect was a frightening.

He was on the run, branded a terrorist.

He would probably lose the greatest girl he had ever met and his soulmate.

He was penniless. He was in relatively strange territory. He was hungry and tired. He was wanted for murder at home. He was fucked.

"You bollix" he thought as he downed a half litre of vodka he'd found in a cupboard in the caravan that had now become his home.

CHAPTER 34

NOT RETREAT BUT TACTICAL WITHDRAWAL

DOM QUICKLY SAW THE situation was above their job description, this was the work of a tout, they'd been set up, it was a trap. The Irish Republican movement had always been riddled with paid spies and informers but he was 100% positive it wasn't any of his colleagues, so the rat must have come from the other side. Anyway he couldn't dwell on that now. In this situation there was only one sensible course of action, get away! They could fight, die, have a hero's funeral and be quickly forgotten but he thought it would be much more productive to simply get away.

So he gathered his ASU and told them to take the lorry to Dundalk and burn it ASAP, he himself would stay and observe for a while. So when the others had departed and he was left on his own he prowled that backstreets of Clogherhead and couldn't help but laugh as he crawled around the "Ripe Chestnut" and remembered the great time him and Dualta and the rest of the lads had before his life became crazy! He felt lucky enough that the local town was still relatively deserted in the early hours and the early season, in fact the only person he saw was an elderly man dressed in what he could only assume were clothes from a local charity shop. The old man was acting quite strangely but he dismissed it and began to formulate an escape plan.

CHAPTER 35

GO SOUTH DUALTA

HE COULDN'T GO NORTH (or he'd be arrested for murder) so his only option was to head South, he'd get to Dublin and make his way to London, get a flight back to Canada and leave it all behind, sound plan. He still was not sure what he would tell Sofia about where he had been but a quick analysis of his options left him thinking the truth might be the best way forward. He doubted Fred would ever get to invent any lies against him so the truth would be his salvation or downfall depending on her reaction. The worst thing that could happen to him now is that he would lose her, so his plan had to revolve around getting back to her and rolling the dice on him telling the truth and her potentially accepting it .

CHAPTER 36

GO EAST DOMINIC

WHEN DOM FINALLY GOT to a safe place on the Avenue Road in Dundalk he called HQ and relayed the events of the morning but he was not met with the sympathetic voice he might have expected. He was told to report to an address in Dundalk and await further instructions. It always annoyed him that although it was himself and his colleagues out in the field, taking the risks, he always felt judged by the "The voice on the end of the phone". He could not help but wonder how often the "voice" had ever been out on active duty. Somehow, he doubted it. However, in life there are those that sit behind a phone and order others to do things they would never do themselves. Then, there were leaders who get out there and no matter how scared or worried they themselves are, they never show it and they lead by example never ever asking their colleagues to do something they wouldn't do and taking the first and biggest risks themselves. However, he quickly shoved these thoughts away thinking one day he might meet "voice" in person and explain his feelings on it personally. He was still mulling over what that meeting would potentially go like, when the lorry driver he had managed to flag down dropped him off in the centre of Dundalk town.

It just so happened his safe house he had been directed to was very near to an old flame and although he knew he shouldn't have, he couldn't resist paying a little visit to a girl he remembered with extreme fondness. Anyway, he was certainly glad he enjoyed this distraction as he was told the next day to get on board the next ferry bound for London.

CHAPTER 37

LONDON CALLING –
A STRANGE PLACE

WHEN YOU NEED TO disappear off the face of the earth there really couldn't be a better place to do it than London. London is huge, sprawling, cosmopolitan and vibrant but it's also dark, concrete and oppressive. London is the Promised Land but is also the biggest graveyard for hopes, dreams and aspirations. Dualta soon realised he was invisible. A bedsit in Plaistow and a labouring job down at the docks kept a few quid coming in and he found with his Irish accent his English neighbours of all colours and creeds avoided him like the "plague". A few months and he'd have enough money to buy a plane ticket back to Canada and he could put this nightmare behind him.

The daily grind in London was exhausting, up at 5am, walk to the underground, catch the train from a crowded platform and make three train changes before work which started at 7am. He found it strange that a lot of men he saw on the tube and trains who were dressed in suits and carrying briefcases often arrived on his building site only to change into work clothes and become a tradesman or labourer for the day, but each to their own as his mum would say. Life became mundane but he needed to keep a low profile, head down, save and get his ticket out of there and back to the life he loved and wanted back.

One morning he felt particularly cheery, for some unknown reason and he actually spoke to his afro Caribbean neighbour. To his shock and dismay he was immediately met with a "Fuck off Irish". Which, to be honest, he found strange, as he really thought he might find common ground with a fellow ethnic minority but perhaps she had been in England too long and now saw bad manners as acceptable, he mused.

He tried to be positive but it was hard being so isolated and alone. On the walk from the job to the train from work he noticed an Irish pub and often thought how nice it might be to just go in once, for a few pints and talk to someone from home, but he couldn't risk it. Better to just keep the head down and not arouse any suspicion. He worked, ate, slept and repeated until he nearly had the price of the coveted ticket back to Canada, he often wanted to ring Sofia but he daren't for her sake more than his. He wanted to learn more of Fred's fate before he could begin to tell his truth. But it was so lonely.

One Friday as he was finishing work on the site a work colleague tackled him "What's your problem lad?" in a very unmistakably Irish accent.

"Nothing" replied Dualta

"Since when does an Irish lad not speak to his own kind?" replied the accent he presumed was from at least as far south of Ireland as Kildare, definitely below Dublin anyway.

"Look, we don't give a fuck who you are or what you're hiding from lad but for fuck sake, we can't see you being so miserable here every day! Come out with us and have a drink tonight, no questions asked, the offer is always there lad just don't think you don't always have friends here "even if we are behind enemy lines "he laughed.

Dualta was stunned not by the gracious offer of unsolicited camaraderie, as that is a given for all Irish natives worldwide, but the fact he had been noticed, when he thought he was keeping a very low profile being invisible.

"Oh Bollix"

Dualta thought about the offer for a few weeks but dismissed it every Friday on the grounds that he probably shouldn't but Jesus he was so lonely in that one room bedsit, but what if he met someone from home? He couldn't justify the risk of being caught for a few hours of fun.

His existence followed a mundane pattern with total focus on that air fare to Canada and a reunion with Sofia keeping him going in his dark hours. He wished he could phone her but knew he shouldn't until he knew the whole picture of what she knew.

He had considered ringing Sofia again but he thought it would be best to leave it until he was at least at the airport. The doubt had crept in.

"Did she really love him, like he did her?" "Would she wait for him?"

"Had she moved on?"

"Has Fred survived and poisoned her against him?"

The doubts swirling round his head actually hurt sometimes. When those thoughts get ingrained in your head, they won't leave, won't leave you alone, won't let you sleep, it was constant, but he still had to get up and get out to work.

As the bottom of the workforce hierarchy it was the Irish and black labourers who were ordered to the most back breaking and menial jobs on any building site. The work was hard and exhausting and very dangerous, Dualta often wondered if they had ever heard of health and safety in any of these jobs but then again if they had it would be reserved for those well above his pay grade and station in life.

In the words of Christy Moore who had so eloquently put into words and music the plight of the Irish.

"In 1986 there's not much for a Paddy but swinging a pick or lifting the brick"

Dualta felt like an extra in one of Christy's songs as he worked and toiled in the dirt and muck of the foundations of what would soon become another sky scraper in London's affluent docklands area. When the awards were presented to the architects and engineers at the plush Hilton Hotel ceremonies, there wouldn't be any of the labourers present. The thought of it was quite funny.

On the next journey into work he was still thinking about it when his new found Kildare mate caught his eye on the last train into work. "It's Friday lad, you finally going to come out after work for a drink?" he shouted over the heavy throng of the packed train.

CHAPTER 3 8

A DAY TO END ALL DAYS

"MAYBE I JUST WILL" Laughed Dualta as he struggled to hold on to the handrail as the train lurched forward again.

On arrival at the site Dualta's alarm bells were on red alert straight away. The foundation was huge, at least 20 or 30 feet deep and there were absolutely NO safety precautions being taken, the shuttering on each side of the trench was (at best) bolted together very tenuously.

Working down there Dualta could actually hear the creeks, moans and shifts of the barely secure wood as gallons upon gallons of liquid concrete were poured into the shuttering. It was very claustrophobic and stifling down in the bowels of this building but increasingly it was terrifying working in an environment where you were only a moment away from tragedy.

***

Over the coming weeks in hospital, he wasn't exactly sure of what happened but he did remember the fear was present quite a while before it happened.

The rivets in the shuttering were probably the size of a grown man's fist. On that morning the moans and groans of shifting timber were different than other days, it seemed to be almost screaming to the men "get out, get out!" The atmosphere was palpable; no one was comfortable. Dualta was working in the hole with Matus and Bartek who without getting over friendly with had been the mainstays of his shift and the lads he felt closest to in this environment.

His memory of the first explosion was pretty straight forward. It reminded him of a time when he had been sitting in a doctor's waiting room opposite a very fat man wearing a tight fitting shirt (not a pleasant sight) but Dualta had thought frivolously, "If that man breaths out, that button will burst and it'll have my eye out".

But today the fat man was replaced with a 60x40 foot sheet of wood shuttering and the button was a rivet the size of a fist.

***

Back in the foundations on that fateful day the mood was so sombre with an air of foreboding. The noises, creaks, cracks, strains and moans were almost prophetic. The noise was scary enough but when the shuttering started to actually rumble, 30 men down in the foundation trench had exactly the same thought, get out of here now.

Dualta looked to the possible escape routes and they consisted of two rickety ladders and a broken cherry picker that was stuck in an extended position (thankfully). And that's how it was when the shuttering finally yielded its pressurised load just like the fat man's shirt in the doctor's surgery it burst out like a barrage from an Armalite rifle and instead of taking Dualta's eye out it took Bartok's head clean off his shoulders. For a split second time stood still and Dualta wondered "How the fuck can one wee head contain so much blood and guts?"

He was still wondering how far all the innards could actually reach to when he quickly came to his senses and realised the shuttering had all burst and were flooding the foundations with rubble, liquid concrete and earth. Very soon they would be completely buried beneath this capitalist concoction of cheap industry and corner cutting. It was really just a situation of survival, most lads still alive at this stage were forming a very disorderly queue for the two rickety ladders but Dualta thought his best chance might be trying to scale the disused cherry picker. The climb might be more difficult but thinking time was of the essence and was pushing him totally in this direction. But the cherry picker was not designed to have desperate workers using it as an escape valve and while Dualta was making great headway towards the surface the cherry picker crashed downwards and all on board had a toll free roller coaster thrill right down to the sodding earth below. Thankfully the feeling of fear was quite fleeting and the next step was oblivion. Maybe that's what it's like when you die? Nothing, blackness, darkness and then suddenly Dualta was awake covered by bright, white, over starched sheets. He thought he might be in the afterlife until he realised he didn't believe in an afterlife and that he was actually in a hospital.

"Oh bollix"

"Carnage" that's a strange word mused Dualta, but it totally described the scene down in the foundations when the shuttering burst, flying debris, wood, metal and concrete everywhere. This was how the news reported it, apparently four were dead and twenty six were in hospital experiencing differing degrees of suffering.

His suffering amounted to stiches, bruises, soreness and a blinding headache but compared to Bartek, whose head was now a permanent fixture in the foundations and earth of the latest sky scraper, he was remarkably ok.

On his first day able to leave his bed he found Matus in the next ward. His right arm had been severed above the elbow and his hip had been snapped in almost a straight line. So walking was going to be a struggle for the foreseeable future. Matus would never labour again, so no money would be going home to Poland and his wife and kids would go hungry. There was no insurance for an illegal immigrant. Such an unfair system when the large companies would soon move into their nice, shiny new offices but no one would remember Matus, Bartek or even himself, when that happened. Dualta surmised the empires of the world were built off the blood and tears of the working class and their lives didn't really matter, and for the first time in a few years he was annoyed and felt anger. He was really pissed off that the "system" meant some lives were unimportant while others were precious, all depending on how big your bank balance was. Surely that shouldn't be the root of everything? But the more he thought about it, yes it was.

He had to stay in hospital for a few days and then he stayed for a couple more to help support Matus, who had nowhere to go now Bartek was dead and gone as was his bedsit in which Matus was an unregistered guest. His gut reaction was he'd have to bring Matus back to his flat and at least put a roof over his head. His good intentions were still intact when he arrived back to his now home and was met by a red letter from the landlord saying he was in arrears with the rent, "I'm sure he'll realise I was in the docklands disaster and would give him some leeway on the rent". NO, NO, NO, NO, NO. No money, no rent, no bedsit. The landlord gave him a week to get out. Where was he going to go? What would he do? He had nowhere near the money for the flight and he was still too scared to ring Sofia, (oh he longed to ring her and tell her where he was and how much he missed her, but it was too dangerous). What if the mob were still considering her a target? What if they were annoyed about the botched gun running? He felt confident they wouldn't take it out on Sofia as long as he was still at large and then when he got back to Canada he would sort it all out and everything would be ok, he didn't want to think of any other scenario.

But then there was Matus, he needed him, he had nowhere to go and no one else to rely on. Matus was going to be released from hospital and Dualta needed to take care of him but he was going to be evicted so neither of them had a place to call home.

CHAPTER 39

WAR ON ENGLAND

DOMINIC UNDERSTOOD THE REASON behind escalating the war in England. They believed that such bombing would help create a demand among the British public for their government to withdraw from Ireland. The principle was sound, "bomb them into submission." The theory was flawless, however the practicality of the bombing was that those volunteers planting the bombs were almost certain to kill innocent people, possibly even children and this was extremely hard to reconcile in Dominic's mind. He had no problem shooting British soldiers or bombing security force members but bombing shops and pubs was a necessary but none the less evil enterprise. Best not to think about it too much and just get it done.

The practical aspects of working in London also meant that the minute himself or one of the ASU spoke then everyone knew they were Irish and that carried a huge deal of suspicion so best to keep your eyes open and your mouth shut and have no communication with anyone that wasn't relevant to the mission, which is quite difficult when you need to eat or drink. Just being Irish had the potential to get you arrested under the "prevention of terrorism act" so they had to be on their guard constantly. English justice had no sympathy for anyone suspected of being in the IRA with even suspicion of that getting you 15 years in Brixton prison with your guilt or innocence being irrelevant.

Their target was a large corporate tower block being constructed in the docklands area. The plan was to get in, plant the device and make their getaway so they would be long gone by the time the bomb exploded. Dominic was delighted it was a corporate target and as long as they were able to give a one hour warning the building could be evacuated and there would be no casualties which made this type of mission much easier on the conscience. Getting in was proving to be the problem on this particular job as security was water tight and there had been some sort of accident in the foundations of one wing resulting in a couple of workers deaths so everything was in lockdown.

Their reconnaissance showed that the workers entered through a heavily manned mobile hut and each had a photo ID lanyard round their necks. But the security guards didn't always check the ID's and sometimes there was just a nod of recognition. This was perfect, the guards were getting lax and not following their proper security protocols and that's just the opportunity the ASU would need to get inside.

The IED (improvised explosive device) could be easily enough assembled with the switch, fuse, container and power source easily obtained. The problem was acquiring and carrying the explosives which was the dangerous parts of the mission. Their contact for the supply of this meant a long and arduous trek across London on the underground which had its own risks. They needed to travel separately and be very vigilant and then there was the storage of the explosives until the IED could be assembled. For this they needed to find somewhere disused, abandoned but with a potential electric source that could still be used or fed into. They looked around warehouses and old shipyard areas and found a few potential sites where they could store and assemble their deadly calling card.

CHAPTER 40

"LET ME TAKE YOU BY THE HAND AND LEAD YOU THROUGH THE STREETS OF LONDON"

"NO BLACKS, NO DOGS, no Irish"

Well, to that old adage you could add "No Poles" as Dualta and Matus tried unsuccessfully to barter some accommodation for a couple of nights, Matus still couldn't work so they had only Dualta's wages and savings to live on and that was rapidly running out so the accommodation's viewed recently had been squats and abandoned buildings. They were heading to one such building when they stopped at an all- night café for a warm cup of tea before they bedded down for the night. As they left the café Dualta saw a wad of cash lying on the ground tied up in an elastic band. There must have been hundreds of pounds there and to be honest he was very tempted to put it in his pocket and walk on but then he thought of the poor fella that must have lost it going home to his wife and kids without his hard earned cash and maybe them having to starve for a week, so he instinctively walked back into the café and asked did anyone drop a bundle of cash.

"Yeah I fucking did you thieving bastard. Give me that" said a brash cockney as he snapped it out of Dualta's hand.

"You see that, you Irish prick" he roared in the most arrogant East End accent ever.

"That's nothing to me, I earn that in an hour, I can spend that in one night and not give a fuck. I'm loaded you pathetic Irish shit" he laughed as he took off a £20 note from the wad and threw it at Dualta.

"Here go and buy a Guinness, you Irish prick"

"Oh bollix" thought Dualta. He realised he was now going to hit this moron but would have little support from Matus and he has three mates with him, when an accent he remembered spoke up from behind his head.

"Who the fuck are you calling an Irish prick?"

He had no opportunity to investigate the source of the accent before "loadsa money" was getting punched repeatedly in his smug face and Dualta joined in gladly using rights, lefts and uppercuts and a few boots to be honest against anyone with an English accent who was standing with this cockney bollix.

It wasn't until the fight subsided that he was able to source the origin of that recognisable accent and then his world stood still.

Time froze, he didn't think he would ever be able to take a breath again, but it came and allowed him to utter a word to his equally shocked, avenging saviour.

"Dominic? "Dualta?"

And time stood still.

CHAPTER 4 1

REUNION

CONFUSION MUST HAVE BEEN the outstanding reaction to the inhabitants of that café as the two Irish lads, after beating the shit out of four cockney assholes, were standing embracing and crying for what seemed like an eternity, until the moment was punctuated by one of the gang Seán Óg.

"What the fuck is going on?"

"We better get out of here before the cops come"

At that Dominic shouted, "Come on with us"

Dualta paused, "What about him?" pointing to Matus "Who the fuck is he?"

"Come on then both of you, we have got to get out of here!"

The five made their way through back streets and alleyways until they came to a small 2 bedroom terrace house which had long seen better days and no one spoke until they were inside and the door safely locked behind them.

Matus was beginning to suspect there was more to his Irish friend "Doolta" than he had realised. Dualta was beginning to suspect Dominic's hurried demeanour and desperation to get away was not merely to do with a bit of a punch up with a cocky cockney.

The house was sparsely decorated and really only had make-shift beds and chairs. Dualta knew enough to know this was a safe house but why was Dominic here and who were the two quiet men that took orders without question? But Dualta realised he had a lot of explaining to do himself. As Dominic asked the two lads to give them a bit of space and Dualta told Matus to look upstairs and find a bed where he could have a much appreciated rest.

Finally, the two friends were alone and with so much to talk about, neither knew where to begin.

CHAPTER 42

DOMINIC'S VIEW

"I THOUGHT YOU WERE dead" he said almost immediately.

The pause was palpable, he thought he was angry but if the truth was to be told he was just so happy to be with his friend again it didn't really matter. For anyone who's ever had a real best friend they'll understand that it's not really about quantity, it's all about quality. But he wasn't about to let Dualta off totally scot free so he asked as aggressively as he could manage.

"Where the fuck have you been?"

So Dualta spoke in detail about how he killed the Christian Brother and how he was suddenly on the boat and the confusion and how he'd ended up in Canada, and his new life, his changing opinions and philosophies and falling in love with Sofia and wanting to stay there but being forced into coming back and joining the gun run escapade and how the wee shite had touted and got them all nearly caught and how he didn't know where they were now and what was going to happen to him and whether his choice was to be jailed for murder in Ireland or shot by the Canadian mafia?

He barely drew breath for about an hour and probably hadn't even told the whole story.

"Holy fuck" thought Dominic, that was a lot to take in but he felt he had to interrupt him and explain.

"You didn't murder the old bastard! You stopped his fucking paedophile plan" he screamed. "Everyone thinks you are an absolute hero"

"Oh for fuck sake Dualta, for once it's you whose the bollix"

"We had a remembrance service for you after we found out, it was all over the news and papers"

Dominic explained "But that was when everyone thought you were dead and although I heard it I never really deep down believed it was true" he paused for a moment "Cause I knew deep down inside if you had really been dead I would have felt it" and again the friends embraced, being apart for so many years doesn't stop your best friend being your best friend.

CHAPTER 4 3

DUALTA'S VIEW

WHEN HE WAS LISTENING to Dominic speak he felt an overwhelming sense of grief and guilt. How could he have spent so long away and not really thought about how much it would affect his loved ones.

Obviously he was relieved he wasn't going to be jailed for murder and the paedo had got what he deserved but he was hugely guilty about not at least trying to contact home and tell them he was ok and he felt very close to Dom now probably closer than ever knowing what he had put him through.

And when Dominic recounted the years gone past and how his dad had been shot and how he had failed in his sporting career and failed in his political career and also his personal life where he had lost his love and family and how life had pretty much kicked the shit out of him Dualta felt huge regret and loss at what he had done to his best friend. This wouldn't have happened if I'd been there, he thought.

The friends drank and talked and sometimes cried, all night till they were rudely interrupted by Seán Óg who burst into the room saying

"We need to go Dom"

"Go where?" said Dualta and it occurred to him at that point that they had talked about literally everything except what Dom was now doing in London with these two quiet lads.

"Where do you need to go?" ventured Dualta

"Ah never worry mate, just something we have to pick up, it's fine" continued Dom.

"What are you lads going to do today?" Dom said in a bit of a patronising way.

"Sure I've to go to work" replied Dualta

"Oh nice, good stuff, sure we'll meet up after, where do you work?" said Dom as if he couldn't be less interested.

"Canary Wharf" said Dualta and number one quiet guy almost choked on his half pint of carton milk and Dom looked stunned.

"Is that a problem?" said Dualta

Dom, "No no no, that's great!" but now quiet guy number 2 was staring fiercely at him and it was really awkward.

Dualta, "What the fuck lads? Is there something I don't know?"

Dom, "Look Dualta! Come back here tonight after work, I think I maybe need to tell you something."

As time was getting on he probably thought it was best to leave it for now. "What about Matus?"

"He'll be fine" said quiet lad 1, Seán Óg and Dualta really believed him! On his way to work that morning Dualta wondered what the hell had just happened? In a city of 6 million people he had met his best friend and they had talked for hours and hours and a million questions had been answered and he should have felt brilliant but he didn't, something wasn't quite right. Why is he here? Who are the quiet lads? What's going on?

CHAPTER 44

DOMINIC REFLECTS

ON HIS WAY TO pick up the Semtex explosives. Dominic's head was spinning in circles, his best friend in the world was alive, his whole reason for being was turned upside down now that Dualta was back.

He thought "What am I doing? Where am I going?"

It seemed to him that now Dualta was back he was in some way complete again and he remembered the person he used to be. When did he become a killer? When did he take death so lightly? When did he stop giving a fuck?

Yeah it wasn't all because of Dualta's disappearance but things certainly started to go wrong at that point. His frantic thoughts stopped abruptly when they pulled up to an abandoned warehouse and Seán Óg brought him back to earth with a thud when he said "We're here, this is the lad with the Semtex"

The deal was done pretty quickly, product accepted and money exchanged.

The English lads selling the product never asked once what it was for. With everyone in London on high alert, these lads were more than happy to sell Semtex to a few lads who they must have known were Irish and at war with their country but obviously to that end they didn't give a shit.

Had money replaced their patriotism? Or maybe a country full of people who had colonised and conquered all over the world had become very confused in its identity and something very wrong had happened that these children of England were now dressing like fascists and giving Nazi salutes to the news cameras.

Dom couldn't help but reflect that the music culture of the time was the Ska movement, a Ska beat of music that was produced by bands full of black and white musicians who sang songs of political significance like the Special, UB40 and Selector. Dom loved their music and appreciated that there was a genuine push for change in England but by the same token there were Nazi's and fascists who seemed to forget about their identity parading with their skinheads and DM's and braces and shouting racist chants and then there was these lads who were happy enough to sell a few kilos of Semtex to a few Irish lads without asking what it was for, some patriotic confusion right there.

He and Dualta had had a great talk last night but while they had cleared the air and felt at ease with each other, Dominic had stopped short at explaining why he was in London and what he actually did now. He especially didn't really feel he could tell him of his immediate reason to be in London. He had so much going on in his head that he thought it would burst but as they pulled away in the Ford Fiesta he couldn't help but admire the stoic nature of the 2 volunteers he'd been assigned for this mission and he knew for certain that these lads would never waver in their patriotism, never compromise it and never fail to carry out their mission even if they should have to make the ultimate sacrifice. These were men chiselled out of granite and stone faced in their Irish identity and patriotism. They weren't going to swap their identity for a fascist/Nazi flag.

He knew when he'd get back to the house that he'd have to talk to Dualta and tell him the truth. Come clean and explain everything. Dualta was a Republican, he'd understand.

CHAPTER 45

DUALTA REVIEWS

WALKING THROUGH THE SECURITY at work that morning Dualta nodded to "Aul Hughie" on the gate and exchanged that knowing glance that only Irishmen know, that bond that literally just comes from being Irish. He was sure "Aul Hughie" had been in England for a long time but he also knew that he was still a proud Irishman and would never forget his roots. If he'd had a quick look into Aul Hughie's life he'd have realised it centred round his wife, children and the Irish identity that he celebrated in his local GAA club and Irish social club. He may have left Ireland out of necessity but as Dualta guessed, Ireland had never left him.

Hughie asked after Matus and Dualta suddenly lied and said he'd gone back to his family in Poland probably more for Hughie's peace of mind than his own.

What Dualta didn't know was that quiet lad number 2, the man with no name, who had kindly given them a lift to work that morning, had witnessed this exchange with interest.

CHAPTER 46

DOMINIC'S DIVORCE

OBVIOUSLY, NEVER HAVE BEEN married or close to it (well maybe once). Dominic had never had the "It's not you, it's me" talk, but now after only being reunited with Dualta, he was going to have to come clean and tell him what was going on, tell him why he was in London, he knew Dualta well enough to know he was suspicious already, he knew something was up.

He was a bit annoyed that although he knew Dualta would be ok he was inwardly questioning his loyalty to the ASU, but then he had to remember Dualta wasn't part of his ASU and he never had been.

Matus was proving a welcome distraction as he was quite a good singer and knew a few Irish tunes. The atmosphere in the house was beginning to mellow to an extent where they were getting chilled after work and taking a few beers home and for the first time in a long time 5 lads with totally different agendas in life, sat in the room of a shitty house in a foreign country and laughed for a while and sang for a while. Even the 2 quiet Irish lads relaxed and joined in a chorus of Sean South from Garry Owen, coupled with "Mazurek Dabrowskiego" from Matus, which the lads couldn't sing along to but definitely appreciated his enthusiasm.

In fact, things were so good in the house Dominic wished he could just postpone the inevitable but he knew time was running out and it was either fight or flight. So less than 3 weeks after reuniting with the best friend he'd ever known or would ever know, he decided this was the time to come clean. So when Dualta arrived home from work the next night Dom said

"Do you fancy a pint? There is a pub round the corner, think it's an Irish one so we'll be ok" he laughed.

So off the two mates went to a pub to have a draught Guinness together for the first time in many years and although Dom wanted to come clean, he couldn't help relax initially and take in the atmosphere and enjoy the craic, Irish songs and plenty of beer were the recipe for a great night as always and to be honest Dominic wanted to freeze frame life and enjoy the time together that they had been given. One night led to two and then three and it soon turned out all five inhabitants of the house were enjoying the craic in the local Irish pub especially when Liam Óg and his Birmingham Band were doing requests and telling tales of home. Dominic just couldn't pick out the perfect moment during that perfect spell in time and perhaps he never would have until one night in the pub a crowd of lads from Kildare walked into the bar and immediately recognised Dualta and screamed like excited school girls at him.

Dualta was drunk and relaxed and he welcomed this intrusion into their closed world with relish, but then Dualta didn't know they were living in a closed world. The Kildare lads from the building site represented a turning point for Dominic and it also meant a realisation that the honeymoon was over and the inevitable had to happen.

That very night after they sang songs and drank Guinness with all the Kildare lads and threw chips at English lads in the all night café, Dominic pulled Dualta aside as the rest of the lads made their drunken way to bed.

CHAPTER 47

DOMINIC REVEALS ALL

AS THEY WERE STILL laughing and spreading mouldy cheese on out of date bread Dominic got serious.

Dom, "Mate I've got to talk to you"

Dualta, "Oh Jesus, don't tell me your gay and going to run off with the fiddle player from Kildare" he laughed

Dom, "No mate, this is serious shit" Dualta, "Fuck off, you bollix" he laughed

Dom, "No mate, this is serious! You've got to get away from here"

In his drunken state Dualta was trying to make light of his confession but he suddenly realised Dom wasn't messing about and he braced himself to engage in this conversation.

So clutching a tin of beer Dualta listened intently as Dominic explained exactly what he had been doing and why exactly he had come to London. To say Dualta was shocked was an understatement, he felt a bit nauseous and light headed as Dom revealed details of things he had done and what he had seen since they had been apart, but the most shocking revelation was the reason why they were now here in London! Suddenly it started to make sense to Dualta, the two quiet lads living with Dom, the fact none of them appeared to have jobs but were always off doing things and had money to buy stuff. And as if an avalanche fell on his head, Dualta affirmed in his mind that Dom was on active duty in London with an ASU and their target was the very building he was working in! Was this a coincidence or had he planned this?

"No, of course not" Dom tried to reassure

"Do you think if I'd known you were here I wouldn't have come to get you home?"

Dom, "It is what it is Dualta, I'm sorry but that's all I can say, take Matus and get the fuck away, just forget about me again there's no future in it" he paused, "Just maybe fuck off and leave me alone like you did the last time, it would probably have been better if we hadn't met again, so just please go, take your man upstairs and go."

"I'm in this, me and the lads here are in it. There is no going back for us but you can get out and head back to Canada, save yourself please, just fuck off and leave me alone"

Dualta, "But we are brothers, we're one for all and all for one, we always swore that"

Dom, "Oh for fuck sake Dualta, that was children's stuff, we're not children anymore. I've done stuff that can't be undone. Just go away and make the best of what you can. Go on just fuck off and take that Polish prick with you before I chin him"

Dualta, "Stop, stop, stop being such a dick. I've done things too I know what it's like. I've lived with myself as a murderer for years, I know you Dom, that's not you."

At that, the friends we so mixed up between aggression, emotion and exhaustion they felt like hitting each other but ended up hugging each other. Their bond now was just so inseparable they may as well have been born twins. Nothing could ever divide them or split them apart. As they hugged in the living room of the dingy house, childhood memories swirled around of how happy they had once been and how their bond had been born and forged in steel.

"He has a pass, an ID pass, they both have" Quiet lad 1, Seán Óg, said.

"In fact they both have, the Polish lad has one as well" he said it as a remote observation with no recognition of the moment that was happening between the best friends in the room but he said it with a determination and conviction to his statement.

He sat down beside the lads and said, "That's how we'll get in. They've got passes, they can get through the security, they can take it in, plant it and leave, we won't even have to be there"

Without taking a breath Dom jumped up, "No way, no fucking way, we're not getting these lads involved, it's our job not theirs"

He almost had Seán Óg by the throat as he shouted, "No, no, they won't be involved"

Quiet lad Seán Óg wasn't at all annoyed at being grabbed by the throat, in fact he held and pushed Dom's fist away like it was a child's. "We've fucked about here long enough. Time to get this job done" he said very matter of factly. "If you don't sort it, I will "Dom and Seán Óg were about to fight as Dualta desperately tried to stop them. Dualta, "Fuck sake lads, we're all on the same side here" he shouted "Stop for fuck sake stop"

By this stage all other members of the house were awake and standing in the small living room and after thirty minutes of talking everyone was up to speed with what was actually happening in the house, in fairness it would probably have been 15 minutes if Matus hadn't needed a few translations here, there and everywhere.

CHAPTER 4 8

A COMMON WAY FORWARD

DOM WANTED DUALTA AND Matus to leave. Quiet lad 2 and Seán Óg wanted them to stay and to use their passes to get on site, Quiet lad 2 actually wanted them to take the bomb through. But Seán Óg was happy to take the passes and use them himself. Dualta was stunned, Dominic was still annoyed. And if truth be told, Matus was quite excited, especially when during the long and arduous nights conversation he realised the boys had guns in their possession, and thought this was a wonderful thing.

"Not if you don't know what to do with them" said quiet lad 2 "But I can teach you"

CHAPTER 49

THE LONG DEBATE

DOM WAS STILL INSISTING that Dualta and Matus leave, but Dualta was insisting he stayed, stalemate!

Dualta thought he had a compromise.

"If there are no risk of casualties and there is going to be a warning, we'll get you in, but once it's done we're going home and you're getting out of this, you've done enough! Sure why not come to Canada with me?"

Dom laughed heartily but also genuinely, "There's nothing I'd like better my friend, it's a deal" and there and then they shook on it.

CHAPTER 50

OPERATION FREEDOM

DUALTA AGONISED, HIS COUNTRY had had 800 years of British rule and that hurt, he couldn't justify killing anyone but at the end of the day it was only bricks and mortar and two fingers up to the British capitalist imperialist system that he hated so much, and after all there wouldn't be any loss of life so he felt he could cope with it. They started doing "walk throughs" in the house. The two lads knew if at least one of the security guards on the day was "Aul Hughie" then the rest of the operation should be straight forward, no one needs to get hurt or injured let alone killed, so Dualta was happy enough with the arrangement.

A walk through on the blue prints on the kitchen table looked very straight forward and reasonable.

- Wait until "Aul Hughie" is on duty.
- Dualta and Matus walk through and Dominic walks in with them (Hughie shouldn't be suspicious) but if he is they will say he is a new start with them and he hasn't got his ID yet.

Seán Óg will hover outside the security office a little out of sight with the gun, which obviously was only going to be used as a "frightener" was according to quiet lad. It wouldn't even be loaded

159

(except for the one that always remains in the chamber). So just use it to threaten and everyone will behave.

They went over the plan at least a hundred times, and probably a hundred more, and after a few days intense preparation they decided they were ready.

The day for the operation came quickly and the lads were all well drilled.

- Dualta, Matus and Dom walk into the security hut.
- Banter with "Aul Hughie" and get through with the rucksack
- Plant the IED in an optimum place.
- Leave the site on the pretext that Dom has to get some paperwork.
- Seán Óg will watch the door to make sure everything is ok.
- Quiet lad will be outside to drive the unit away in his hire car. Perfect.

The night before was a bit tense as obviously it was an attack at the heart of Britain's economic regeneration area and a huge statement from the IRA that they will fight on forever. But Dualta relaxed himself in the knowledge that there wouldn't be any civilian casualties and with that he was able to rest easy, well easy enough.

So when the alarm went off Dualta had been awake for a long time. They ate a basic breakfast and got into the car which was waiting outside the house driven by quiet lad. Seán Óg had the rucksacks in his arms, one for each of them and then he flashed the hand gun he was obviously carrying.

"Just for frighteners" Dualta said into himself, "just for frighteners" So with a deep breath Dualta asked Matus for one last time did he know what was happening and what they were going to do and have you listened to every instruction.

"Yeah, it's good" he assured, but Dualta doubted if a lot of this shit hadn't been lost in translation.

So quiet lad pulled up to as near to the security hut as he possibly could and the lads headed into the clearance zone where "Aul Hughie" was working.

Hughie, "Ahh lads, good to see you, and Matus how are you after that awful accident? You poor man, are you ok? Do you need a coffee, sure I'll bring you one down later. Grand lads, oh wait whose this?" Referring to Dom who had tried to remain anonymous throughout this exchange.

"Ahh that's Paddy, just started today but he hasn't got his pass yet." Said Dualta as matter of factly as he could. Inside he was saying "please just fuck up and let this slide."

But Hughie wasn't playing ball. "Ahh lads I'll just check the register here and see where he should be going." Said Aul Hughie.

Dualta, "No, it's fine mate, we'll show him where to go, for sure"

Aul Hughie, "It's not a problem, I'll just check the rota here, no worries"

For fuck sake thought Dualta, don't pick today to get conscientious about your shitty job. "Honestly Hughie, its fine, we'll show him where to go" said Dualta getting so tense that he could feel his muscles contracting. "Please Hughie just leave it to us"

But Hughie wouldn't leave it and he picked today of all days to become Mr Diligent. Aul Hughie dithered about so much that another guard began to get inquisitive and wandered in and asked was there a problem.

Aul Hughie, "I'm just looking for this young lads new start papers"

Second guard, "There isn't anyone supposed to start this morning."

Dualta now as tense as a cannon ball, "Look lads, no worries, we'll just take him in and show him"

Second guard, "No, you can't do that. Do you mind if I look in those rucksacks? Big lunches today lads?"

How did he know there was a bullet in it? But Dualta knew he was about to explode.

"Please just chill out lads" said Dualta, "we're fine". But the younger security guard was determined to check the rucksacks and as soon as he reached for the first one, Dom hit him an almighty punch to the side of the jaw and pulled him down to the ground with a choke. Aul Hughie looked stunned and couldn't even speak as Dualta tried to calm him down, which he was just managing to do when Seán Óg burst into the room brandishing the pistol and pointing it at Aul Hughie.

Dom, "Chill the fuck out lad! Its fine, everyone be fucking cool. No one wants to hurt anyone."

Seán Óg had the gun pointed at the guards so Dom said "Give the gun to Matus and Dualta, you talk to the guards and keep them calm, keep talking to them."

Dom, "Remember everyone, just keep calm and remember what we told you about the gun lads?"

So Dom and Seán Óg headed down to plant the bomb in the foundations but it took such a long time and things were getting so tense in the office Dualta tried to speak quietly to Matus.

"Take the cartridge out, the gun is just a frightener, remember just slide the cartridge out, they won't know any difference, just take it out." Matus' hands were shaking but he managed to slide the bullets out and Dualta breathed an almost audible sigh of relief, now the gun is a frightener and no danger.

In what seemed like an hour the two lads appeared back in the security hut.

Dom, "Right we are sorted, now listen lads" talking to the guards, "We are going to calmly walk out of here and you lads are going to lie on the floor and count to 1000 before you even lift your heads and even after that if you do lift your head, Matus here might come back and shoot you. So just chill and forget about us" he calmly stated, "OK?"

But it wasn't ok, for whatever reason Aul Hughie decided to take a last stand against his fellow countrymen.

Aul Hughie, "No lads, I'll not let you do this. Stop now and it'll be ok, stop, please stop". And then Aul Hughie fell to the ground and mumbled incomprehensively about how England had given him a living and how he owed them and "blah blah blah" until Matus was getting annoyed and screamed.

"For fuck sake Hughie, the gun isn't even loaded" as he pointed it to his own head and pulled the trigger by way of demonstration.

Obviously forgetting one piece of a soldier's main job. Listen to instructions. "Remove the cartridge but remember there's always one bullet left in the gun chamber"

Dualta thought this piece of advice might be a little too late after Matus' brains redecorated the security hut in a crimson tide.

The gun shot almost deafened Dualta and it created a surprising amount of damage to the security hut wall as well.

As Dom and Seán Óg ran out telling the lads to run, the situation was so incomprehensible, Dualta froze, just froze and stood still. The other lads were long gone when he came too and grasped his current predicament with Matus' blood splattered all over him, he could barely walk.

At that moment Dom reappeared and grabbed him roughly around the neck and started to drag him out the door. He could hardly keep his feet when a car screeched up on to the footpath within their reach. But the car was followed by a police car with a screaming siren and flashing lights and as "quiet lad" skidded to a stop they opened fire and blew him half way across the street.

Seán Óg had now taken refuge behind a Vauxhall Corsa and was returning fire on the British police.

Dualta, "Did you phone in the warning?"

Dom, "What? What?"

Dualta, "Did you phone in the fucking warning? You said you would."

Dom, "Yeah, but I didn't think your mate was about to blow his own fucking head off? No, I didn't phone a fucking warning. When did you think I had the fucking time to do that?"

Dualta fell back towards a wall and breathed out, he was losing control of every emotion he had but the fact he was about to get shot woke him into a reality and he realised Dom was screaming at him.

"Get behind that fucking wall, the wall, now, get behind it."

His hearing was still impaired from Matus' gun shot when the loudest bang he had ever heard literally shook the very earth beneath them.

The bomb had gone off, and the very sky had darkened.

Dualta, "The warning, was there a warning?"

Dom, "No, how the fuck could I have given a warning?"

Dualta fell back onto the pavement and lay there. Dom grabbed him and started to run with him.

"We've got to get outta here" as he broke the driver's seat window of a parked VW Golf and started it with his pen knife. Dualta fell into the newly opened passengers seat and put his head in his hands just as the shots started to pierce the vehicle.

"Drive" screamed Dualta, "Drive."

Dualta kept calm as best he could until he felt a warm sharp, stabbing pain in his torso, he never spoke for another few miles until he folded over the redundant seatbelt. Dom was manically driving the car on adrenaline alone despite feeling as if he needed to throw up.

Eventually he had to stop before he was sick, his stomach felt nauseous and he pulled the VW to a stop down an alleyway and vomited his guts up. He fully expected to be shot and to be honest at the exact point in time he honestly didn't give a shit if he was.

He spilled the contents of his guts on to the carpark stones and threw his head back in despair. He was about to give up when he realised Dualta could be dying in the car. He came to his senses and quickly dragged Dualta out of the car which he was sure they'd be looking for and put him into a fireman's lift and ran as far as he could away from the car.

Finally, exhausted he found an empty garage lock up behind a block of flats and lay Dualta on the floor. He wasn't responding and was obviously losing a lot of blood.

He must have passed out or fallen asleep, cause the next thing he knew it was dark. He startled to and quickly felt for Dualta's breath, he gently tried to wake him but Dualta wasn't responding. Now his breath came quicker and quicker as he began to panic.

"He's going to die if I don't do something"

"But if I take him to hospital, we'll both die in prison"

"Think, think, think"

And then he realised he knew two people in London.

He was pretty sure the Prime minister lived at 10 Downing Street but he doubted he'd be taking house calls at this time of night, and then he remembered his cousin, Nigel. He blindly staggered to a nearby phone box and lifted the book on a million to one chance that his number might be there and holy fuck it was.

He had no money so he made a reverse call to the number beside the name which was the same as his cousins. Nigel was his dad's twin brother's son. However, the twins were not that close and in fact his uncle had moved to England as a young man to seek employment and had only come home for summer visits and holidays.

Dominic and his cousin Nigel had known each other all their lives, however Nigel was English, Nigel was military trained and despite the fact they had enjoyed some really brilliant holidays together at their Grannies house in Dublin, they were really polar opposites.

"Ring ring, ring ring, ring ring" he was about to hang up when a voice cheerily replied.

"Hello Nigel speaking, what can I do for you?

Hello, hello" Dualta, "Nigel" he whispered, "its Dominic"

Nigel, "Dominic? Dominic, holy fuck, how you are man, long time, no hear. How are you man?"

Dominic, "Actually bro I'm not great I'm in really, really deep shit, I need your help."

Nigel, "Where are you man?" Dominic, "I don't know"

Nigel, "Ok, calm bro, don't worry I'm gonna find you."

CHAPTER 51

THE RESCUERS

NIGEL WAS SURPRISED TO get the phone call but not shocked, he was no orthodox man and years of working in security had taught him that people's actions were not that shocking anymore or was it that he had just seen everything. He was a loner and preferred the company of his dogs to most humans. He lived a relatively carefree life and looked after his working dogs on a compound that was very isolated and "far from the madding crowd". His home was a small but impeccably clean mobile home without a TV or very many mod cons. He liked it that way, reading and listening to music was his release and he was content with his lot in life and his only indulgence in an otherwise sparse existence was his passion for motorbikes. He had 3 and they held almost the same place of reverence in his heart that his dogs did.

He was a very clever and resourceful man; he read voraciously and kept up to date with current trends and technological progressions but simply chose not to indulge in many of them. He could fix any engine that came his way and knew more than most people about politics and philosophy and history. He was a huge man and had done some strongman competitions in his time as was evidenced from the size of his biceps. His preference for a shaved head yielding to a dark long beard was perfect for his work in security and put a sense of fear into people which generally suited him as they tended to avoid conflict with him in favour of an amicable solution and his full arm tattoos (even before they were trendy) marked him out as a renegade but what people couldn't see was that below that granite surface was a very gentle, thoughtful and caring person.

He had worked in all aspects of security (once for a couple of years he had been responsible for the security of a girl band on tour). He hadn't spoken too much about that job but had promised himself he'd write a book about it someday. Nowadays he was combining the knowledge and expertise on all matters security with his love of dogs. He trained and sold the dogs into all aspects of the industry from the police to night watchmen but if there was any insight into the fact that this man had a soft heart under that hard exterior was the fact he had so many pet dogs that lived not in the kennels but in his home. Some dogs got so close to him that he just couldn't sell them on, even though he lost a lot of money by keeping them. Currently he had 4 pet dogs and 10 working dogs, mostly Alsatians, in his kennels.

Through his work he'd seen so many things and been in so many difficult situations that he'd become hardened to a lot of life's challenges. He'd been bitten, punched, glassed, spat at and insulted but he'd never been stopped from doing his job. Now he cared more for the safety of his dogs than himself, but he was still the best in the business when it came to security matters.

Of his identity he would say he was Irish but obviously he had been born in England and lived there all his life but his heart was Irish and growing up he had spent every summer there with his parents and relatives and there were a lot of them, happy times and he enjoyed spending time with his mum's family but it was his dad's family and Dominic that he had a particular bond. Because of his accent he wasn't able to speak much in the border county that his cousin lived in but he loved the atmosphere in the homeland, he felt at home there, he had an unbreakable bond with the place and summers chilling out by the salt water pools and chatting up the girls. He'd remembered one time when himself and Dom had met two girls near their grannies house and brought them out for a few drinks. Good times!

He often thought he might go home to live there but he was probably too big and scary looking now to blend into any rural villages in Ireland he mused. He was content here, near the coast and the quiet life suited this deep thinker.

CHAPTER 52

NIGEL EXPLAINS LENNY

AND WHEN LIFE GOT too dull he always had Lenny. Lenny lived next door on a plot of land that was a cross between a farm and a warehouse. Other than a few sheep, pigs and cows and a multitude of dogs, cats and goats Lenny always seemed to be busy in his warehouse. In an age of synthetic drug progression, Lenny was still cultivating the best crop of weed in the area.

Lenny really was never strictly legit but he was a great lad and great company, although like Nige (as he called him) he preferred the isolated life and the two neighbours got on like a house on fire on the times they chose to be together. If truth be told, Nigel had often been drawn into less than legal activities in an attempt to help his mate next door. On the odd time Nigel went down the local pub with Lenny, he soon realised he was a local legend or some others would have called him an urban myth. One night in the local pub Nigel had heard a story that a local bobby (cop) had surveyed Lenny a few times on his journey home and took an increasingly unhealthy interest in Lenny's nocturnal activities and followed him home from the pub on a few occasions.

One night he pulled Lenny over and accused him of erratic driving and asked him if he'd had a drink. Lenny replied, "Yes constable! I've had 8 pints of bitter and 4 whiskeys"

Constable, "Oh is that right Lenny? Well would you mind blowing in to this wee breathalyser" he said smugly.

Lenny casually asked, "Why? You bastard. Do you not believe me?"

Someone also once recounted a story about Lenny going to a bar/ off licence in the city with a transit van and sat down with the two kids and asked the bar manager to fill an order for a significant amount of beer and spirits to be placed in his van while himself and the two kids sat in the bar and had a pint and coke and crisps respectively.

After about 20 minutes Lenny told the barman he was going to check if his order had been appropriately loaded and could he give the kids another coke and crisps, which he duly did but watching the clock he realised Lenny still hadn't come back after 20 minutes, he asked the kids, "Where's your daddy?"

To which the reply came, "He's not our daddy, that man just asked us if we wanted to come in for some coke and crisps".

Needless to say a check in the carpark revealed Lenny had indeed disappeared with a rather large supply of drink from the off licence.

Although Nigel's favourite story was the time when Lenny stormed into the local shop electric holding a huge TV saying he bought it in a local market and screaming that it didn't work and they'd told him to come to this shop to uphold the guarantee. It wasn't until 15 minutes after the manager had literally thrown Lenny plus the TV out the door that they realised the showcase TV on display in the window, near the door, was gone.

So whether the stories were true or not it gave Lenny legendary status in the area and Nigel liked and respected his neighbour and friend and often enjoyed his company. For his own part Lenny was glad to call Nigel his friend. It was like having your own security guard on your side that would protect you no matter what and could definitely be relied on in an emergency.

Like the time he frantically rang Nigel and said he was in a bit of bother with a couple of lads that were trying to break into his "weed" shed using a quite vicious Doberman dog to ward Lenny off and Nigel appeared from the darkness with four huge Alsatians and went full crocodile Dundee laughing "That's not a dog, these are dogs". The lads couldn't get out of there fast enough.

So it was no surprise that Nigel's first stop after getting the phone call was with Lenny. He explained that his cousin was in deep trouble and needed help and because it was an extremely dangerous trip, the only one he could trust to help him was his resourceful neighbour.

Lenny didn't seem to have ever been political but just in case he didn't tell him the whole story that they were going into London city to extract two Irish lads, one of whom had a gun wound and were being searched for and chased on the very day there had been a huge bomb in the docks area. No organisation had claimed responsibility for the bomb so Nigel had a small hope that maybe they weren't involved but somehow his gut told him that that was wishful thinking.

A quick discussion between the two resulted in a plan that would see them both go into London on bikes together and extract the lads and bring them out separately as to reduce the risks of being caught or followed.

They were also aware that Dom's mate was wounded so this would provide an extra challenge so they decided that Nigel would carry the wounded man on his bike as he had a vague idea that he might be able to get him treated without arousing too much suspicion.

The plan seemed manageable but they weren't completely sure how severe the injuries were so it could run into all sorts of complications. Among other accomplishments, Nigel, had spent many years in his early career as a courier, so he knew every nook and cranny of London's back streets. If you needed a parcel or letter delivered ASAP in London, then Nigel was "your man". So pulling out the map of London Nigel planned their joint route in and their simultaneous different routes back out. He had managed to gain a grid reference on the phone box from which Dominic had called so he could narrow down their location to within at least a 100 meters.

They were in a lock up so it shouldn't be that difficult to find them, the difficult part was going to be getting them out.

So while they finalised their plan and made their final arrangements, Nigel made a mental note that Lenny had never once questioned his motives or who their targets were. Now that is loyalty he thought. Just before they left, he grabbed Lenny back by the arm, "Mate, you don't have to do this?"

"It's dangerous, you could get in to trouble or hurt here mate. And you don't even know these lads, you're doing it for me and I don't want to see you get hurt for that."

And Lenny looked up at him and said, "Sure you didn't ask me in for a game of Monopoly" and he laughed.

CHAPTER 53

LENNY'S VIEW SEEK AND DESTROY, NO! SEEK AND SAVE

LENNY HAD ALWAYS LIVED under the radar. He had served in the military with distinction and was an expert in undercover ops. Those that generally met Lenny through his regular buying and selling activities often mistook his placid demeanour and innocent looks for a bit of a fool but that suited Lenny in his current endeavours.

He grew his "weed" and did some wheeling and dealing and he got on with life as best he could, but what most people, including Nigel, didn't know that Lenny had been trained (elitely), utilised (brutally) and then discarded (shamelessly).

He had been in many "black ops" where it was only the ruthlessness of his unit that got them through alive so he knew what life was about and how it was precious. He had also learned that he wasn't fighting for "Queen and Country", he was risking his life to ensure that the Capitalist Oligarchs of the Western World kept their hold on the oil and precious metal supplies from all corners of the globe. So when he was "honourably discharged" with a tiny medal and an even more paltry pension, and one lung, Lenny realised ultimately we are all on our own unless you are born into some wealth or aristocracy but he also remarked he had never met any of that class on his particular battlefields.

He never met any Sandhurst graduates in a ditch in Argentina but yet he watched them getting medals at ceremonies on TV in their bright shiny uniforms. But he wasn't bitter, he honestly wasn't. He had volunteered his services so he wasn't about to whine about how he was treated, that was just the way it was. He remembered his mum saying, "Dry your eyes Lenny, we have no time to feel sorry for ourselves, we have to make a living."

And Lenny made a living at whatever he could. His dad had long gone when Lenny was taking paper rounds and delivery jobs, not long out of Primary School. His work ethic was unparalleled but this meant his scholarly opportunities and education suffered. His mum often said, "Lenny, you can be whatever you want."

And possibly she was right but Lenny was too busy earning a few quid to put food on the table. If he could have attended school he would probably have been the Prime Minister by now but he was stuck at home on a tenth story flat looking after a mum who was a whole lot more interested in drink and drugs than she was in the career path of her only child. He actually had some great entrepreneurial ideas when he was based in London. Due to the high percentage of crowds coming to soccer matches he bought, sold and traded hats, flags and rosettes for any team that had the biggest support. He also traded in crisps and chocolate and one particular season he had a great little earner "minding" parked cars in dangerous areas near the stadiums.

He managed to steal a bus conductor's cap and would approach supporters hurriedly parking their cars and formally announce he would, "Mind your car for £1 mister." And most supporters were happy enough to part with £1 to ensure the cars safety but would always have told anyone in the local pub that he remembered on one distinct occasion when a particularly arrogant and dismissive Tottenham fan replied to his question.

"No, I don't need you to mind my car" smugly, "Can you not see my minder in the back there?" he laughed pointing to a huge Alsatian dog in the back seat.

Lenny let him walk on a bit before calling him back, "Here mister?" The Spurs fan turned around obviously agitated and annoyed,

"What?"

"Can your dog put out fires?"

Needless to say, Lenny could have been the next Alan Sugar, if his mum hadn't upped and died when he was just turning 16, so rather than entering the care system he joined the army.

He blazed a trail through the ranks and his bravery, courage and resourcefulness marked him out as a future leader. Without anything else in his life Lenny went for it and was soon being promoted on a yearly basis and soon he was a target for the "Special Ops" brigade. He duly joined and spent many years not knowing his name or his location but getting his job done to the best of his very skilled ability. He was a hugely appreciated team member until he took a hail of bullets during an extremely "Black ops" situation and suddenly after all he had given, he was six weeks in hospital before he even knew what was going on. His army family had disappeared overnight and now he was alone again without any money or family or friends or one of his lungs.

Still in what he called his bewilderment phase, he was ordered to dress up in his dress uniform and appear at an event where a tiny nickel medal was pinned to his chest and some upper-class, non-combat major told him he was indispensable and promptly dispensed with his services.

He was devastated and incomprehensible but soon he realised that his role, however skilled or dangerous it had been, was just as a "pawn in a princely game" to quote the Bard himself.

So he did what he always did, he dusted himself down, took a deep breath and moved on. He moved away from anything connected to the army. They encouraged him to get a local job and join the "British Legion" where he could avail of half price pints and discuss the glory days with other veterans who had served in the forces and play some snooker and darts and share stories of how tough you were in a previous life, but the truth of it was these lads weren't so tough, like he was!

They signed up, did basic training and were sent into the scariest situations ever. Without any experience or combat nuance, they were forced out on to the hostile streets of Belfast, Derry or South Armagh, where they had no idea who their enemy was or where the next bomb or sniper attack might come from. The native population in these areas were hostile, stoic and tough. Like the US discovered in Vietnam, these people would not be beaten and also like the US learned in Vietnam, you can't beat an army you can't actually see or identify.

When Lenny served his first term in Northern Ireland he was blown away by the resilience of the indigenous people. The areas like West Belfast, Derry and South Armagh who wanted to be free from British rule. Lenny understood this completely but it wasn't his job to understand, it was his job to contain and stop or destroy any attempt to prevent this. He hadn't been deployed in any Loyalist areas but he knew they wanted to stay within the British Union regardless if the majority wanted it or not. "Seek and destroy" was a philosophy he lived by or would have died by if he hadn't. While he admired the stature and resilience of the Nationalist people, he also knew that those involved in the Guerrilla warfare against them were fundamentally ruthless and would kill him in an instance but he also knew he couldn't obviously identify his enemies within the general population so he learned to hone his skills and be vigilant one hundred percent, to watch, to observe, to listen and to learn. He'd seen so many of his colleagues shot, killed and wounded and never once seen who did it. He often thought

"How do you fight an invisible enemy? How do you shoot at a target you can't see?"

One time he remembered doing a foot patrol past a house in a very normal housing estate, when they came across a kid's bike wedged into a gate and blocking the whole footpath, so he ordered an inexperienced private to move it while he kept an eagle eye on where any potential attack might come from, and while he was examining the roof tops, skyline and horizon unfortunately "Private Inexperienced" was blown to bits by whatever explosives were packed into the kids bike. "They don't teach you shit like that at basic training." Thought Lenny.

After 4 tours of duty in Belfast and South Armagh, Lenny was actually relieved to be posted to "Las Malvinas" "Argentina" "Falklands Islands"

Initially it was a relief to know who the enemy was and the fact they wore a uniform and were legitimate targets was something he appreciated until he lived through the 74 days of actual fighting, which saw 255 British Soldiers and 649 Argentinian's lose their lives and after being involved in the Battle for Goose Green and hearing stories of how the British Army lost more ships including the sinking of the "Belgrano" he realised this war was no less dirty or pointless than the one in Ireland. Here he was risking his life for an Island. 5,000 miles from England? Why?

Lenny wasn't one for dwelling on things and he quickly realised he could get busy living or get busy dying. So he used his meagre pay off to buy a small mobile near the coast. He loved being near the sea, he actually hated being "on the sea" where he experienced profound sickness but in a strange way he loved the whole atmosphere around a sea side town so he chose to relocate near Brighton and he wasn't disappointed, he loved it, everything about it, (except being on a boat). He loved the smell of the sea, the look of the sea, the harbours, the dinghy's, yachts and trawlers (from a short distance). He loved swimming in the sea, walking on the beach and sitting for hours taking the advice of one of his favourite singers, "Just sitting on the dock of the bay, watching the ships go by. " he just didn't like boats.

His life was fine and dandy but when he met and got close with his neighbour "Nigel" he was glad. He was the first person Lenny had felt a kindred bond with since he left his army family. Himself and Nige were okay just to chill and talk about normal everyday stuff and not get heavy about any shit, which suited Lenny perfectly. As he soon realised Nige was a tough strong lad with Irish roots and he liked him even more. The fact that Nige seemed to want to look after him was a little amusing but he ran with it and Nige became his "big brother" and protector. Lenny was happy for once to sit back and not worry if his back was covered, cause now he knew it was. He knew it was with Nige and the two lads became close without, ever once invading each other's personal space. They got on "easy" and that was perfect for both of them. So their relationship was a very mutually beneficial experience and so it was when Nige asked for his help with this current delicate situation in London. Lenny was happy to say very little but he wasn't stupid and he knew if 2 Irish lads were stuck in London (one with an injury) on the very day there had been a huge explosion then they weren't boy scouts who had missed their bus home. Did he feel compromised? No. Did he feel angry? No. Did he feel a sense of anger at this attack on his country? No. Why? Because he'd been in enough situations to know that each country has their legitimate reasons and in fairness his own country had less than a chequered history of colonisation, plantation, plundering and conquering so he realised they were really reaping what they had sowed for many, many hundreds of years. Anyway he liked the Irish, they were great craic and he often wished he had been born one of them.

So he had no other thought than to help his best friend.

CHAPTER 5 4

ONLY FOOLS AND HORSES, DUALTA IN LONDON

DUALTA WAS UNCOMFORTABLE BUT not in any real pain, the wound was probably superficial, it stung and he felt exhausted but he knew he was not going to die. What worried him most is how it had come to this and how him and his best friend were living in a lock up in Peckham or somewhere like extras from the "Del Boy" comedy.

Only there wasn't much laughter in this episode.

"What the fuck is going on Dom?" he sighed, "What is going on?"

Dominic didn't answer, he continued his sentry duty at the garage door.

Dualta, "Remember when we were young? We were going to rule the world? What happened to us?"

"Shut up he'll be here soon" Snapped Dom.

"Who? Your big cousin? Who used to beat the shit outta me? Was he not in the British Army? Oh, jeez, he's gonna hand us over, not help us" "Don't be a prat! He's ok, he's on our side." Said Dom lowering his head.

"And what side is that?" Said Dualta, "Cause I haven't a clue what's going on here or what I'm even doing here? I didn't chose this Dom! You did." He continued.

"Matus, didn't chose it either." He started but stopped when he remembered his friend's brains being liberally splashed all over the security huts walls.

"Matus was a feckin fool, he was told about the gun but he was being a dick." Dom unconvincingly offered.

"For fuck sake Dom, he didn't know what the fuck was going on. Do you think he wanted to blow his own brains out? No he fucking didn't!" He was getting angry now. "You brought the gun into his life. Up until a few weeks ago Dom, I never thought I'd see you again and now we're lying in "Del Boy's" garage and I've been shot. Not exactly the reunion I hoped for."

Dom was getting frustrated, "Well what did you expect? A red carpet?"

"Well I expected to be able to recognise my best friend not this "Che Guevara" looney I see now. What happened to you mate? This just isn't you, I know it's not"

Dom seethed and boiled, "What happened? What happened? You fucking happened. You happened to fucking disappear. Do you know how painful it was for me not knowing if you were dead or alive? Not knowing how my life was going to continue without you. Not knowing Dualta! I was terrified, I was distraught, I was crushed." His fists were clenched now. "Yeah this isn't me but you didn't care then? Did you?" He turned away.

"You knew you were alive, I didn't! But you chose not to tell me!" Now he was fuming. "You were off, having your best life in Canada and fair play to you, go after it and enjoy it, but you didn't care about the mess you left behind, you didn't give a fuck about us who spent every single day wondering and worrying. Yeah this isn't me! Cause you took the old me with you when you left and you left me as much for dead as that fucking Christian Brother"

By now Dom was so angry he had almost unknowingly approached Dualta and had his closed fist on his shirt, he didn't hear Dualta gasp and struggle for breath, and then suddenly he came to his senses and fell off him and back to the floor. With his head in his hands, he said almost in a whisper.

"I missed you so much Dualta, I was alone and lost without you, I didn't know what to do or where to turn, when you left a lot of me left too and it never came back. I'm Sorry I grabbed you, are you ok? Oh shit, I forgot you've been shot, I'm sorry for getting you shot."

Dualta composed himself and straightened up in his sitting position. "It's ok, I'm sorry Matus ruined your bomb plans." And the two best friends and soulmates sat together and were quiet and slowly Dualta, through his pain found Dom's hand and he squeezed it, that was enough, no words needed to be said. They sat quietly like that until a loud crash brought them back to reality.

Dom quickly jumped up forcing Dualta to slump back on his side causing considerable pain, "Arghh" he groaned through gritted teeth, "What is it?"

Dom was straining to see but he was almost sure some kid's from the adjoining estate had found their abandoned get away Golf and were burning it.

"Fair play boys, you would make good Irish lads in a riot."

Dualta started laughing and it turned into one of those situations like in Mass or a strict teachers class, where you shouldn't laugh but that just makes it worse and you laugh till your stomach hurts, and you actually feel sick or you might pee yourself, but you can't stop laughing and then Dom joined in and it wasn't that he wanted to laugh but he was just infected and the friends just lay down on the ground and laughed and laughed until they were rolling around with tears streaming down their faces.

And so it was when a knock came to the door and Nige whispered, "Dom? Are you in there? It's me Nigel, are you there? And it brought the boys back to their senses, well just about.

CHAPTER 55

RENDEZVOUS TIME

"HI CUZ, LONG TIME no see" Said Nigel as he grabbed Dom and gave him a huge hug.

Dom extracted himself and gave the introductions, "This is Dualta, you might remember him? He's been shot so he's not much craic but he remembers you."

"Yeah" says Dualta trying to sit up more upright. "The last time we met, you had me pinned over a railway bridge, you weren't much craic then to be honest."

"Sorry mate" excused Nigel, "I thought we were having a bit of fun." And Nigel began to look at his wound and examined it closely and applied some medicated water and bandages to clean and seal the wound. "I think you'll live but you do need a few stitches" Dualta objected, "I'm not going to any hospital for stitches." Nigel smiled, "Who said anything about a hospital?"

So while Dominic and Nigel discussed their plan for their evacuation.

Dualta tried to get himself upright and set his gaze on Lenny. "Alright mate?" Said Dualta.

"Yeah, you alright?" Replied Lenny. "Yeah" Dualta felt a little bit of Déjà vu.

CHAPTER 56

THE LEAVING OF LONDON

AS AGREED, THE LADS decided to split up to give them a better chance of escaping the city. The security presence was intense to say the least so it totally made sense to split up. It would give them the opportunity to get out of central London without rousing too many suspicions given the numerous road blocks and security checks that were springing up all over the city.

The problem was that Dualta was losing blood and consciousness and couldn't ride pillion so Nigel was going to have to pilot the bike from behind him and hold him upright as best he could. Neither Lenny nor Dominic were happy about this but they couldn't come up with a better option so that's how it was going to play out. Also for the best chance of getting out they knew they were taking different routes so there couldn't be any quick "call the cavalry" missions if things should go wrong.

In that moment before they left there were strong emotions in the air but no one was willing to break the awkward silence and say something that might make them sound weak.

It struck Lenny that he had been through this so many times before but he gained a new found respect for his new companions when he realised they were no less soldier material than he was. He found them to be calm, professional and thorough. In that moment he had probably his first glimpse into the mind set of his enemies.

Now for once he was in the away "changing room" and gaining an insight into how the opposition's mindset worked and he was probably a little surprised that it was exactly the same as his was when he was in special ops. And he meant special ops cause he thought these lads had a steely determination that you didn't often come across in the lower ranks of the army, who probably were only there to escape their unfortunate circumstances or poverty, neglect or lack of opportunity to progress their lives in any other situation.

These young lads were what they now referred to in the army as cannon fodder, a reference to the lost generation who needlessly marched across no man's land in WW1 and were slaughtered because of the arrogance of their leaders who were nowhere near the frontline but happy enough to send an unending parade of doomed youths to their ultimate destruction.

Lenny appreciated that these lads were also dedicated to their cause which a lot of his compatriots weren't and were just pawns in a bigger game being played out among the elite nations of the world.

So with this in his mind he welcomed Dominic onto the back of his bike and they set off to hopefully make it back to the coast without being stopped, questioned or shot. But he was shocked at how he had already bonded with this "kindred spirit" and wanted to help him as best he could. So he left the lock up and headed into the unknown and for the first time in his life he was at odds with the British Security Forces after having been one of their champions for nearly 20 years.

CHAPTER 57

DOMINIC LEAVES THE LOCK UP

DOMINIC WAS STILL CONFUSED when he finally slid onto the back of this lad's huge Honda 750.

To be honest in the short space of time he'd met this lad he actually felt at ease in his company and trusted him despite the fact that for all intents and purposes he was totally his "enemy". He was everything he had been told to fight against, he was British, a Soldier and Dom didn't know why he had bonded with him. He was not a Unionist who flew the Union Jack and burnt Irish Tricolours on the 11th July but he was an English soldier who was just so probably unfortunate that he had to join the British Army just to make ends meet. This guy was English, and he probably in all possibility cared as much about Ireland as he did about the Middle East, Africa or the Falklands or anywhere else he may have been stationed.

For Dominic, he realised there was only ever one fight or one alternative but he did feel sorry for this lad who probably had never been brought up like he had. So he decided there and then to trust him and he literally put his life in his hands (or motorbike) but this was made easier by the instant bond he had made with him.

So they headed off through the London skyline and tried to make their escape. Lenny was obviously skilled on a motorbike as he weaved his way through the incessant London traffic but the first real test came when they reached a large checkpoint just before the motorway and when they were about four vehicles back in the checkpoint Dom thought they were fucked as he had no ID, so if it was called for they were going to be in big shit.

The wait seemed interminable for Dominic but when they finally reached the checkpoint Dom was actually stunned by how easily Lenny got them through it. A small part of him thought if it had been him he would very easily give up the Irish bomber on the back of his bike but in reality he knew he would never do that.

When they pulled into the checkpoint, Lenny handed over his ID and began a bit of banter, with the Police on the line and was still laughing when he rode through it with Dom still mounted on the back of the bike.

And with that they rode right through the barrier and headed straight back to the South Coast without so much as a hiccup.

CHAPTER 58

DOG DAY DUALTA'S SURGERY

DUALTA OBVIOUSLY REMEMBERED NIGEL and the childhood visits he made to see Dom. In truth he hated Nigel, viewed him as a huge bully who had used his size and strength to harass and annoy all those younger and weaker then himself, but in this situation he hadn't many alternatives but to trust what Dominic had said and literally place his life into the hands of someone he thought he hated.

He knew he wasn't going to die but the "wound" hurt like fuck and was constantly bleeding so he was feeling very tired and nauseous. Obviously he had never been shot before but it was as sore as he ever could have imagined it could be. He was trying to put a brave face on it as Nigel was roughly loading him onto the bike but in all honesty he was literally a rag doll in Nigel's huge hands.

Nigel placed him on the front of the bike and then strapped him to his own waist under a huge black and blue biker jacket. It would all work perfectly unless they were stopped and the security forces would see them strapped together and of course this would set off alarm bells. So it was really an "eggs all in one basket situation" and in the circumstances he couldn't help but feel nothing but admiration for Nigel who was quite obviously risking his neck if not his life for him right now.

He probably didn't fully realise how grave their situation was and to be fair he was totally as weak as water and didn't imagine he could be of any use anyway if the situation got out of control.

Nigel was receiving updates on a "CB" radio through his headset so he was doing a terrific job of avoiding the checkpoints that were coming through the dispatches. He zigzagged through London as if it was his back garden and he rode the huge mechanical beast as easily as if it was a tricycle, Dualta was very impressed as he was doing it all with an injured Irishman strapped to his waist.

At one stage they could see flashing lights coming over the brow of a hill and Nigel calmly slowed the bike down and seamlessly reversed them into a side street while the police car drove past with full lights and sirens blaring before coolly driving back out and on to the road. At that point Dualta realised there was more to this guy than the huge foreign bully who hung him by the feet over a bridge back when they were young. He'd always hated this man but now here he was literally saving his life, he thought this just doesn't add up and there is definitely something more to this lad "than meets the eye".

So after a couple of close scrapes they were actually out of the city confines and it occurred to Dualta that without Nigel he would've been shot or at least caught and looking at a life sentence in Wormwood Scrubs. The more they drove on the more Dualta realised how much this lad had put his neck on the line for him and now already he was eternally grateful cause like most people when faced with their own mortality, they pretty soon start to count their blessings. And in this situation being without religions guidance Dualta firmly believed if he was ever going to ever have a saviour then it was going to be the very man behind him on this motorbike right now.

He was maybe still groggy or semi-conscious but he felt safe and was definitely impressed with Nigel's performance. The next thing Dualta realised that they were slowing down and the bike was slowing down over gravel or stones.

Coming back into consciousness Dualta could feel the pain more then he previously had but he also realised that they were reaching the end of their journey, whatever that had been because he'd slept through the most of it.

As his eyes focused on the lights in front of him he realised they had definitely arrived at some sort of turning point or place. He subconsciously thought that it must be the hospital Nigel had mentioned earlier but he had also told him that he wouldn't be able to get into any hospital without arousing suspicion. Soon the bike had stopped and Nigel was lifting him off and undoing the belt that had joined them together during the last few hours. He couldn't actually say it was a relief because it released in him a sudden surge of pain that literally laid him low and he fell to the ground and rolled around in agony, he was so grateful he was obviously very close to getting near a doctor and possibly some relief from his current predicament and pain. Nigel lifted him up in one scoop and carried him through a glass door and planted him roughly but securely on a bench in what he presumed was a waiting room. He was beginning to feel a little better as Nigel gave him some water and a Twix bar which surprisingly lifted his spirits enormously. He tried to touch the wound but it was too sore so he left it alone.

Feeling better he lifted his head up and began to take in his surrounding and his first reaction was a little confused because there seemed to be an inordinate amount of dogs in this waiting room, all of them greyhounds (those skinny dogs that run races and lads bet on) being held precariously by a very scrawny looking disinterested youth. He could see them but his brain still couldn't process why they were in the doctor's office. He curled up and drifted off again as Nigel came back and sat down beside him and in doing so lifted the whole row of seats up by at least six inches. "We're next" said Nigel and Dualta felt a surge of relief and began to regain his senses.

"Why are there so many dogs in this hospital? Said Dualta

> Nigel just laughed, "As I said before, who said
> anything about a hospital"

For Dualta there was good news and slightly less good news. He was indeed in a surgery with a doctor. The slightly less good news was that he was potentially Dr Doolittle "Veterinary Surgeon MRCVS"

"Oh Bollix" said Dualta.

"Well what did you expect? I could hardly explain your injury in our local causality on the day that's in it, now could I?"

Doctor Doolittle wasn't at all happy to have Dualta in his surgery but he obviously was a friend or a onetime friend of Nigel as he grumpily set about fixing the wound Dualta had taken during the getaway. The vet didn't think it was particularly bad as it had taken more of the flesh away than anything else and other than some scorching and bleeding his prognosis was that it had luckily missed any vital organs or veins. So fixing him up would be pretty straight forward said the vet and then "could they get out of his surgery ASAP, before any questions had to be asked or any suspicions were aroused."

However, the logistics of the situation raised a number of impractical issues.

"What weight are you?" asked the vet.

Dualta, "About 11 ½ stone, why?"

"Cause these greyhounds aren't and I don't know how much anaesthetic I need to knock you out to clean and sort your wound, also I've never operated in here on anything heavier than those dogs so I don't think you're going to fit on my table." Said the very worried Dr Doolittle.

"Anything your size is normally lying on a barn floor or a shed!" he said without showing any signs of sarcasm.

So Dualta braced himself as the vet gave him instructions on what he was going to do with the wound to make sure it was clean and sterile and, blah blah blah.

Suddenly Dualta didn't feel very well and a tingling in his toes became a blur in his brain and suddenly, everything went dark.

When he woke up Nigel was laughing hysterically and the vet was furiously scurrying around the surgery picking up medical equipment and trying to clean up an almighty mess.

Dualta forgetting the stabbing pain in his side long enough to ask, "What the fuck happened here?"

Nigel tried to explain through his tears of laughter that Dualta had fainted and fell straight onto the instrument tray and every sharp scalpel and knife- like object had flown through the room and nearly decapitated the poor vet which spooked the remaining greyhounds who ran amuck through the surgery while Dr Doolittle had to quickly inject Dualta and do the operation before he woke.

"Funniest thing I've ever seen in my life" Choked Nigel.

As Nigel was finishing speaking to Dr Doolittle, Dualta realised he hadn't eaten since yesterday morning and since it was now dark he realised that this was the end of his second day (except a bite of a Twix) without food. Yesterday's events weighed heavily on him but he guessed he wasn't focusing on the enormity of what he had been a part of and probably wouldn't be until he had started to feel better.

As he climbed on to the back of Nigel's monster bike his thoughts raced back to Canada and Sofia and where he had, just for a short while, felt true happiness and contentment. As the bike careered around several sharp corners he came to his senses and realised that it probably was just going to be his lot in life to never find that everlasting happiness.

He was still feeling pretty sorry for himself when he realised the bike was slowing down outside a "Wimpy" and he perked up thinking a burger might help him feel a little better.

Nigel was not a man that could easily blend into the background of any situation so Dualta felt everyone was watching them as they took a seat in the booth nearest the door.

Dualta was feeling surprisingly well after his ordeal and as the two men sat down to a veritable feast of a slab of beef stuck deliciously between 2 bread buns, he looked at Nigel across the table in a completely different way than he ever thought he could. After all, this had been the Brit bully who had dangled him over a bridge and generally tortured and annoyed him at any opportunity when they were younger. He had actually hated him at times but he was Dom's cousin so he had to put up with him but he would never have envisaged a situation where they were both sitting, eating together and he was so grateful that Nigel had just saved his life on at least on 2 occasions. In that light you start to look totally differently at someone and Dualta could only describe his feelings towards "Nige" as admiration. So strange how people's views can change so quickly. Maybe the old adage of "first impressions last" was a load of old bollix thought Dualta.

"So seriously Nigel? What's going on? Where'd you learn all that shit? I think you're a wee bit more than a security guard.

Nigel sat back and laughed," I do ALL kinds of security, in a lot of different situations."

Dualta, "I knew it, you are a British Soldier"

Again he laughed, "I'm honestly not but I do have a lot of experience of security at a lot of different levels. I might be employed to kick drunks out of a bar but I also know how to keep spies out of a country." Dualta didn't press him anymore on it as it was obvious this lad has secrets he was definitely not going to discuss.

> Dualta, "So what about the vet? How'd you pull that one off?"

> Nigel, "Part of our security business are dogs, security dogs, I train them, work them, sell them, he treats any medical problems they have. They work in all sorts of situations in the military and the private sector. You would be stunned at how many people have secrets to keep and are willing to pay a lot of money to me to help them keep them."

> Dualta, "Jaysus, so you're like a special agent or some shit, do you work for the government?"

> Nigel, "Sometimes? Mostly with dogs going into bomb squads or drugs divisions."

> Dualta, "Holy Shit, that's crazy, you are a bad ass."

> Nigel, "Not really 90% of my job is just to watch, observe and note. You'd be surprised

how many people never open their eyes or observe anything further away than the end of their nose."

Dualta, "So the vet is part of your secret operation? He fixes the dogs and turns them into killers? Does he train them as well? Is that how you got him to treat me? Is that what he does, goes out and treats wounded men undercover?"

Nigel belly laughed again, "The vet, Dr Doolittle, as you called him when you were a bit spaced out?" Nigel continued through his laughter, "No! I just happen to know he's shagging his wife's best friend's wife, so I kind of had him by the balls."

He continued, "But what about you?" Nigel said, "Why are you involved in all this? I remember you were more into your music culture? Were you not for going to live in Donegal to speak Gaelic?"

Dualta, "I was mate, I honestly was but now I realise life sometimes serves you lemons and you can't always make lemonade, I tried mate but it just wasn't to be, and now here I am."

Dualta, "What about you? Is this where you thought you would be? Are you happy? You got a girl?"

Nigel, "No mate, no time! And not really the best time to bring a kid into this world! Plus I spend a lot of time on my own, if the truth be told mate I prefer the company of dogs. They are kind, friendly and loyal and they won't betray you."

Dualta and Nigel sat for the next hour and forty-five minutes and discussed the roads that had led to this moment in time and both felt very comfortable with this even though neither would have ever been described as "big talkers".

By the end of their "Wimpy" experience the two men left with a hell of a lot of mutual respect for each other.

As they left the restaurant and walked towards the carpark. Dualta ventured in the spirit of their new found friendship, "Can I steer the bike?"

Without breaking his stride or looking back Nigel replied, "Not a fucking chance"

CHAPTER 59

LENNY'S DILEMMA

LENNY WAS AS EASY going as they came. He had experienced numerous "combat zones" and "war situations" and had served with honour and distinction but very few people would ever know based on the few military medals he was able to display on his uniform. He had seen some things that were so disturbing that he had never spoken to any other individual about them and didn't think he ever would.

That's why he had chosen to remove himself from the hustle and bustle of London life. In his current life he was happy. He did a lot of wheeling and dealing and he got by, his overheads were low and his view from his mobile were honestly breath-taking. Yeah he was a happy and content man, or at least he had been until Big Nigel had rang him a couple of days ago.

Sometimes he'd had nightmares and woken up covered in sweat and the memory of his comrades blood and guts spread all over his face but in general he had been able to control those traumas and when he smoked a bit of "weed" with his mates he knew that he had found a way to get through it. In fact, so much so he found he was able to cultivate a bit of the stuff himself so he decided that this was where he was going to stay, at least in the present. Lenny had what the Irish called "the gift of the gab" which meant he could talk to people and always had a bit of banter. He was able to make a living buying, selling and cajoling. In fairness he didn't need much to keep him afloat so he didn't feel his activities really hurt anyone or left them in much hardship.

So his life was pretty free and easy. He had a good relationship with most of the community and quite often enjoyed a few pints in the local pub. He'd met Big Nigel a few years ago and immediately felt easy in his company. The lads had shared a few drinks and conversations before they realised they were kindred spirits. Nigel had a sketchy past but a lot of dogs which was absolutely fine. The dogs were like pets until Nigel showed him what they were capable of and jeez these dogs were absolute beasts. One night Lenny had a break in on his little "weed plantation" and the perpetrators had a huge dog with them so he thought rather than taking one of his guns out he would see if a;; Nigel's talk about his dogs was actually true.

So he called Nigel in a pretend panic and sat back to see what his reaction would be. He wasn't disappointed when Big Nigel burst through the side hedge with four huge Alsatians and sent his potential robbers scattering in the wind. "You call that a Dog?" Nigel laughed " No, these are Dogs!"

Life was actually pretty perfect for Lenny until he got Nigel's last phone call and for the first time in many years Lenny was faced with a dilemma.

Even though he had long since fallen out of love with the British Government's agenda he still felt part of the army family and the comrades he had stood and fought with and yet here he was risking himself for someone that could only be seen as his enemy and that brought back a lot feelings and memories that he didn't care for. Although Nigel hadn't told him who these lads were or what they had done he wasn't stupid and he quickly made the connection between these two Irish lads and the bomb in London. So having a potential IRA volunteer on the back of his bike was an uncomfortable situation. However, another part of him realised that the lad on the back of his bike probably wasn't much different than him.

When they arrived back at Nigel's yard, it was in complete darkness so they drove on to his own mobile where he offered

Dom his humble hospitality which consisted mainly of a large whiskey and an even larger spliff. There was an awkward silence as both men were trying to work each other out until Dominic ventured, "Why did you help us?"

"Cause Nigel asked me to" he shrugged. "Do you know who we are?" asked Dom.

"No, I didn't ask." said Lenny

"So you just followed blindly? Do you know what we did?"

"I could guess" he replied.

"And still you helped like you were just following orders, are you a military man?" asked Dom before taking a large mouthful of whiskey and a long drag on his home made cigarette, "Ever serve in Ireland?"

"Yeah, South Armagh" said Lenny matter of factly and Dom nearly choked on his drink.

"Holy fuck" and he started laughing and Lenny joined him, a huge belly, weed induced laugh that neither of them could control.

They both laughed till they were sore and then laughed some more and the tears rolled down their cheeks for what seemed like an eternity until Lenny blurted out, "What are we laughing at?"

And they started again almost falling off the chairs they were sitting on. Eventually Dom raised his glass and giddily proposed a toast to the "best of enemies" He asked, "Have you anything to eat? I'm starving" And that set them both off laughing again.

So it was that the ex-British Special Forces operative and the provisional IRA volunteer got drunk and stoned together and bonded over the search for anything edible in the bare cupboards in Lenny's mobile.

The next morning Nigel still hadn't returned so Lenny took Dom down to a local café for a bite to eat even though a cup of tea and some toast was all Dom could manage as his head was absolutely bursting with the worst hangover he ever had.

As they left the café Dom tripped over a homeless man's collecting hat and immediately apologised as Lenny lifted the hat and gave the man an extra few quid. Lenny turned to Dom saying, "He's a good guy."

"Do you know him?" asked Dom.

"No, but look at his dog, its well looked after, a good measure of that man in my book."

And as they walked away a random man in a suit behind them followed them to tell them the homeless guy took drugs and would probably spend the money he gave him on those.

"No shit Sherlock" replied Lenny, "We thought he sat on that corner begging because his life was sorted and he was in a great place. I don't give a shit what he spends it on if it makes his life a little easier." And right there and then Dominic knew his "Best enemy" was a really decent man.

CHAPTER 60

OH WE DON'T LIKE TO BE BESIDE THE SEASIDE

WHEN NIGEL AND DUALTA arrived back the other lads were waiting, Dom was so delighted to see Dualta he totally forgot about his injuries and hugged him tightly causing him to wince and push him away.

"Are you ok?"

"Yeah I'm fine. Just been to see Dr Doolittle"

Dom didn't understand but laughed nervously anyway. Nigel filled the lads in on how they had got out of London and sought the safest medical alternative he could think of.

Dualta was tired and groggy so he went to lie down as Dominic and Nigel discussed their immediate plans. It would be too risky to attempt to leave the country until the heat had died down a little and in any case Dualta was too weak to do anything other than rest. And to be honest Dom thought there could be worse places to hang out for a while. This coast really was a beautiful place which surprised him a little cause in his youth he always associated England with the British occupation of Ireland and that always conjured up unpleasant images of colonisation, plantation and brutality. Ugly horrible images of waste, murder and destruction.

He expected all of England to be "ugly and horrible" like the parts of London he had lived in so it was quite a shock to his system that he found this place so breathtakingly stunning. He'd never seen anything like the sheer chalk cliffs and lush green hills. It really was a stunning place and in different circumstances he would be happy to spend an extended period there.

He didn't want to stay any longer than he had to as that would put Nigel and Lenny at risk and they had already done enough for them. In addition, during his conversations with Nigel and pouring over the newspaper article, he now knew that there had been civilian's deaths caused by the explosion and while he himself had long since understood that could happen in a war situation he knew Dualta was going to take that news very badly. He didn't want to tell him until he was a little stronger but he also knew it was a conversation that had to happen sooner rather than later. So after a few days while they were walking on the Pier near the harbour he stopped and asked his friend to sit down.

"I need to talk to you."

"Ok, what is it?" asked Dualta experiencing one of these pit of stomach sinking moments, "It's about the bomb isn't it?"

"Yes" said Dom, "Remember you asked about the warning?"

"No, not really, I can't remember very much after the shooting to be honest."

"Well you asked me did I get to phone the warning in and the answer is I didn't and a couple of workers were killed in the explosion" said Dom, feeling pretty ashamed making this admission.

"Ah fuck Dom, no, no, no, you promised. You said it was a legitimate target and there would be no casualties" screamed Dualta as his hands cradled his aching head.

"You fucking promised Dom and now I'm a murderer you've made me a murderer, who died? Who? Where? Why?"

"I don't know" said Dom quickly.

"Who the fuck were they?" roared Dualta

"I don't know" he repeated but a lot louder now that it raised and turned the heads of many bystanders. "I think they were Irish,

I think they were from Kildare" and at that Dualta was like a broken man.

"Kildare? Kildare? I know those lads, they were good decent lads, my friends and I've fucking killed them".

He rose to his feet and went one way then the other and eventually froze not knowing where to go or what to do, his tears were uncontrollable as he sobbed.

"I fucking killed them. We fucking killed them. And for what Dom? For what? For what Dom?" he finished. His grief, overwhelming as he sat back down and curled into himself.

Dom stood off initially but closely edged closer to his best friend and tried to reach out his hand with which he touched Dualta lightly on the shoulder. He thought about hugging his friend until Dualta jumped up and angrily pushed his friend away.

"Fuck off Dom, don't touch me, don't put your fucking hands near me" and he walked off in the direction of the town.

Dom thought it best to just leave him and give him some space, its not everyday someone has to deal with the responsibility of someone else's death, even though if Dualta had been willing to stay a little longer he'd have heard Dominic take full responsibility for everything and put his arm around him and tell him it wasn't his fault and it was all down to Dom and he was sorry and he wished he hadn't met up so freakishly, wished his life had been different, wished no one had to die. With his head in his hands and here in this beautiful place overlooking the crystal clear water and the stunning cliffs and the good looking people, he thought it's all just glossed over, it's all a myth, the world is just an "ugly and horrible place" because it is owned and inhabited by ugly and horrible people who have no humanity towards each other.

He followed Dualta up the Pier and across the harbour at a distance when he accidentally bumped into a handsome young man in a blue boating jacket, white shirt and chinos who had obviously just parked his Porsche before walking to his Yacht with his gorgeous girlfriend.

"Sorry" muttered Dom before moving on

"Oi! You! How dare you! I've a good mind to give you a thrashing" said the young, obviously rich and well-heeled gentleman, much to the delight of the young lady on his arm.

"Not today asshole!" said Dom as he placed a well-aimed uppercut under the lads chiselled jaw line.

Dom was pretty sure that he wouldn't drown before the good people surrounding the harbour wall were able to get him fished out of the sea pretty quickly.

CHAPTER 61

REGRETS, I'VE HAD A FEW

AS HE ARRIVED BACK at Nigel's compound Dualta was nowhere to be seen and Nigel was cleaning and feeding the dogs.

"Come on over, they won't touch you" said Nigel.

Which is the most patronising thing any dog owner can say to someone who isn't comfortable around dogs.

"Have you seen him?"

"Nigel, "Yeah, he's gone down to Lenny's, he doesn't want to see you. Cuz, I'd just leave him alone for a while if I was you."

And Dom knew he was right but he couldn't help but want to talk to him, so he thought he'd give him the rest of the night and talk to him tomorrow.

"So do you need any help with the dogs?" He enquired more out of a sense of responsibility than an actual desire to be near these beasts.

"Yeah" says Nige, "Take Pebble out and let her have a run round the yard. Then put the hose on her and let her roll around."

Dom was nervous, "And she won't attack me?"

"Not unless you're a bad man" Laughed Nigel, just a second before Pebble grabbed Dom by the arm and shock him like a rag doll.

Nigel seemed to see a funny side to this episode and said laughingly, "Jesus cuz, you ARE a bad man"

"Don't I fucking know it" said Dom with no hint of humour or even sarcasm.

So Dom spent a very uncomfortable evening at Nigel's place having a couple of beers but being overwhelmed by what conversation he was going to have with his best friend in the morning. It wasn't that he didn't enjoy the company of his cousin but he would just have preferred to have been with his best friend.

Nigel sensed his discomfort and regaled him with a few stories of their youth he remembered and those tales were particularly pleasant memories for both of the lads.

Back in the days when very little else mattered except a great day by an outdoor swimming pool or a dip in the ocean followed by a pre-packed chicken sandwich and a Victoria sponge bun in the nearby shopping centre café, those memories were golden.

The beer turned into whiskey and the cousins had so many memories to reminisce and discuss that by the time they were finished the dogs were howling for their morning attention.

"Oh jeez cuz, you'll have to help me this morning, I'm not in great shape." He remonstrated through what wasn't quite a hangover yet but still a drunken point of view.

Dom was quite upbeat due to his alcohol consumption so he replied, "Of course I will but keep that Pebble beast away from me."

They had spent the day working on the dogs when Lenny appeared in the yard and whilst he stood there clicking his heels and looking down at his toes, Dom knew he hadn't got anything pleasant to say. So he nodded his head in his direction.

"Yeah"

Lenny, "He won't see you mate, I'm sorry. He says when the coast is clear he is going home on his own."

Dom was suddenly fully aware and very sober and depressed, how long would he remain angry for? The answer he thought was "a long time"

So the days started to take on a routine whereby Dominic helped Nigel with the dogs and even went with him on a few jobs where there wasn't a risk that he'd been seen. Then he'd walk down to Lenny's to see if Dualta would talk to him but inevitably

Lenny would shrug his shoulders, look at his feet, shuffle around a bit with his hands in his pockets and then shake his head saying, "Sorry, he doesn't want to speak to you."

CHAPTER 62

DUALTA'S TURMOIL

WHEN DUALTA LEFT THE harbour he could hardly breathe, he just needed to get away from Dom and try and digest what he had just found out that,

- He was a murderer and
- He'd actually killed two decent lads and great Irishmen

He actually didn't blame Dom, once the initial anger had subsided, but he didn't want to see him cause he was a reminder of the fact that Dualta was now a murderer and responsible for families not having a father to welcome home. That was a lot to reconcile in your mind. He had taken part in the operation, he hadn't been forced, he also had thought that there would be no casualties but that was naïve of him as they were planting a bomb, so deep down he knew things could go wrong.

So his time at Lenny's was all about trying to get his head back in the mind-set of moving forward and ultimately getting back to Sofia but in this darker moments he doubted if she'd ever speak to him again let alone love him.

Dominic called everyday but he really just didn't want to talk to him as it would be too painful. The physical scars were healing very well and he was feeling stronger day by day but mentally he was at a low ebb and didn't feel he had the mental strength for a philosophical debate with Dom.

He found a little relief in helping Lenny around the town. Lenny seemed to be a totally free spirit and that was a big bonus for Dualta right now. Lenny always had a scam on the go. Dualta honestly thought he could have sold "snow to the Eskimo's".

Dualta enjoyed spending time with Lenny but he knew this couldn't go on indefinitely so one night over a "hand rolled ciggy" and a few whiskeys he decided to open up to Lenny. He told him about the bomb and how Matus had died and the escape and how he was emotionally eaten up by his feelings of guilt. Lenny listened, which is a very good trait to have, Lenny really listened and that was brilliant because Dualta normally found when you pluck up the courage to talk to someone about your "feelings" they normally listen for about one minute before they start telling you about how they or their family had just as bad an incident (if not worse) which normally ended in Dualta spending half an hour listening to their bullshit. But Lenny was different, he really listened and as someone who Dualta now respected that meant an awful lot.

For Lenny's part he was happy to listen if that helped someone but as for him opening up and talking to someone about his own experiences or emotions? That was a can of worms he was nowhere near ready to deal with. So Lenny continued to wheel and deal and live a simple life that normally also provided him with a bit of craic.

After listening to Dualta and then helping him to bed between the bouts of drunken vomiting the only real piece of advice he had to offer was, "You really need to talk to your friend."

He wasn't sure if Dualta could take that on board in his drunken state but it was all he could offer.

CHAPTER 63

THE REGATTA OR YACHTING

AS AN IRISH PERSON, unless you lived in the most afflu-ent unionist communities you would never have known what a "Regatta" or "Yacht race" was. Certainly Dominic had no clue what Nigel was talking about when he briefed him on the day's work ahead. So in layman's terms he told Dom they were going to look after a lot of rich guys who were going to show off their rich toys to other rich guys.

"Oh, oh" Thought Dom, "Do they have long memories?" recalling his meeting with the chino guy on the Pier.

To be honest the "Regatta" was hugely impressive. It was a lovely sunny day and the ocean looked fantastically blue and despite his wish to hate most things British, Dominic was most impressed by the whole occasion. The pomp and ceremony were really intoxicating and Dom actually loved the spectacle of it all.

It was probably British Pageantry at its best but if truth be told Dom thought it was fantastic. His job was to direct traffic and basically make sure parking regulations were adhered to while Nigel oversaw the event, ensuring everyone's safety on the shore and then the RNLI would do likewise on the sea.

Dom was happy and enjoying the day until he saw Dualta and Lenny arriving at the harbour to set up a stall selling sweets, drinks and confectionary. At this stage he hadn't spoken to Dualta for at least 10 days but he desperately wanted to. But he fought off those feelings and went back to his duties in the car park. But he couldn't help but check every so often how the "confectionary stall" was doing.

The day turned out to be a perfect occasion and the patrons and guests all had a fantastic time. No one parked where they shouldn't and Nigel debriefed his team in a very positive note, and while handing out the envelopes he also had one for Dominic.

"Give this straight to charity" He thought, he didn't want to take money off him after all he had done for him.

"What about a pint?" Said Nigel.

"Why not" he replied, "As long as you're buying?"

So the lads strolled into the huge pub that overlooked the beach and with its huge vista window it was just the most fantastic view Dominic had ever seen. It had been a great day and now they were starting to unwind, Dom felt very relaxed for the first time in ages.

Himself and Nigel and a few of his workers were enjoying a well-earned pint or two in an amazing marina bar with a most spectacular panoramic view of the ocean, anyone would feel at ease and peace in this situation. And so it was for the lads until a commotion started down on the Pier on the harbour and even the most relaxed patrons couldn't help but notice the crowd that had gathered and the ambulance that was slowly making its way through the crowd. The lads moved out onto the balcony and watched the events unfold with morbid curiosity as everyone does. Word was coming through that a family had stopped to take a few photos and the pram with their youngest child on board had rolled backwards off the harbour wall and fallen into the sea in what would have been a huge tragedy if a young lad hadn't dived into the sea and managed to release the babies harness and bring the baby back to the surface. By all accounts it was a very lucky escape and a very heroic rescue.

CHAPTER 6 4

NO TIME TO THINK, JUST ACT

AS DUALTA HAD BEEN restocking the stall he took a little break and wondered towards the end of the Pier. It really was spectacular. Everyone seemed to be radiating happiness and there had been no expense spared in the glamour stakes. He passed a young family taking photos and thought ruefully that he might never get to experience that joy and that made him sad but he was quickly brought back to reality by the most painful shrill scream he had ever heard. The agony in the scream scared and terrified him in equal measure, as he quickly turned to see its source and at that split second he realised the child's pram had fallen off the Pier and was rapidly descending to whatever depth was down there. So without thinking Dualta, not for the first time in his life, found himself submerged in the waters of a harbour. Luckily, the sea today was crystal clear and although blurred, he could manage a pretty good view of what was happening under the surface. If there was a God, he was on duty and working hard today as the prams handle had caught on a boats mooring rope and was dangling precariously above the unknown depths below.

Dualta tried to lift the pram but that was going to be too difficult and dangerous and he doubted if he could swim up holding it above his head. So the only alternative was to try and release the harness which was extremely difficult as he needed two hands to work on it and then he found it difficult to swim. Jeez, he thought this is taking too long, the baby can't breathe, "Fuck sake. Open you bastard" but it just wouldn't open and he was about to despair when he was joined in the attempt by Lenny with the biggest knife he had ever seen which quickly cut through the harness and released the baby. Dualta was then able to grab the toddler and swim to the surface where first aid could be administered. Luckily "Regatta Day" had no shortage of Doctors and the child was soon in a stable condition.

Dualta tried to slip away but was quickly grabbed and hugged and thanked and hugged some more as himself and Lenny tried to make their excuses and leave but there was no chance they were going to do it easily and suddenly they were being grabbed and shoved into photos by the many photographers that were there to cover the "Regatta". This made both men extremely uncomfortable but they just couldn't get away.

"Way to keep a low profile" thought Dualta. People were recognising Lenny and Dualta was begging him to leave but people were swarming all over them. So when the family and rescued baby disappeared in the back of the ambulance after many profuse thank you's and genuine gratitude, Dualta and indeed Lenny were both relieved to get the attention off them.

Later that night he heard Dom at the door as usual but to be honest he was just too emotionally drained to talk to anyone let alone enter into the conversation he knew he'd have to have with Dom someday. So Lenny wisely sent Dominic away as usual.

He knew Dom would be back the next night and the night after that but tonight his dreams would be filled with the terror of knowing that if that pram hadn't hooked on to the rope, he'd never have been able to get the child out and that thought terrified him and made him sick to the pit of his stomach. He declined the fish and chips Lenny had put out on the kitchen table and went straight for the whiskey bottle.

"Only way I'll be able to shut my eyes tonight." He ventured to Lenny and the reply was not unexpected.

"Fuck it, make that two glasses."

CHAPTER 65

LET'S LIE LOW THIS TOWN AIN'T NOTHING BUT A GHOST TOWN

NIGEL TOTALLY RESPECTED THE lads intervention in the harbour rescue but also knew it was going to draw attention to the group, so he knew it was time the lads moved on for everyone's sake. Dom knew it too and that night they started to formulate a plan to get the lads back to Ireland. Probably the most difficult aspect of the plan was going to be getting Dualta to actually start speaking to Dominic again so that was going to require a careful strategy. Until that time Nige thought it would be an idea for the lads to keep their heads down and avoid attention, Lenny totally agreed and it so happened he had been contacted by the owner of their local pub who had a few odd jobs and deliveries for Lenny so that should keep them occupied and busily out of the way for a couple of days.

So Lenny and Dualta headed down to the "Stags Head" and started to empty out the cellar and load Lenny's van for a trip to the dump. By lunchtime, they were ready for a break and the landlord Gary told them he would have a bite for them up in the bar at 1pm. So it was turning into a good day as they worked away in the sunshine very much minding their own business.

Just before lunch the lads wandered up to the bar and Lenny joked they might get a few pints as the lounge was quiet and lit up a "spliff" just as they were entering the bar, Lenny laughed and said, "Chill mate, there's no one here" and offered the ciggy to Dualta who tentatively accepted just as Lenny opened the door and Dualta entered the lounge area taking a large drag of the "spliff".

Before he could exhale, Dualta's breath stopped in his chest and almost choked him as he looked, stunned at the scene that greeted them. Lenny was equally shocked and his metaphorical jaw not only hit but probably went through the floor of the bar.

Although neither probably counted accurately, what greeted the two lads in the "quiet bar" that lunchtime was in the region of a dozen fully uniformed Police Officers, and some other less startling civilians all in a circle facing the two lads as Dualta tried to stub out the "joint" he was literally smoking in front of a multitude of coppers. Neither lad could speak but through their shock they realised the police and others were clapping and loudly cheering. Looking behind them the lads realised that the cheers were for them. At this point Gary, the landlord, interjected.

"Sorry to trick you lads but the parents wanted to thank you personally for saving their child's life." And again everyone cheered and clapped.

It turns out "harbour baby's" mum and dad were both off duty cops out for a nice stroll when the "incident" had happened and had very quickly realised that years of careful training counted for nothing when emotion takes over and to that effect they were eternally grateful to Dualta and Lenny for reacting so quickly. Their colleagues from the station were equally impressed and thought the uniformed "guard of honour" was just the exact way to show these two heroes the respect they deserved.

When Dualta was finally able to exhale the smoke from his joint, he was literally unable to form any words let alone sentences and was greeting each handshake with an "mmm" or sometimes an "aagh" but with regards to actually uttering a word from the oxford dictionary, not a chance. However he did inwardly muse on the irony of the situation where a drug smoking, terrorist murderer was receiving a standing ovation from a group Britain's finest Bobbies.

Lenny was equally off put and his brain was spinning so much that he thought he might actually pass out. Luckily most of the cops had to return to work so the situation calmed quite quickly and the lads were able to escape out the door and back down to the cellar.

This turn of events had to speed up the evacuation plan and Dualta, Dom and Nigel all knew the lads had to get out of the town after all this publicity.

Nigel, "Look lads, we can't do any more for you here, it's just too dangerous"

Both lads agreed and knew it was time to go back home or at least try to. This was the first time Dualta and Dom had been together since their fall out on the Pier but there was no animosity between them, neither was there much empathy from Dualta.

"Okay" he said, "Let's just do it"

Nigel's plan was to get the lads up to Holyhead and get them on a ferry to Dublin, with a bit of luck they'd be able to slip through any security and then make their way across the border.

"Then you'll have to deal with your own shit up there" says Nigel.

So all was agreed and the lads were secreted into the back of one of Nigel's trucks and headed to Holyhead. The gang of four arrived in coastal Wales without any incident and soon it was time to say farewell. It was awkward cause generally men don't ever know what to say in these situations. But men equally realise the importance of these events and would all like to say something. In a very short space of time, the four had become very close and that had to be recognised now it was coming to an end. So as men often do, everyone suppressed their actual feelings and emotions and gave each other a quick hug which probably had as much feeling as they could have articulated anyway.

CHAPTER 66

DON'T PAY THE FERRYMAN

AS DOM BOARDED THE ferry he felt a mixture of sadness and relief. He was sad and annoyed to be leaving Nigel but also that Dualta would barely speak to him and was obviously just going through the motions of being civil to get through their journey. Dom wanted to talk about it but would wait until Dualta was ready. So they boarded the ferry without any incident to be honest and were given a key to their berth which was designed for four people and was more than adequate. Dualta's answers were still monosyllabic so Dom decided to head to the bar and see what was going on. But what was going on was about ninety school kids from Ireland on their way back from a Manchester United match who were totally hyper and manic and running around the ferry like they were on fire. Not that Dom was resentful but he was envious of their joyous youth as he felt his had been snatched away from him when Dualta had disappeared.

So here he was sitting watching "Match of the Day" on a cross channel ferry thinking "How come I never got the lucky break?"

Dualta hadn't come down to the bar/restaurant area so Dom just thought he'd just sit and drink a few beers and head up to the cabin when Dualta was asleep to prevent any awkwardness. Match of the Day was non eventful and Dom thought "I'm better than those boys" but it was what it was and by the time he slipped back into the cabin he presumed Dualta was asleep and despite the fact the school kids were still running wild around the corridors, he was tired enough to still think he could sleep.

And sleep he did at least until he heard loud banging on their cabin door which caused him to wake up startled as he made his way to the door. As he tentatively opened the door expecting the full might of the British law enforcement he was actually quite taken aback to see a very scruffy, very belligerent man asking if this was the "party cabin".

Dom told him to "fuck off" but as he made his way back to bed he realised every other cabin on this floor was occupied by school kids, so he thought he might just take a look out on the corridor but as he did "belligerent" guy had disappeared. "That was quick" thought Dom, "Maybe I'll take another look."

As he walked up the ships residential corridor he noticed one particular rooms door was wide open and there sitting proudly on the end of a child's bed was "drunk belligerent man" claiming he'd been invited for a party. Dom quickly went back to his own cabin and told Dualta to "get up" and follow him.

Now he thought "This has to be done delicately" so he tried to gently talk to "drunk guy" and get him out of the room and tell him to come with him as there was a much better party going on down the corridor and although "drunk guy" was a little slow to leave the cabin when he did he was very quickly able to choke him out very easily, all thanks to his Brazilian Ju Jitzu memories from his ace coach Marty.

Whilst holding him in a choke hold he told Dualta to alert the ships bursar to get this predator locked up. Maybe he was just too drunk and wasn't a total paedophile but Dom wasn't going to take any chances.

So after the drama had died down and the ships authorities taken over, Dom and Dualta had walked down to the bar area to see what was happening. To their surprise "drunk guy" wasn't locked up but was sitting comfortably in the day lounge and although he was being watched by the bursar he wasn't under "ships arrest" as was promised he would be to Dom.

He got up to walk towards Dom and offered a hand but Dom told him to "fuck off" and pushed his hand away.

"You were in a kid's room. Are you a paedo?"

"Drunk guy" moved forward and threatened Dom but was immediately hauled back by the ships security team. Dom told the ships staff exactly what he thought of them and when he was eventually assured the "drunk guy" would be locked up he agreed to go to bed.

Even after this episode, throughout which Dualta had his back, they still hadn't really talked or communicated.

They walked wearily back to their cabin and went back to a restless slumber without really talking. At 6.05am the ships siren blared out that the ship was docking and if you had booked breakfast you had to make your way to the restaurant area and vacate your cabin by 7.00am.

Dom didn't even bother talking to Dualta as he was really losing his patience and couldn't be bothered apologising anymore. So he showered and got dressed in silence and walked down towards the breakfast area. Although still tired and lethargic he was immediately stunned to see "drunk guy" at the bottom of the staircase he was descending with two full Irish breakfasts. Dom was confused as to why this potential paedo was walking around freely and he immediately addressed the man.

"What the fuck are you doing out here? Do you remember me?" Drunk guy, "Aye, now fuck off out of my sight or I will kill you"

Now mostly Dom was a fairly tolerant and easy going fella but even for him this was too much and as "drunk guy" walked up the steps towards him he laid him out with a sweet yet forceful straight right. It only took one punch and as he delivered it he realised Dualta was right behind him, where he always had his back.

"Drunk guy" tumbled down the staircase, his breakfasts scattered in the process. But what happened then stunned both Dom, Dualta and any unfortunate innocent that was in the area as "Drunk guy" fell and on his way to the floor his leg flew off in the complete opposite direction. Time stood still while everyone's brains started to compute the information until the silence was broken by someone shouting, "He's got a wooden leg?"

Luckily ships security were quickly on the scene and he was scooped up and taken away very speedily. Dom stared at Dualta. Dualta stared at Dom. And then Dualta started to laugh hysterically and soon Dom joined in and they sat down on the ships staircase and laughed until they thought they would wet themselves.

"You beat up a one legged man?" Laughed Dualta.

"He was a paedo" Explained Dom, through the laughter.

As the laughter continued, Dualta noticed the man's prosthetic leg was still lying on the floor and quickly raced to lift it.

"What are you going to do with it?" Asked Dom.

"Let's see if it floats?" Laughed Dualta and they both rushed out on to the ships deck and Dualta fired the leg into the sea.

"Oh, it does float" And the friends laughed again. "Fuck him, he deserved it"

As the laughter subsided the lads both knew an in-depth conversation wasn't probably going to be necessary as in that moment they both understood each other a little better.

"I'm still very pissed off with you." Added Dualta.

"I know but come on, we're nearly home."

"I don't know if I can go home Dom" said Dualta quietly, "Everyone thinks I'm dead. The only one who knows I'm not is my ma as I wrote to her from Canada."

Dom said matter of factly, "Sure its ok, you'll be a miracle like that lad Larry Ross we learned about in school"

"Who is Larry Ross?" queried Dualta.

"You know that lad in the Bible, come back from the dead, we learned about him in Religion"

"You mean Lazarus, you bollix?"

"Oh yeah, that's him, come on Larry" "What's home like now?" Ventured Dualta

"Shit, since my dad was shot" Dom

"Jamesy is dead?" Dualta was stunned, "What happened?"

"Long story, my fault" he continued, "I also have a son but I fucked that up too and don't see him much now. I've fucked up mostly everything mate"

"So have I mate but it's not too late, is it?"

"What's his name?"

"Jude, he's better off without me" said Dom, "The patron saint of hopeless cases, and I'm certainly a hopeless case" Dom continued, "He's a great kid, I'm just a shit dad"

"You'll make it right, get out of all this shit you're involved in and start over. If Sofia will have me back I'm still planning on going back to Canada. You and Jude could come too."

"I had a girl too, not Jude's mum but a good girl and I really was starting to fall in love but I fucked that up too" said Dom in a way only realising it himself for the first time. "Mate I've made a mess of everything, and now I've got you involved in my disaster, I'm sorry mate I shouldn't have got you involved."

Dualta thought, "You didn't force me, I agreed."

As the ferry's horn sounded the last call for passengers to disembark, both lads felt quite low even though they were back on home soil.

The only thing that brightened the mood was "drunk guy/paedo" being carted off by the Garda shouting, "Where's my leg?"

So the lads made their way into Dublin on that DART and thanks to the money Nigel had given him, they had enough to lie low in the city and make a plan to get back across the border. As long as they didn't use any main routes they should be able to avoid any major check points, so they thought they might just chill in Dublin for a couple of days and prepare for whatever might lie in store.

CHAPTER 67

THE GREEN GREEN GRASS OF HOME

DUALTA'S MUM HAD ALWAYS been a huge Tom Jones fan and she constantly told Dualta that he was number one in the charts with a song called "The Green Green Grass of Home", on the day Dualta was born. She always loved the song and on the surface of it the song was pleasant enough, all about a man returning to his longed for home where he could meet his parents, family and girl after being away for a while and their reunion would be warm and precious.

The line in the song, "The old home town looks the same as I step down from the train" resonates with a lot of travellers but Dualta knew the song paints a picture that is pretty joyous and sentimental until the end when if you listen closely enough you realise the guy in the song is actually in a death row prison and rather than getting his joyous reunion the only "green grass of home" he'll see is in his imagination as soon he'll be buried six feet under it. The ominous feeling he had now about coming home matched the far from joyous words at the end of the song and the feeling he had in the pit of his stomach and the nagging, dark cloud hanging over him. He would of course be happy to see his mum, family and friends but it just didn't feel right. To be honest he wanted to be thousands of miles away in Canada but he knew he'd have to go home first and sort things out before he could follow his dreams.

He thought it was ironic how his life had changed. When he was younger, he thought his Irish culture was his identity but now he realised it's what is inside that matters not what surrounds you. He thought it strangely odd that that was how Dom used to be but now he'd gone full Michael Collins and was going to revolutionise the whole Island. He couldn't help feel responsible, at least partly, for that as Dom's change had occurred when he thought Dualta was dead so maybe something had died within him as well and changed him cause he knew Dom wasn't happy but was stuck very rigidly down a very bad path that he had chosen to travel down more by default than clarity of decision.

He remembered reading somewhere that "True friends love you, despite who you are." And this was definitely the case with Dom as Dualta didn't like what he had become but he still loved his best friend and always would. He hoped he might turn his back on his present life and perhaps he might even come to Canada with him and make a new start. He decided he wouldn't give up on his friend but first he had to get his own house in order and that meant trying to re-establish a connection with Sofia and see what mess had been left behind by Fred's activities. He wasn't even sure if Sofia would even talk to him but he knew he had to try.

When they eventually crossed the border and got back home it was pretty awkward for Dualta. He really didn't want a fuss but he knew they story of the "Prodigal Son" and guessed because his side of the story was common knowledge that he was a bit of an enigma and a hero. His mum cried and he felt guilty that he hadn't seen her for so long (even though he had made sure she knew he was still alive). He saw his sister and he felt guilty cause he now had a nephew and two nieces that he had no idea about. He met his friends and he felt guilty cause he didn't feel any connection to them. He walked through the town and he felt guilty because he compared it to the wild beauty of Canada and it couldn't stand up against it.

CHAPTER 68

TIE A YELLOW RIBBON

DOMINIC WAS NERVOUS ABOUT coming home. The London operation had been a disaster in terms of execution and PR. So he was fully aware he'd have to answer to "command" for that as being an officer in any military organization, albeit a lower ranking one comes with responsibility. At least he'd had the sense to get out quick and no one was ever arrested or questioned so the IRA could claim they knew nothing of the operation.

On the way home he thought about a song his mum had listened to when he was young.

"Tie a yellow ribbon round the old oak tree" was an American song by a lad called Tony Orlando, it spoke of an old tradition where returning prisoners would be greeted by yellow ribbons tied to a tree on the entrance to the village.

Dominic had grown up with that song and songs like it. Like most Irish children of his generation he had gained a certain amount of his morality from the church but also a large proportion from Country and Western music, which tended to not only entertain but also give a good clear message on how to be a general "good aul boy". If you were happy enough to ignore the racism, sexism, ageism, sectarianism, colonialism, imperialism and bullying, then country music was a hell of a moral indicator. In this case, the "Yellow ribbon" meant forgiveness and you were welcome home with no questions asked.

Dominic remembered the sentiment as a youngster but also realised his journey home would not be met with a yellow ribbon or much less "The hundred ribbons" the particular gentleman in the song had experienced at the end of his journey, but then he assumed the young prisoners indiscretions were not on the scale of his own.

After the initial excitement and questions when he arrived he moved back in with his mum but found it very difficult. In truth she hadn't gotten over his dad's death and he soon realised she never would. They had been childhood sweethearts and probably had never had a night apart in all their married life. Dominic soon realised that his dad had done all the banking and controlled all the money in their relationship and his mum had struggled without him. His sisters had obviously helped as best they could but they had their own lives and children now and although they welcomed their mum into their homes for as long as she needed, she could never settle and developed what Dominic diagnosed as a "broken heart" but the doctors described as "depression". He was actually stunned when one of his sisters told him his mum had been on "anti-depressants" but to be honest with himself he struggled to know what to do about any of it and with his sisters so busy dealing with all their own children, he struggled when left alone with his mum. He had had an initial meeting with the Commanding Officer of the Brigade and although he had escaped with a rebuke, he knew that there was going to be any riding off into the sunset to Canada with Dualta.

Jesus he would have loved to but once you are "sworn in", it's not a simple matter of leaving.

He knew he had fucked up in London so it made complete sense that he would have to make up for it. It hadn't gone unnoticed that he had brought Dualta home with him and the rumours and whispers were already circulating that he had helped out on the London mission but Dom had nipped the idea he would "swear in" as a complete nonstarter.

"No way, just leave him out of this" he emphasised at length.

But in doing so Dom realised he was hardly ever likely to escape his current position. So he went back to work and the first few missions were pretty much formalities. A bomb in a ditch here or a shooting over the head of a policeman was really all they were doing as the Politicians were taking over and making good progress at the negotiating table. So Dominic and his Active Service Unit were serviced with applying just enough pressure for everyone to realise "they hadn't gone away" but also to indicate that they could stop if necessary.

Routine missions were really just a "show of strength" and not really intended to harm anyone which was a great result for all involved. Maybe, just maybe Dom could see a light at the end of the tunnel and possibly a way out of his situation. He couldn't really talk to Dualta about it but for the first time in a long time he was feeling positive that this great conflict might actually be over soon, what joy!

CHAPTER 69

YOU'RE ONCE, TWICE, THREE TIMES A LADY

DUALTA MOVED BACK IN with his mum and began to establish a relationship with his nieces and nephews, which was great but his main mission in life was to re-establish communications with Sofia in Canada.

Since their arrival on the "Gun run" he had tried to ring her a few times but knew that he couldn't risk talking to her as it was too dangerous. But somewhere in his heart he knew that she knew it was him on the end of that phone line, so she knew he was still trying.

Sofia had always been a "lady" and just different from any other girl he had ever met. She had also supported him against her "bollix" of a brother which in his eyes made her "twice a lady" in terms of a song he'd remembered so his absolute prayer was that she'd be "three times a lady" and take him back.

He dialled the phone number a hundred times but when he heard her voice he hung up, partly out of fear for her safety and partly because he didn't think he could face her rejection. So he made a few enquiries from the local press and tried to piece together some of the details from the incident from the beach in Clogherhead and what had happened and for all intents and purposes it seemed that there were no records of a Canadian involved in the incident.

So Dualta thought he might have better success writing a letter to Sofia and trying to explain everything and what actually had happened.

He thought he might as well tell the truth, the whole truth and nothing but the truth and as his granny had always said, "If it is for you it'll not go by you" (A good old Irish saying).

But he also remembered what his dad used to say, "Better be hung for a sheep as a lamb".

The fact Sofia was even engaging with him was a good sign. He was very prepared to be patient and give her space if it meant that he would win her back, then he would take as long as was necessary. He decided to write a letter every day to convince her of his love and commitment and in the meantime he needed to get a job. He was enjoying living in the bosom of his family and if he managed to reconnect with Sofia, he thought she'd be "three times a lady".

Working in the bakery was tough. His boss Shane was an absolute gentleman, who had gone outside the parish to marry so he took his fair share of banter but he was everything anyone would have wanted in a boss. He was kind, gentle and compassionate and everyone in the bakery thought the world of him and Dualta thought "this is a really fantastic place to work". Also his work partner was a Lithuanian guy called Vincent and they both got on so well that in different circumstances Dualta would have been happy to work here indefinitely. He couldn't help but notice that some bosses are absolutely terrible people and show no respect for their staff but Shane was different and would often come down and talk to the workers to make sure they were doing ok. Dualta was very impressed and thought maybe if the world had people like this looking after it, then it wouldn't be in such a fucking mess. Himself and Vincent became close and worked very efficiently together and it must be said very happily, but Dualta was just biding his time till he could get back to Canada and he knew Vincent also had huge plans to live the best life he could.

One day after a particularly long and tiring shift that had started at 5am, they decided to go for a pint in the mid afternoon. Himself and Vincent sat and talked and drank all day and they realised how much they had in common and how two lads from totally different countries and contrasting politics could suddenly bond over a chat and a few beers.

One pint led to another and then a few shots and Dualta felt comfortable enough to open up and tell Vincent a little bit about his situation and how he wanted to be somewhere else and the response he got stunned but also inspired him.

Vincent, "You're feeling lost? I come from Lithuania and we come here to survive, wise up Dualta! Go and experience life, make yourself better with new experiences. Meet amazing people who are like minded or maybe even a few steps ahead of you. The reason you're feeling lost is either you're not doing what you really want to do or because you are surrounded by toxic people that are bringing you down because they are too insecure to follow their own dreams."

When Dualta woke up in his sister's house the next morning with his young nephew crawling over his chest he couldn't remember very much about the previous night. But one thing he was absolutely sure about was that he really liked that Lithuanian guy Vincent.

At work the next day himself and Vincent were out on an early morning delivery and they got to talking again about where their lives had taken them up to this point and Vincent said, "Our lives had been mostly dictated by the concerns of other people's judgments."

Dualta could really relate to this and he began to enjoy the company of Vincent more and more. His relationship with Sofia has started to improve, she had started replying to his letters and in her last letter she had sent him a Polaroid of herself. So to be fair Dualta was in a pretty good place whilst pursuing his dreams. He wasn't one for words but Vincent seemed to be able to say and articulate everything pretty straightforwardly.

"Simple thing is my friend, have your goals and your visions and just go and get them then and have a beautiful life."

Himself and Vincent would sit for hours and discuss life and living and Dualta always felt better for being in his company.

He was spending less and less time with Dominic and again he was probably feeling guilty about that and he brought the issue up with Vincent one night and after many beers and a good few laughs he remembered a very poignant thing Vincent had said that night through a drunken slur he clearly said, "Dualta, it's not about whether you've stood with the great, it's about whether you've sat with the broken."

CHAPTER 70

YOU'RE STILL YOUNG THAT'S NOT YOUR FAULT

IF DUALTA HAD EVER asked then he would have realised Dom was actually very close to "broken".

His mum was causing concern, she was always fecking sick or wanting to be sick. He and his sisters were trying to look after her but he couldn't really cope. She was still a relatively young fit woman but she just wasn't herself.

Dominic would like to have had time to look after her but he was obviously on active duty and still owed a lot to the organisation.

He would have appreciated spending time with Dualta and talking to him about his mother but they were still not on great terms and he knew he was still trying to build his life up again and get back on good terms with Sofia so he was giving him space. As for himself he had re-established a line of communication with Jude and his mum and he had hopes they might try to reconnect so he was trying to be understanding and taking that relationship one step at a time. He had listened to the song "Father and Son" and he knew it would take time for Jude to regain his trust, but he was so young and there was hope. He still had to complete a few missions even though there were peace talks going on behind the scenes.

On one occasion he has due to be picked up by a colleague and when he was comfortably settled in the back of the estate car boot where he would be able to take a few leisurely shots at the barracks. The mission was never meant to take any casualties but just let the establishment know that during the talk's process, the IRA still had fire power if any ceasefire wasn't respected.

However on this occasion Dominic's driver was quite inexperienced and as they got nearer to the target he panicked and drove out of town at neck break speed which may have been fine other than the fact Dominic had fallen out of the car's boot and was lying prostrate in the middle of the town's square right below the huge army look out post in broad daylight. Dominic closed his eyes tight shut and waited for the bullets to blow him away but after a minute or so he realised he wasn't going to be shot and the lookout post must have been empty. So quickly he gathered himself up and ran to the nearest shop which happened to be a Chemist Shop, full of customers. Dom momentarily forgot, in his haste to escape, that he was wearing a balaclava and carrying an ArmaLite rifle so when the chemist saw him he immediately threw his hands in the air and screamed "Don't shoot me! Don't shoot me!"

Dom had known the chemist since he was a boy and to calm the situation he lowered the Armalite and took off the balaclava assuring the chemist.

"Look, Mark, I'm not trying to rob you, I just need to get out your back door"

At which point Mark started taking notes out of the till and throwing them towards Dom again crying, "Don't shoot me!"

Dom realised the situation was going to escalate and decided on decisive action, "Mark! If you don't calm down and shut the fuck up and let me out your back door. I will fucking shoot you!" He managed to get away and he knew Mark would never tout on him but he resolved to get a more experienced driver the next time!

Dom was getting more and more stressed, his mother's ailing health was a huge concern. One night when he was taking Jude to football up at the local club which was a total safe haven and always a joyous experience he got a phone call from his sister that rocked him to the core.

"Mums in hospital, she's had a heart attack"

To say his brain didn't compute was an understatement, "Surely that can't be right? My mum is a tiny wee woman, heart attacks are for fat men?" But it was true and within a few days he was sitting at her bedside in the local hospital when she passed away. His sisters, nieces and nephews were all of great comfort but it was still a blow that was of the knockout variety.

He wondered in a daze through another wake and funeral and in fairness the kindness and generosity of the local community really helped as they were all kind, considerate and sympathetic. As soon as it had happened he had rang Dualta and throughout the process he had never left his side. Dualta had been his strength. The two friends without brothers had as always been brothers to each other during a crisis and no matter how distanced things had been they would always be together when they needed each other.

An Irish wake is a comforting thing but when the crowds have disappeared and the funeral is over and the loved one has been buried, you start to feel alone with your thoughts and only then do you start to grieve. As the two lads sat in Dom's sisters house where the funeral and wake had taken place. Dominic realised something that every Irishman in the same position would testify to.

Dom, "Dualta, it's not that I don't miss my dad or mourn for him but it's a hell of a lot harder to lose a mum than a dad."

As the days and weeks went on Dom realised he was going to be destined to be on his own forever if he didn't make more of an effort with those closest to him.

CHAPTER 71

KNOCK, KNOCK, KNOCKING ON HEAVENS DOOR

DUALTA WAS DEVASTATED BY Dom's mums passing. She'd been like a mother to him from he was three or four years old. It made him want to be closer to Dom but it was still difficult between them. So he took a huge leap of faith and said, "Come and stay with me brother. It'll give you time to relax and take it easy for a while."

Dom was in no position to turn down such a good offer and was delighted to be back in close proximity to his best friend.

Dualta still hadn't come to terms with how badly their relationship had gone but he was also glad and comforted they were now back together. They could maybe start planning their future in Canada.

"I've even a spare room for Jude"

Just like it was meant to be the two friends hugged, cried a bit, then pushed each other off and had another drink. It is always strange how Irish deaths unfailingly bring people together.

CHAPTER 72

WHAT A GOOD YEAR FOR THE ROSES

THE LADS ACTUALLY MADE good housemates. They could both cook, both could tidy, Dominic could iron and Dualta knew his way around a brush and mop. If either of them had brought a girl back to their bachelor pad, she would have been well impressed, however the lads only visitors were their families and in particular Jude and Dualta's nephew Jimbo. Great craic was had with the boyos and life was beginning to look up.

Dualta was communicating regularly with Sofia and by a stroke of luck Fred had simply disappeared so although he felt bad for him, he couldn't help but think it had excused Dualta an awful lot of explaining. In Canada they assumed he was off on one of his drug deals and was reaping what he had sowed so when Dualta explained the story without including Fred, it made sense in a way and he could feel Sofia was starting to forgive him. For the first time in a long time both Dualta and Dom were beginning to smile again.

Vincent had taken his own advice and was now enjoying his "beautiful life" in Dubai but Dualta still enjoyed the work in the bakery so he was content where he was at in his life until such times as Sofia was ready to welcome him back to Canada. Big Hank might take a bit more convincing of his return but he knew Sofia was working on him.

Even better news on the home front was there was now a ceasefire so Dom was not active anymore and that was a huge relief to Dualta who kept working on him about coming to Canada and making a fresh start. Jude could time share between here and there.

"Will you at least think about it?"

Dom laughing, "Yeah, now leave me alone"

CHAPTER 73

A DOG IS FOR LIFE, NOT JUST FOR A CEASEFIRE

DUALTA'S NEPHEW GOT A puppy for his birthday, vicious wee Yorkshire terrier but Jimbo loved it and insisted on bringing the dog on every visit and sleepover. Jude was also badgering Dom and his mum for a dog but Dom wasn't having any of it until a dog appeared at their door out of nowhere and now their small house resembled Crufts at times. They'd take the dogs out for a walk and they would attack every other dog and dog owner in the town, it was becoming embarrassing but most people were understanding, if a little bit annoyed.

But one day there was a car that drove dangerously close to them and a couple of lads in the car seemed to be giving Dom a bit of abuse. Dualta thought it was a little strange but Dom assured him it was nothing so Dualta put it to the back of his mind but it did worry him and it was a little concerning because he knew Dom so well, he could tell he wasn't being 100% truthful when he said it was nothing but he didn't want to upset the kids so he let it go. He had started to notice a change in Dom's mood of late, he seemed distracted as if he had something on his mind. Something was preoccupying him but Dualta didn't know how to approach it so he decided to just sit on it for a while. He had received a letter from Canada and things were definitely looking up on that front and he was quite hopeful that he'd soon be going back to his "Spiritual home" in Canada. Of course he'd miss his family especially wee Jimbo but they could visit and of course he would come home regularly to see everyone. So Dualta was pretty happy with life at the minute and felt things were finally going right. But there was still that continuing nag at the back of his mind that something was bothering Dom.

CHAPTER 74

THE IRISH PEACE PROCESS

DOM DID HAVE A lot on his mind. Talks between Sinn Fein and the SDLP had led to a belief that the "Troubles" might be brought to an end and when it became clear that the British Government had also been in talks with the Provisional IRA then the way had been paved for the Peace Process. However it would never be a simple matter when the Unionist population viewed it as a "sell-out" and the principle of consent was the only way forward and it seemed very unlikely they would consent to anything remotely Irish.

The "Cessation of Military operations" was hugely supported by nationalists but there were also a minority of nationalists who would not accept anything less than a 32 Sovereign Ireland. So not only was there the bigger stumbling block of the Unionists vetoing every progressive step but also the ever increasing threat from dissident Republicans who were apparently receiving funds and arms from supporters in the United States and the Balkans and possibly also acquiring arms and materials, namely Semtex.

From Dominic's point of view his main concern was that dozens of rifles, machine guns, pistols and detonators had been stolen from the "Arms dumps" of the Provisionals and this was going to allow the dissidents to continue to wage war on the security forces in Northern Ireland and scupper the Peace Process. Internal tension within Republicanism, splits and feuds made this whole situation a nightmare and meant that Dominic couldn't relax and enjoy what could be a peaceful new start for everyone.

As a face in his home area he was commissioned to try to deal with any immediate threats from the ground to the Peace Process. The command wanted things to run smoothly so this might require him to use methods that were strictly not within the confines of the Anglo-Irish agreement but it had been a Guerrilla War so the peace process was never going to be free from dirty tactics.

Realising that a significant amount of weapons and munitions were missing from their arms dumps was a huge set back but also a personal slur on Dom as he realised it must be someone he knew, someone from an Active Service Unit. The problem with secret movements were they were so often infiltrated by spies and informers. So, yes, Dom was preoccupied, worried confused and paranoid.

"Who was the rat? Who was giving away secret details? Who was stealing the weapons?"

He was thinking so hard it hurt but he couldn't work it out, he saw everyone as a threat. Trusted no one (except Dualta) and became very paranoid and distracted.

One thing he had always possessed was good intuition and he had noticed a few of the young lads around the area acting out of character and possibly getting ideas above their station, so he started to observe more closely and take a keen interest in their activities. They tended to be all from a similar area of the town, living within a close radius in the same housing estate.

So Dom began to track their comings and goings and saw these group of lads beginning to show some muscle around the area and he didn't really know who they were except for one lad who he thought he recognised from the botched gun shipment fiasco. He had a meeting with command and although it was against normal protocol he was given the name of the young lad who was involved in that operation. So Dom started to piece things together and soon had a good idea who all these lads were.

After observing the lads for a while it became quite clear that their motives were completely unrelated to any desire for Irish freedom but instead they were using the dissident threat as a cover screen for their illegal activities which included smuggling and distributing many substances, including to the detriment of their own community a lot of drugs.

Kids from the area were now regularly turning up at the local hospital on deaths door due to the scant regard any of these dealers gave to the health and wellbeing of their clients. Stories of rat poison, arsenic and horse tranquilisers were probably more truth than fiction but a lot of the youth of the area were being drawn into this cycle of destruction. So whilst allegedly standing as pillars of the nationalist community, these thugs were using their Republican identity as a means to control their local areas and bringing nothing but pain and misery to its inhabitants. He was gathering a lot of "intelligence" on these lads and the organisation they claimed to represent.

On one occasion he had heard about an incident in a local High School where a young lad was taken out of a school assembly and knee capped by a group claiming to be the "IPLO", the "Irish Peoples Liberation Organisation" which apparently had noble Republican objectives but really was just a front for a drug dealing organisation who had discovered a way of taking over the neighbourhood now the Provisionals weren't there to monitor things. So Dom spoke to the youth in question and he was happy enough to talk to Dom about his experiences with the men who were supplying the drugs. He told Dom he had been given a certain amount of drugs to sell but if he met a certain quota he could keep the rest and do whatever he wanted with them (which in this case was consume them ASAP).

Dom had a friend who taught in the school and he told him it was absolute carnage in the assembly hall that day when the Priest was giving a general blessing and absolution to the pupils when the IPLO burst through the assembly hall doors and ordered everyone onto the stomachs, hands behind their necks, on the floor. The next thing the shots of gunfire resonated around the building.

When the teachers finally were confident enough to go and check on the list of pupils who had been called out to report to the school foyer, what they saw was a blood bath. Three pupils of 15 years of age had been shot through the back of their knees as some sort of warning from the very men that were employing them in the communities that they were purporting to protect.

This annoyed Dominic so much. His decision to become involved in the conflict was centred around Dualta's beliefs and Dom's innocent dad had been an accidental victim of these troubles so it made his blood boil that these thugs were using the name of republicanism to make money and terrorise their localities. So he had to do something about it and he decided he would have to take some action to be honest to his principles.

His investigations had probably alerted some attention from the young dissidents, it'd be hard not to arouse suspicions in the relatively small town but their attitude was quite cocky and confident as if they were untouchable. Given that their motives were hardly honourable he suspected their methods would be equally unethical. So rather than confronting the dissidents head on and risking an open conflict he decided to keep investigating and try to find out where their weapons were hidden and cut off their arms supply there by making them impotent.

The only problem was they now realised he was on to them and would be watching their moves and at times actually taunting him as they drove past. He met with "Command" and he was instructed to observe but not to take any action for the time being.

CHAPTER 75

THINGS CAN ONLY GET BETTER

DUALTA NEVER CEASED BEING amused by the difference in his hometown in the ten years he had been away. It was absolutely remarkable how things had changed in that time. The peace process had permeated every aspect of life in the town and the community. When he looked around the town now he saw prosperity, development, expansion and hope.

Old derelict buildings from his youth were now vibrant coffee shops and cafes. Where once there was only a supermarket and a fish and chip shop there were now hair salons, beauty salons, flower shops, designer clothes shops and on street dining. It truly was just amazing, the town seemed brighter, more welcoming and successful. The residents seemed younger and less stressed as well. People stopped and chatted, smiled and laughed with each other but he clearly remembered it certainly always hadn't been like that, he hadn't forgotten the dark days before "French cuisine" and "Pizzerias".

He remembered watching out of the living room of their flat which overlooked the town centre and seeing actual gun battles between the British army and the Provisional IRA when a group of local volunteers would roar into town in a white van and start peppering the British Army Barracks with a hail of bullets after throwing a few sand bags on the ground. In that moment what he was actually he was witnessing was a group of part time soldiers and full time farmers, joiners, brick layers and builders taking on the best of the British Army and holding their own.

Dualta was amazed at how a bunch of local lads with a fire in their belly could fight against the British Army. Obviously they had very little training or experience of how a war like this might work but the one thing they didn't lack was courage and determination. He clearly remembered sitting with his dad and watching a few volunteers firing homemade mortars at the British Army base and wondering "Who are these men?"

The truth was they were his neighbours who by the day just went about their business as usual but by night they fought against the British Empire. Years later when he saw "Star Wars" in the cinema, Dualta wasn't that impressed as he had seen the whole scenario played out right in front of his own eyes and it was much more remarkable than anything that he could see on a TV screen.

One night Dualta remembered sitting in the living room of the flat which overlooked the town centre when a gun battle started in the middle of the rosary, and for anyone of a certain age they will understand how important the rosary was in Irish Catholic families.

Anyway, Granny was kneeling up on the good armchair with the rosary beads going hell for leather and Dualta and the siblings were trying not to laugh out loud when a gun battle started and everyone evacuated to the safety of the nearest concrete wall when they realised Granny was stone deaf and couldn't obviously respond to either the gun fire or the desperate cries of his mum. Then all of a sudden a hail of bullets ripped through the living room window and bounced around the walls until they embedded in a stud wall and missed Granny's head by about a millimeter.

It probably said a lot about how life was lived then that they often told this story to get a bit of a laugh and never really considered the consequences of what might have happened if Granny had been an inch taller. However life was like that then, people seemed to be more resilient and tough. It seemed to Dualta that people were more accepting of their situation and they didn't moan or complain as much as they did now.

He also remembered that people and in particular kids, didn't need as much when he was young. It seemed to him that wee Jimbo and Jude wanted everything that they saw when they saw it and were prepared to have a huge tantrum if they didn't get it. He quite clearly remembered the time when any tantrum would result in quite a slap from your mum as she threatened "Next time I'll tell your dad" and "Then you'll get a real hiding" or another good one was "If I see you crying, I'll give you something to cry about."

Everyday life was also very different back when he was a child. He remembered there were only three channels on the TV and there was no remote control so to change the channels you had to physically get up and press a huge button on the TV. Every house he had ever been in as a child had one living room and one TV and this meant a lot of sibling rivalry as to who got to watch their programme or indeed sit on a chair cause anyone brave enough to make the arduous trek to push the button and change channels, often found themselves enjoying their selected genre from the comfort of the living room floor, as every house he had ever been in only had a sofa and at most two chairs. He laughed to himself as he thought of the youth of today struggling through life with only one TV and no remote control.

He also remembered when the new and exciting initiative called Channel 4 was a ground breaking journey in one's televisual experience. They had a little red triangle on the corner of the screen late at night when they were going to show adult themes and possibly nudity. At that point, every young man alive was praying that his parents would go to bed as there was probably no worse shame in the world as being in the same room as your mum and dad when a pair of boobs were being majestically flaunted in front of you. It was at that moment that time stood still and everyone was frozen to the spot until dad either ordered you to bed or managed to put his cigarette down, without burning himself, quickly enough to get the channel changed. And the agony may not have ended there as mum might have suggested a quick decade of the rosary before bed.

Seeing kids walk around the town with mobile phones was crazy, considering in his youth there were barely phones in people's houses and sometimes he would answer the phone in his own house but the call might be for some lady who lived three doors down from them. He also observed that the town now didn't have any phone boxes anymore.

Another thing Dualta observed was that young kids didn't smoke anymore. In his day at the Friary CBS smoking was a rite of passage, you weren't really a "man" until you had inhaled the toxic poison of a huge cigarette. He remembered one particular occasion when he was in 1st or possibly 2nd year at school when during a visit to the toilet he happened to share the space with a legendary 6th form student, Lenny Tunny, who was about to have a trial with a Premier League soccer team and Lenny actually spoke Dualta's name and offered him the last drag from his cigarette. Dualta's huge man crush meant he took the cigarette and inhaled deeply. After Lenny had left the bathroom Dualta could barely walk straight as he staggered back to class bumping and thumping into every sink, wall, door and window on the way back to his seat in science. He felt sick as a parrot but it was all worth it as he realised Lenny Tunny knew who he was.

Dualta thought a lot about his upbringing and history during his period at home before he was due to leave for Canada, which he now knew would be a permanent move as he realised it was what he wanted to do and his new life with the woman he loved would be the beginning of something refreshing and brilliant.

He chuckled heartily one day, when he remembered himself and all his mates having a snowball fight with the Brits that got way out of hand. Things had started quite light hearted until someone obviously put a huge rock into the snowball and fired it directly at an RUC man accompanying the patrol and then things became a bit more serious. Apparently an incident resulting in an RUC man losing his hat requires an immediate arrest and on this occasion there were no shortage of options for such an operation and this resulted in an altercation that Dualta remembered as being a moral victory since it really was a boys versus men situation. Despite their valiant fight, the whole gang ended up incarcerated and up in court soon after. After a farcical trail the judge dismissed the case as he British Army couldn't really prove snowballs were a "threat to life".

Dualta soon realised that his regular walks around the town were in essence his last goodbye to the place he loved so well but would now never live in again. During these walks he realised every building, every corner, every shop and street brought back a hugely poignant memory for him and despite the troubles and extreme hardships that they had all experienced on a daily basis, his memories were all warm and positive.

Whilst walking through the graveyard of the local chapel he was reminded of a pet dog his family used to own who would often cause quite a stir. His sister had somehow persuaded their dad to let her have a puppy despite the fact they lived in a small flat on the 3rd floor of the building and had no garden or outside space. The agreement was based on the condition that it would be a "Toy dog" that was tiny and able to live in a small flat. And that is exactly what was duly delivered as his sister brought home an absolutely tiny dog that fitted right in the palm of her hand and was the tiniest living thing Dualta had ever seen, job done! Box ticked.

The problem was within 2 months the dog was absolutely huge and a visit to the seller revealed it actually was a cross between a red setter and a Doberman pinscher. The dog became huge, restless and hyperactive so much so his sister lost interest and it was left very much up to Dualta to take the dog with him everywhere he went and try and tire it out, which always proved a difficult task. Although the dog was huge and appeared fearsome he really was a big softy and was hugely loyal to the family and hated to be left alone. During his visit to the chapel Dualta couldn't help but smile when he remembered the dog, who his sister had embarrassingly named "Smartie", burst into the congregation during Sunday Mass looking for Dualta's mum and ending up dry humping the Priest on the altar as Dualta's mum tried to slide under the pew in a fit of mortification and the Priest asked if anyone could come and claim the dog that was humping him and take it away, "Oh bollix". It was a funny memory now but certainly wasn't humorous that Sunday.

He also clearly remembered the day he came home from school and realised the dog was missing only to be told that daddy had sent the dog away "to a farm" where he would be able to enjoy open spaces and not be confined within the flat. Now even at that young age Dualta knew that "the farm" was a euphemism for "I've shot the bastard" so it came as a huge surprise to him a couple of years later whilst himself and his mates were walking home in the early hours after a night out at local carnival when there in the middle of the road there was a very intimidating dog approaching them. All of a sudden all fear was set aside as Dualta realised it was in fact his very own "Smartie" who actually now did live on a real farm but obviously hadn't forgotten his former pal and was now in the process of licking him to death. It was very emotional when he had to leave and Smartie obviously wanted to come home (a fact signified by his tight grip around Dualta's leg). "Oh bollix" thought Dualta and he had to send Smartie away with a tear in his eye.

The town was booming now but Dualta couldn't help but remember there were many dark days in his home and that defines a person and who they become and you can never forget or never should forget where you come from. But despite the hardships most memories were very positive and that was a testament to the resilience and strength of the local community that despite the occupation by British forces and the daily grind and hardships they faced, the people of his home town were always upbeat and positive.

Being stopped and searched had been a daily occurrence, bombs and bullets were common place and death and destruction were part and parcel of the fabric of life. Yet these people moved forward and thrived despite the overwhelming crushing nature of their lives. And an overriding factor amongst all the darkness was the ability of his community to laugh and smile through the trials and tribulations. Humour was a great tool that kept so many people sane during those dark days.

He remembered, as a child, listening intently as one of his dad's friends recounted a story of his "active service" in the town. This particular man's objective that day was to open fire with a semiautomatic weapon on one of the many look out posts that occupied vantage posts throughout the town. Well things started to go wrong for the volunteer when, rather than a van, his associate picked him up in a bright lime green hatchback car. After a debate which centred round the cars suitability for a covert mission it was decided they must just go ahead and the volunteer ended up secreted in the boot of the lime green hatchback with his ArmaLite in hand and a bale of hay for cover. One wrong turn later and a hasty U-turn from the hatchback resulted in the volunteer lying spread eagled on the road of the town facing a looming outlook post full of British soldiers, with a rifle in his hand and a balaclava distinguishing him as very different than the majority of townsfolk going about their normal Friday business. After saying his prayers and preparing to meet his maker the volunteer soon realised he was still alive and indeed the "post" was empty of enemy forces and he had had a very lucky escape. So he quickly got up and ran into a house where although he was a huge surprise to the house-wife within, she quickly ushered him out the back into an alleyway and into the custody of her neighbour who quickly took his coat and replaced it with a non-descript duffle coat and sent him on his way. These were ladies used to the struggle and did what they had to do regardless of the consequences.

"Oh bollix" Thought Dualta, that's a brilliant story.

The more he thought about his childhood and upbringing, the more he realised they were a special people, a breed apart, a brave and noble spirited nation that would never be defeated.

CHAPTER 76

BOMBS, BULLETS, BLOODSHED, IMAGES FROM A DARK AND PAINFUL PAST

THAT WAS THE HISTORY of his hometown but it didn't tell the whole story. Inside the obvious "war zone" children went to school, lived routine lives, enjoyed themselves and engaged in very normal children/teenage activities and grew into quite normal adults. If anything the "troubles" made them better people, more resilient tougher and stronger. Dualta couldn't help but think the kids nowadays didn't have those qualities and always had an excuse for their failings and misgivings. He clearly remembered growing up and taking part in riots as a 14 year old where the RUC would open fire on the crowd and parents being absolutely terrified and trying to deal with these life threatening issues but today he thought there might be an even bigger issue in the house if "Wee Jonny didn't get his latest video game". How times had changed!

CHAPTER 77

IT'S ONLY A GAME.
DUALTA'S GAME

THIS NEW FOUND PHILOSOPHY really manifested itself when Dominic started back playing with the local football team and persuaded Dualta to join him. Although both lads hadn't played for a while they were both quite useful and at underage level they had won many championships and awards. Indeed Dualta was a County Prospect and underage player for their year before his life took a different turn.

So without so much as a training session Dualta found himself lining out at full back for the reserve team in a quite important fixture so Dualta thought, "I'll just do what I used to do and burst this lad's nose the first time he moves".

So as the ball is thrown in and this young lad starts to sprint and run all over the pitch, Dualta thought "Holy fuck" he couldn't even get close enough to the lad to even hit him. Dominic was playing out the field but could do little to help his mate in his agony. The young lad scored 1, 2, 3, 4, 5 points, jeez Dualta was losing count, so when a sub was being warmed up he instinctively knew it was his number that was going to be held up.

Back in the social club, it was open season for his non playing mates to take the piss out of him but it was also good craic and Dualta realised this was totally his comfort zone. To be honest he was loving life at home at the minute and although he 100% saw his future back in Canada, in some of his more drunken moments he did contemplate, "Would Sofia ever come here?"

Cause now he was an adult and more mature he could see the bigger picture and the advantages of living in a hometown that you actually loved. But in all honesty he knew Sofia wouldn't thrive in his community and when all things were considered he knew he would follow his heart and go to Canada. In fact the only thing stopping him going now was the football championship. Himself and Sofia had talked it out and she was now ready to welcome him back and if truth be told he had the money for the ticket and a few pounds besides, to tide him over until he got back to work out there. But, the team was now going into the Championship season and despite his inauspicious start in the league he was now playing well and against all the odds, the team were beginning to play well. After a couple of victories and a few mandatory drinking sessions which obviously included the singing of a few rebel songs in the local pub, Dualta never felt happier in his hometown environment, but he knew it wouldn't last, or would it?

The team went on to have a winning spree and with himself and Dominic now starring on the first 15, the town was buzzing at the prospect of winning the Championship for the first time in ten years. A bit of luck with a penalty in the quarter final and then an extra time win over the much hated local derby team found the team in the Championship final. Dualta was absolutely torn, Sofia had forgiven him and wanted him back, but while he knew this was the right choice for him, he knew he couldn't leave before the final or he'd regret it forever. So he spoke to Sofia on the phone and pleaded and begged with her to try and understand his situation which he totally knew was unrealistic. There he was asking her to understand that sport was such a driving factor in his life now and within the community. He felt even more guilty because he had been involved in gun running and a lot of other operations which she didn't even know about.

CHAPTER 78

DOMINIC'S DEFENSIVE DUTIES

SINCE COMING BACK FROM London, Dominic's life had been a mess, to be honest he didn't know what end of him was up or down. Meeting Dualta and bringing him home was just crazy, absolutely beyond comprehension but the truth was now they were back and it seemed to be working well. They were friends again, all was forgiven and they were living together. Although he still had a huge problem with the dissidents in the area, life was good and he actually felt relaxed for the first time in a long time. He was relaxed so much that he even felt chilled enough to go back to his first love, Gaelic Football.

When he started back training he knew everyone was accepting of him and welcoming him back and that meant so much. Only the Irish can offer a "Céad Míle Fáilte Romhat" every day, "One hundred thousand welcomes". This is what sets the Irish apart from the rest of the world, Dominic thought. He was very emotional and humbled at how readily he was accepted back into the local GAA Club but then he should have known that's just how it works.

Getting back in touch with his roots was a huge learning experience for Dom as well. Through this simple movement Dom realised that his fight for Irish freedom was just a plain cry to Britain to "Leave us alone." Ireland didn't want to plant or colonise or grow or expand, Ireland just wanted to be left alone. "Let us be Irish and leave us to do it on our own. Let us sing, dance, play, work, educate, learn and love. But let us do it on our own, we are not British and don't ever want to be!"

This was how Dominic was feeling, but he also knew that they wouldn't just let them go and that many of the people in the "province" did want to be British and wouldn't let go so easily. However politics could deal with these people, as a far more pressing concern for Dominic was the Dissident Republican threat who were using the guise of Irishness to cover for their illegal drugs trafficking and general dirty underhand endeavours.

Dominic had had a few run ins with the "Dissidents". They were young and precocious and didn't take advice easily but he hoped they had respected the warnings from the "Provisionals" to back off while the peace was being brokered.

Things had been going so well that Dominic was enjoying playing football again and had persuaded Dualta to join him back at the club. At first Dualta didn't want to as he'd been away for ten years but when he saw his picture was still up on the wall of the social club as a former player and award winner, he finally agreed to come back and give it a go. Dominic almost wet himself when he saw Dualta throwing punches all round him on his first appearance and getting "roasted". In fairness by the next match Dualta had set his stall out and now a bit fitter the young lads weren't going to get by him so easily. Momentum was gathering and soon the lads were in a championship final. Dominic was ecstatic and the craic and buzz around the town was amazing.

He had had to leave the celebrations after the semifinal early as he had to pick up Jude but he was still buzzing as they both entered the house with a huge pizza. It was just before he entered the house he noticed the crowd of lads hanging about who obviously weren't there to congratulate him on his championship success. The "Dissidents" were flexing their muscles and pushing a few boundaries but he wasn't actually worried as he knew these were only the foot soldiers and he was confident he could talk to the leaders as they had once been in it all together so surely they would listen to reason.

Other than these thugs on the street corners life was good in the town and the community and excitement about the team getting to the championship final. He knew Dualta was still going to move to Canada but he also knew he wasn't going to leave before the match so that made him happy. He had picked Jude up from his mum's house and while the pizza was most welcome he also had a little pest of a dog to mind that night and while he didn't hate the puppy he hated the fact he had to lift its mess after he'd done it. Yuck, and jeez this wee doggie was vicious, barking and growling at everyone and everything. He had been nipped and attacked by the dog more often that night than he had been during the match.

He had just got Jude settled when there was a loud sound of breaking glass, which stunned and confused him momentarily. Closer investigation revealed half a brick had been hurled through his living room window. No awards for guessing who this crude message was from.

"Wee bastards growing a set of balls".

Inside he was fuming and wanted to seek retribution straight away but deep down he knew he had to be more calculating and would need to speak to "command" before perhaps making an example of one of these wee shits but they must have some support higher up the chain of command than him otherwise they would have been "kneecapped" by now.

Discussions with his OC (Officer in Command) left him uneasy when he was told things were very delicate at the moment and he was to leave it alone as some of the "higher ups" had been annoyed by the ceasefire and saw it as a sell out and could easily go with the dissidents and continue the fight which would de rail the peace process. A classic "catch 22" situation but it didn't help Dominic's anger at the cheek of these lads coming near his house in a deliberate act of antagonism.

Perhaps they were seeking retaliation from him as an excuse to break the ceasefire and blame him. It certainly led him to have some restless nights. He was also uneasy about his own "commander" being so unconcerned about this situation in the town. Something was going on and he didn't like it one bit. Being left out of the loop was fuelling his paranoia but he was powerless to take affirmative action, unless they came near his house or son again and then he would be acting as an individual, a dad protecting his own and he didn't care what he'd been told. He'd take whatever action he needed to protect his own and he really meant "WHATEVER" he had to do.

Dualta was livid about the broken window but Dominic didn't tell him the truth. He'd got his best friend in enough trouble and he'd be going off to Canada after the match so he didn't need to know any of the shit that was going on. He was just going to concentrate on the match and try to put politics out of his mind for the time being. He went to work during the day and trained at night, as did Dualta and things were generally quiet. He was enjoying the build up to the match but it was also sad as he knew his friend would be leaving again after the final.

He'd grown used to having him around and although they'd had some difficult times lately it was a great comfort having his best friend back in his life and if truth be told he didn't want to lose him again but he also didn't want to hold him back from enjoying his best life which should and would be with the love of his life in Canada. The friends were laughing again and training with all their childhood mates for a County final and the feeling was just priceless.

CHAPTER 79

THURSDAY CHAMPIONSHIP FINAL, T, MINUS 10 DAYS

THE LADS ENJOYED A great session on the pitch, the nerves weren't quite so bad so the coaches weren't busting balls too much if the lads were having a little banter between drills and sprints. The flags were starting to go up around the club house and on local lamp posts so the atmosphere was starting to build and the town was booming. The lads weren't strictly on a "drinks ban" so they decided to head into a local pub for a solitary pint as they knew they wouldn't be getting any sessions till after the final.

Dominic's stomach felt a little tighter when he walked into the pub and saw it was populated by at least five or six of the "Boy scout dissidents" but by the time he suggested they move on somewhere else Dualta already had two pints in his hands and was actually murdering one of them before Dominic could speak. Dualta was all business about the match and speculating on the team selections and whether or not he had done enough to get on the team but his constant chat was really only a muffled noise to Dominic who was watching the dissidents in the corner, who were getting drunker and more boisterous.

Dualta was continuing to chat endlessly about the potential team selection but Dominic was fixated on the nasty group of youths that were now giving an elderly gentleman at the corner of the bar just trying to enjoy a quiet pint some stick. Dominic didn't want to get involved but he wasn't about to stand by and see these pricks abuse an old man who wasn't doing anyone any harm. Suddenly the old man crashed to the floor smashing his head on the bar counter on the way down.

Despite the shock Dominic sprang up like a cat to go to the man who looked like he'd been shot. Confusion reigned in the bar and even the dissident youths seemed shocked which led Dom to believe maybe it wasn't their fault but he still pushed through them telling them to "Fuck off away from him" as he tried to assess the situation.

For the second time recently Dom was stunned and confused as to what exactly was going on until the silence was broken by the barmaid screaming, "He's had a heart attack". At that realisation time seemed to stand still while the barmaid was still screaming "Does anyone know CPR?" At this point Dominic had regained hold of his senses and instructed Dualta to press the man's chest as he applied mouth to mouth resuscitation.

"To the rhythm of, Ah, ah, ah, ah, staying alive, staying alive" shouted Dominic, remembering some course he'd been to on life saving many, many years ago.

After a hell of a lot of blowing into the old lad's mouth, he seemed to kick start and splutter to life again. However what they hadn't told Dominic when he was practising on the dummy was that when the heart kick started up again, everything that was stuck or floating around this old guy's respiratory system came plummeting up into Dominic's mouth and all over his face. It made him baulk but at least the old lad was breathing now and although the cut on his head looked pretty deep, Dom was confident he would survive until the ambulance arrived. The clock was very slow moving that night, every second seemed like a minute, every minute seemed like an hour but still the ambulance didn't arrive. 5, 10, 15, 20 minutes and still no ambulance.

Dom and Dualta were getting weary holding the poor man when the fattest ambulance man ever burst through the pub door eating a huge doughnut and asking "What's up? Did someone fall over after too much drink?" He almost laughed.

Both Dom and Dualta could have choked him but were distracted because they both realised instantaneously that the old man had stopped breathing again and was technically dead. At this stage they both lay back in despair as the ambulance crew took over and despite the best efforts of the health workers, the old lad passed away right in front of them on the floor of the bar.

"Jesus Christ. What took you so long" Said Dualta to the ambulance man.

"Oh, we thought it was just someone who had taken too much drink"

"Oh bollix" said Dualta

Then the barmaid panicked and shouted, "His daughter is on her way here! I rang and told her he had taken a wee turn"

"Oh bollix" thought Dualta, "Did you not tell her to stay away as he's fecking dead?"

At that point one of the young thugs started to giggle and Dualta snapped, jumped at him and grabbed him by the throat and gave him a few swift punches before Dominic intervened and pulled him away saying, "Just leave it".

As the scene played out amidst blue flashing lights and a lot of weeping and wailing, the lads wandered out and towards home without saying a word until after they entered the house with the boarded up window.

Dualta, "Why'd you stop me slapping that wee shit?"

Dom, "I don't know mate, I just thought it wasn't appropriate over aul Jonnies body"

Dualta, "Ok, night" Dom, "Ok, night" Dualta, "You ok? Dom, "Yeah, you ok?" Dualta, "Yeah"

CHAPTER 80

SATURDAY, CHAMPIONSHIP FINAL T MINUS 8 DAYS

THE LADS HAD FELT down over the incident in the local bar but as life has a habit of doing, it moves on relentlessly with or without you. Dualta was off work on the Saturday so went to visit his sister and take wee nephew Jimbo out for a walk. They wondered into the local coffee shop and ordered way more buns than they could actually eat, when a few lads walked into the café and started being really rude and cheeky. The young girl behind the counter was obviously really struggling to deal with them when Dualta intervened and said, "Here lads, wise up and let the girl do her job, don't be dicks"

At that point the young lads said, "Were you in the pub the other night?"

Dualta, "Yeah, why?"

"Well do you want to come and sort me out now?"

Immediately Dualta realised this was the young lad he had big differences with in the bar the other night. Dualta got up very quickly and left the café, he had no problem dealing with this young fella but not when he was with his nephew. As they hurried down the road, Jimbo was screaming, "What's wrong?"

"It's ok mate, no worries, we're just playing a hide and seek game!" Dualta got home and settled Jimbo beside his TV and waited for Dom to come home but never leaving the window. When Dom arrived home he quickly sat him down and told him what had happened, explaining to Dom that there was a problem that they needed to deal with. As he explained everything in animated language and gestures he couldn't help but notice that Dom wasn't becoming agitated or annoyed but seemed to be resigned to it.

Dualta, "Ok, Dom, what the fuck is going on?"

So Dominic explained the whole situation to him and tried to justify to him why he hadn't told him about it before. Dualta was angry but very quickly started to think of solutions.

Dualta, "Let's go to their houses mate"

Dom, "No, we can't. These lads are off limits for the time being."

Dualta, "Fuck that mate, if I ever see one of them again I'm gonna smash him bro"

Dominic didn't sleep easy that night. He hoped that nothing more would happen until after the match and then Dualta would be gone. As much as he wanted to win the championship, he wanted more to get Dualta out of there and back to Canada.

CHAPTER 81

MONDAY, CHAMPIONSHIP FINAL T MINUS 6 DAYS

BOTH LADS WERE WORKING and there wasn't any training that night so they decided to meet up and head to the local leisure centre for a recovery session. Dualta knew all about hot tubs and spas from his years in Canada but Dominic was still amazed by the power of water. After their stretching and wind down they headed to the pool and relaxed with a half-hearted swim and then headed to the hot tub for a muscle hit. Only tonight there just happened to be a pod of really attractive girls occupying the space. The lads were trying to make their excuses and leave when the girls insisted there was space and invited the lads in, Dualta played it very cool and slid into a vacant seat, managing to hold his stomach in while he was doing it and giving off an air of confidence. Dom on the other hand, missed the first step and fell headlong into the tub and managed to save his fall by grabbing one of the occupant's full breasts, of all places. There really was no coming back from that and regardless of how much he protested his apologies and inno-cence, the giggles and laughter just made him feel worse.

If truth be told, Dualta was laughing just as much but trying not to. So when they arrived home they didn't say too much until Dominic asked in reference to their normal sandwich supper, "Do you want a bap?"

And Dualta broke down and went into a fit of laughter. Speaking between gasps of agonising giggle fits he managed to explain.

"I think you've had enough baps for both of us tonight"

Even Dom saw the funny side and both lads put another good day to bed.

CHAPTER 82

TUESDAY, CHAMPIONSHIP FINAL T MINUS 5 DAYS

PROBABLY CAUSE THEY HADN'T been training or playing for a good few years both lads were happy to avail of the clubs offer to go and have a session with a physiotherapist. So both lads secured time off and headed to see the magic physio that most of their team mates called "One Eye Evie"

Dom was laughing when he asked his full back and captain, "Why do they call her One Eyed Evie?"

Captain, "Cause she has one eye, but don't whatever you do, stare at it"

And at that moment, both Dom and Dualta knew that the only thing they would be staring at for the next 2 hours was "Evie's one eye". By the time the sessions were over both lads could hardly contain it any more and they ran out of the clinic falling about themselves with totally inappropriate laughter.

Dom, "Did you see her ass?"

Dualta, "No, but, I did notice her best quality"

Dom, "Oh, eye, eye, what was that?"

The lads laughed so much as they drove downhill through the town they nearly crashed when Dom pushed full throttle on the accelerator rather than the brake.

CHAPTER 83

WEDNESDAY, CHAMPIONSHIP FINAL T MINUS 4 DAYS

DOMINIC ENJOYED HAVING JUDE stay with him the week before the match as it took his mind off things and helped him relax as being a dad is the most full on job anyone could ever do. Unfortunately Jude had brought the dog and while he was totally invested in having his son staying and very much part of his life, he wasn't so keen on the wicked wee terrier he brought with him. It wasn't as if he didn't really like dogs, it was just this particular dog he had issues with. However it was a small price to pay to have his son with him.

After Jude had gone to bed he went to gather up the animal but it had managed to secret itself under his sideboard and was growling lowly when Dominic reached his arm under the furniture to try and retrieve the poison pup. Two or three snaps and bites later Dominic had the miniature dog in his bloody grasp and whilst considering throwing it out the window, he thought better of it for his sons sake and placed the demon dog in its very warm and cosy basket.

As Dualta came home Dominic thought he was relaxed enough to go to bed but he couldn't resist spending a few minutes looking out onto the town square to make sure all was quiet, maybe just habit or a sixth sense but he was always on guard and didn't think he'd sleep much even though he was extremely fatigued.

The next morning Jude was up bright and early and insisting on pancakes and taking the beast for a walk. "Oh great" Thought Dom, "We are going to fall out with everyone out on the road today."

As they walked out onto the street Dom was conscious of a number of youths across the green who were laughing and pointing in his direction. He would normally laugh back at these little brats but it did annoy him that they now had the nerve to do it when he was with his son. In fact it more than annoyed him, it actually made his blood boil.

As he brushed by the biggest lad trying to ignore him, he sent Jude on into the house with the dog and told him to tell uncle Dualta to come out for a wee minute. Jude wasn't stupid and could feel the tension and he betrayed his emotions by starting to cry. There maybe 6 or 7 lads on the wall and footpath outside but luckily Dualta was out very sharpish and the two lads questioned the young men" why they needed to be such dickheads or as Dualta diplomatically put it, "Fuck off before I slap the fecking heads off ye!"

Dualta had a lot of questions but Dom still didn't want to get him involved. He knew that Dualta had a short temper and getting involved in this scenario might get him into trouble and risk his future in Canada. "It's nothing, just leave it, it's ok" insisted Dom, lying through his teeth.

He did however demand a meeting with his CO in the organisation and stressed the fact that this behaviour was getting out of order and he really wasn't going to put up with much more of this shit. However his operative manager was still advising caution with the situation and hoping that it could be sorted out for the sake of the "Peace process". Dom had to accept his orders but he was far from feeling at peace.

CHAPTER 84

FRIDAY, CHAMPIONSHIP FINAL T MINUS 2 DAYS

DOMINIC WAS FEELING A little on edge and not just about the match. He had a knot in his stomach and he asked Jude's mum if he could stay with him again as he just felt a little more comfortable if Jude was with him, maybe it was nothing but a nagging doubt like that at the back of your mind can crucify you.

However his instincts were proving to be quite correct when the next day the youths were back outside his house not really saying or doing very much but obviously making a statement by their very presence.

Dominic was really losing his temper and was about to unload a huge wrath on these lads when a joint RUC/Army patrol entered the scene. The youths were quite quick to move away but a new antagonist entered the picture when the fearless 6 inch pup (as he called him) saw the uniforms and immediately went ballistic and started to bark and growl in Jude's arms at the door (apparently republican dogs know the British army uniform). But soon the dog had escaped the soft clutches of Jude's young arms and was now in full on attack mode against the Jack-booted leg of a British soldier. It was hard to make any sense out of the situation but soon Dominic realised the "inch high dog" was tearing at the soldiers boots with all the might of an infant.

The situation started to unfold in slow motion in Dominic's eye line. The huge Private from the British army aimed his massive jack boot square to the head of the tiny animal. Not only did Dom see red dripping from the poor creatures head but at that point his blood boiled beyond control and he literally saw "red". He grabbed the soldier by the throat and disregarding the fact he was holding a gun, he wrestled him to the ground and proceeded to punch him several times to the head.

The victory would have been his until the patrol sergeant caught him right above the left eyebrow with his rifle and landed him squarely on his back, leaving him completely incapacitated. The fight would well and truly have been over and concluded except for the fact that Dualta was passing the window inside and had witnessed the most recent blows of the altercation.

He immediately sprang from the front door and engaged the leader in a form of hand to hand combat he really hadn't been expecting that morning. Dualta's ferocious entry into the fray really put the cat among the pigeons and gave Dominic enough respite to gather himself and re- join the altercation to at least bring the odds to 2 versus 4 and as long as those 2 were Irishmen, those odds were pretty good.

The flurry of punches, kicks and violence were only brought to a conclusion when the sergeant actually fired his gun in the air and everyone on the ground instinctively stopped. The RUC realised they were as much to blame so no arrests or detentions took place and Dominic was left with the almost lifeless body of the "wicked pup" to bring back to the house and put out of its misery. Jude was distraught and that made Dom very angry.

As the lads arrived at training that evening everyone had heard about the happenings of the day and Dom guessed the manager was pissed off but he ignored it and got on with the job at hand as he and Dualta joined the lads in what was really just a run through and warm up for the big event coming up. The manager kept the tradition of not naming the team until the morning of the match so the lads were still on tenterhooks as to whether or not they would make the starting lineup.

CHAPTER 85

THINKING OUT LOUD

DUALTA HAD A HUNDRED different emotions coursing through his veins that Friday evening before the match. He had been confident of being selected to start on Sunday but tonight the manager spent a lot of time talking to Gerry Toal and he knew it was either himself or Gerry that would start, so he felt a bit deflated. Also it had been a crazy week with the altercation with the Brits and the dog getting killed. However he had also had a great phone call with Sofia and his ticket was booked for 10 days' time so he couldn't help but smile as he thought about how good the reunion was going to be.

As he wandered home that evening he was only considering positive things when as he turned into the estate, he saw Paddy Duane staggering and falling outside his house. This was by no means a shock event as poor Paddy would normally be in a drunken stupor most nights of the week but this time Dualta realised he couldn't get up no matter how hard he tried.

Dualta exhaled and realised that the Samaritan in him couldn't walk by and was going to have to go and help aul Paddy get into the house. So he did so willingly but was a little taken aback to see that Paddy also had a full complement of guests already enjoying the hospitality of his house. Very quickly Dualta realised these were the very same youths that had been outside their house annoying

Dom the other day and when he asked them to help him get Paddy inside, they just laughed and said he'd be fine and just to leave him outside to sober up.

Dualta carried Paddy into the living room and left him sleeping on an armchair but he saw that these young lads were using Paddy's house as a drink and drug den despite Paddy's incapacity to decide whether he wanted this or not. There wasn't much more Dualta could do so he thought it would be better just to leave the place when he noticed an older man sitting in the shadows watching over proceeding with a large vodka in his hand.

Dualta thought he recognised him but he couldn't be sure so he reluctantly left the house and headed home. When he got home he mentioned it to Dom who seemed really agitated and annoyed about it and was all for marching straight over there but Dualta managed to calm him down and persuaded him to wait until morning as little would be gained by confronting them at this time of night and so it was left or at least that's what he thought.

CHAPTER 86

DOMINIC SNAPS

AS SOON AS DUALTA had gone to bed Dominic quietly slipped out of the house and made his way over to aul Paddy's house. They were still partying and making enough noise to ensure none of the occupants of the neighbouring houses would get any sleep and that just made him even angrier. The front door was open and there were people bustling throughout every room, he immediately recognised one of the youths from the last altercation and confronted him as to what exactly they were doing in Paddy's house.

Shouting ensued and Dom knew that he wasn't going to get anywhere talking to these lads so instinctively he pushed one of them hard in the chest and before the second one could throw the punch he was aiming, Dom hit him an almighty punch right on the bridge of his nose which resulted in a huge release of blood that splattered upwards all over the hall mirror.

Dom took up a fighting stance readying himself for an expected all-out assault but what happened next surprised him enormously. The blood covered young lad burst out crying and screaming uncontrollably, "You're dead, you're dead, do you know who I am? I'm gonna kill you, you bastard. Wait till my dad finds out. You're dead and your fucking son too."

Dom might have left it until that last threat, he could handle any threats directed at him but the boy had threatened his son.

Dom struck him hard and repeatedly until he was a mere blubbering, rolled up ball on the floor whimpering and snivelling, "I'm sorry, I'm sorry"

Dom chased everyone else out of the house and told Paddy to get his act together, sober up, change his locks and get a life.

Turning to the remaining youths he calmly said, "Time to leave town for a while lads by order of the IRA. Get away and get yourselves sorted cause the next time I have to pay you a visit, it won't just be fists I'm firing"

Maybe he shouldn't have ordered them out of the town without discussion with command but he was confident they would back his decision given how out of control these lads were and how anti-social they were being not to even mention the drugs they were peddling. He would ring his command contact tomorrow and explain why he did it and he was sure everything would be fine.

However the phone call didn't go that way at all, in fact it was quite the opposite. His OC was quite annoyed about the whole incident and was angry that Dom had made operative decisions without consulting him and was insisting there had to be a meeting to discuss this further. This seemed unusual protocol and not at all what Dom was used to within the organisation. No meeting would ever take place without a code word or security phrase being given.

Dom didn't like this at all, he felt uncomfortable about it and just knew there was something up. His sixth sense intuition and everything within his conscious brain was throwing up red flags on this one.

He didn't even hear Dualta come in and it took him a minute to be aware enough to hear what he was saying, "Sorry what?"

Dualta, "Jeez lad, wakey wakey, I said I saw that lad from the party the other night up at the service station on new street this morning! Someone has given him a right hiding. Looks like he was in the ring with Iron Mike Tyson."

Dom, "What?"

Dualta, "Fuck sake lad, snap out of it, you've a big match tomorrow."

Dom, "We've a big match tomorrow."

Dualta, "I won't start, you will. So switch the fuck on and tune in."

But Dom's mind was racing, "Where did you see him? Who was he with?"

Dualta, "Up at the garage, I dunno who he was with, looked like his dad, I think I saw him in the house the other night too, I thought he was one of your type?"

Dom, "My type? What'd you mean?"

Dualta, "Fuck sake, calm down. I mean he looks like one of your RA mates. Big lad, really dark black hair, looks like he dyes it" he laughed.

Dominic felt sick, things started to make sense now he remembered the lad shouting, "Do you know who I am, do you know who my dad is?" And suddenly Dom had a sinking feeling in the pit of his stomach as he began to realise what was happening. His head was spinning and his eyes lacked any focus as the pieces of this particular puzzle began to fall into place. "Command" was the lad's dad, he was in on it all along. That's why he didn't ever want Dom to get involved, "Command" is a "traitor". He must be leading the dissidents.

Dom almost staggered as he got up and made his way to the bathroom, he sat there for a while trying to assimilate the new information but there was no getting away from the fact that this was the truth. He considered all his options but he wasn't sure if he should act straight away with Dualta so close to getting back to his new life and Jude in the house and the match on tomorrow. So he decided to be cautious but he knew he'd have to do something soon. He went up to the nearest phone box and punched in the numbers he usually did to speak to "command", no answer. Leave a message?

"I know everything you bastard! You traitor, you drug dealing scum, I know, I know it's you"

Hindsight is a great guide and moments later he realised he probably shouldn't have vented and maybe played his cards closer to his chest but it was done now and as soon as the match was over he would go above "commands" head and expose him for who he was. If "command" hadn't already made a run for it as he suspected he might. Weighing it all up, he figured "command" was rogue and had no support within the organisation except for his son and his stupid mates and therefore he didn't carry much threat. Dom now knew he was using his PIRA position for his own ends to make money through illegal activities which included drug dealing. The PIRA would never ever stand for that so Dom was confident that now "command" knew he was on to him he probably was going to make a run for the border or further afield.

CHAPTER 87

MATCH OF THE DAY

DOM TRIED TO PUT his worries to one side to get through the day ahead. It was a huge day for the club, not just for the players but for the whole community. Himself and Dualta headed out to a local café for a bit of breakfast before joining the rest of the squad up at the football club.

As Dualta expected he didn't get selected to start in the match. Dom was picked at full forward and expected to be a huge influence on the game. Dualta wished Gerry Toal well but he secretly hoped he would have an awful game and he'd be asked to come on and replace him (if truth be told every player who ever was dropped to the bench awkwardly wishes his team mates well but secretly wishes he would be injured or roasted by his opponent and he'd get a chance to prove everyone wrong).

Dualta was no different and when the match threw in he was 100% behind his team but he wasn't overly annoyed when Gerry was beaten to the first ball and his opponent scored a point. Dom was having a great game, kicking over 2 monster points from 40 metres as the team took the lead. A quick ball came in across the area and Gerry's opponent turned quickly and took possession as Gerry slid in and seemed to go over on his ankle.

Dualta didn't wish him any harm but he was getting beaten to every ball and Dualta knew he could do better. The match was going back and forward with each team enjoying moments of supremacy and Dom really shining in the forward division. With 10 minutes until half time, Gerry was really struggling to run and it was obvious that he was really hurt, injured and unable to compete. Dualta hoped and prayed that Gerry would be totally unable to continue and he'd be called into action and within 30 seconds his wishes came true when Gerry fell over and was unable to get up.

"Get warmed up Dualta" were the best words he had heard in years. He didn't even have time to do the customary sprinting and stretching before Gerry was being carried off and he was sprinting into the biggest match of his life. He went to introduce himself with the most ferocious shoulder charge he had ever administered but his foot caught on a tuft of grass and he more or less stumbled into his opponents back and almost had to grab his jersey to stop him falling over.

The game was nip and tuck right to the end and with the help of a bit of luck and hard knocks the team managed to pull off a brilliant victory. Dualta couldn't have been more happy and exhausted. He hadn't been a star but he had been solid and his opponent hadn't scored after he came on so he was delighted with that.

CHAPTER 88

THE FINAL WHISTLE

AS THE REF DREW breath and blew the final whistle, Dualta fell to his knees and held his head in his hands. At that precise moment he understood it all.

The seed, the roots, the soil, the earth, the plants, the essence all made sense. Gaelic games was the only sport he knew that grew from the child into adulthood, at that perfect moment all the other crops that had been cultivated had come together and created a perfect result. Whether they were playing, coaching, driving, attending meetings, washing the jerseys, brushing the changing rooms, making tea and sandwiches, it was community victory and no other sport could match that or come close to it. "You don't choose your club, it chooses you."

Even lads from the club who had won honours with the county team would concede that winning with your club is the ultimate honour and the one that means the most. When Dualta raised his head, he saw Dominic coming towards him and they embraced. They didn't speak because it wasn't necessary for in that moment a glance was all that was needed to tell them how much they cared about each other and how much their lives were intertwined. More was said in that momentary hug and glance than could be said in any Shakespeare book.

Their grasp on each other was broken by the ecstatic crowd that were now making their way on to the pitch to share in the joy and happiness of what had been achieved not just by the team but by the whole community. This would be a day and a night, for some a week of celebrations and festivities which would boost the town's spirits for month's weeks to come and consolidate that innate sense of Irishness that only Gaelic Champions could understand.

CHAPTER 89

DUALTA REFLECTS

IN HIS MIND ALL Dualta could think was that no other sport comes close in terms of life and community. No other sports are linked so inherently to their roots as the Gaelic games. At that point he remembered a quote from some part of his education and it really hit home and made sense to him today.

"I am not a product only of my circumstances but also of my decisions."

Life had dealt him a hand and he'd played it as best he could but that line brought him a great deal of satisfaction. He felt when possible he'd made the best decisions that he could in the circumstances that he had faced and he also knew that despite some little nagging doubts, he was 100% behind his decision to move on from the circumstances and head back to Canada where he knew his future happiness would be. And perhaps he'd even dared to dream of having a few kids who would look like him but act like their mum and they would have the world at their feet and be generous, kind humanitarians who would be successful but also care for others less fortunate.

His thoughts were rudely interrupted as the players bus pulled up outside the clubrooms and the team got ready to disembark and meet the supporters who genuinely were just as delighted if not more so than the players were.

There was an awful lot of hugging and back slapping as the squad entered their home club and it really did feel like home. The drinks were flowing and the songs were loud when the boys finally made their way through the thronging crowd to the bar area, where to be honest more drink was landing on the floor than was actually getting into anyone's mouth. Dualta couldn't even see Dominic and every time he went to seek him out he was lifted and thrown around a circle of ecstatic supporters which made him both annoyed and wonderfully happy all at the same time.

Eventually he managed to escape the crowd and get to a toilet to have a pee. Unbelievably it was empty other than another player and they both laughed at the reception they were receiving.

"Jeez Dualta, this is a life changing thing we just did! I know I probably shouldn't cause the lad's will crucify me but I'm gonna go and get the Mrs up here to share this occasion, might be the last time it ever happens. What'd you think?"

Dualta didn't even think twice, "Fucking go for it lad, that's what it's all about. What a night, what a brilliant night, you really do need to share it."

And right at that moment as Big Paul left the toilet he knew he needed to speak to Sofia, "Fuck it" he thought, "I'll run down home and give her a wee ring, sure I'll be back before anyone knows I'm gone."

He was actually quite giddy with excitement about ringing her as he secretly slipped out of the football social club. He thought he'd run down to the house, leave his bag off and ring Sofia, tell her how much he loved her and couldn't wait to see her. Maybe he should propose as well he laughed to himself or possibly wait till they were reunited at the airport. Anyway he was laughing inwardly at how happy he actually was. He had it all now, understanding of his circumstances and an acceptance of his destiny. He'd be back up in the club for the presentation with Dom and the team and as happy as a kid on Christmas Eve after talking to his beautiful soon to be fiancé.

The last thing Dualta was expecting in his state of euphoria was the huge blow he received to the back of his head that spread-eagled him flat across the pavement and the rough treatment he was now being subjected to as a group of yet to be identified people were tying his hands, placing a hood over his head and forcing him into what he assumed was a car.

He was drifting in and out of consciousness when he started to hear voices close by.

"For fuck sake, you stupid bastard! That's the wrong one! That's his fucking friend, you absolute moron, how did you get the wrong man, get out of my sight you wanker"

Dualta was fighting a huge surge of fear and claustrophobia when his hood was pulled off and he was met by blinding light that made it impossible for him to focus or see anything other than lights and shapes. Soon one of those shapes spoke,

"Look, we don't want you! There's been a slight mix up, it's your friend Dominic we want here! So we are just going to get you to ring him and tell him to take your place and you can go ok? We know he's at the football social club so we'll ring him there and you can talk to him and we'll clear this situation up."

Even through his very sore head he was able to formulate his response quite quickly,

"Go fuck yourself"

The voice on his shoulder continued to bend his ear. The voice insisted he was going to ring Dominic and get him to come here and swap places with Dualta or else the voice was going to shoot Dualta. On and on the voice insisted. Dualta's answer was resolute.

"Are you still here? Didn't I tell you to go fuck yourself?"

Inwardly Dualta was terrified, he was tied up and vulnerable to anything these lunatics wanted to do to him and he wanted more than anything for this not to be happening but it was happening and he was absolutely shitting himself but he wasn't going to let them know that.

He could hear three distant voices and it appeared the two most dominant voices were arguing with each other. He was picking up some audio which seemed to be referring to Dom having to pay for what he did and how they needed to take care of him or they would be "fucked".

Dualta started to piece things together and realised this was the lad he'd seen at the house party and obviously now Dom had gone back and been the one who had beaten him up. The older voice may have been a relation possibly a father but were they really doing this because of a beating? No, there must be more to it. He was suspecting that it was IRA related. Anyway he was never about to betray his friend under any circumstances. As he mused earlier, he couldn't control his circumstances but he could control his decisions.

He heard a bigger commotion starting in the next room and a series of doors slamming and possibly a car starting and skidding off. He could make out a shadow moving behind the bright light and attempted to speak and engage the form causing it.

"Have they left you kid?" probed Dualta

"You really don't want to be here, involved in all this shit mate! Do you?" He watched closely as he saw the form shift and move nervously and there it was, fear. The form in front of him was scared! He knew he had to work on that.

"Jeez lad, do you know who I am? I am a commanding officer in the Provisional I, R, A, (He emphasised this point to further scare the lad). They are going to come looking for me and if you are here, they're going to shoot you mate, you're dead!" He continued, "Those other boys have left you in the shite here mate, they've left you to take it all mate, you're as dead as a Dodo" He stopped a while to let the young lad absorb what he was saying, let him get a little more scared, a little more uneasy. "Shut up, just shut up!" he was totally unnerved now, "They'll be right back."

"Will they? Really, do you think so" He said calmly, just pushing enough now to try and push him over the edge.

"I think they've gone and left you to deal with the consequences." Dualta paused again not wanting to go too far but just keep enough pressure to topple him over.

After several moments of uneasy silence, Dualta spoke again, "Look if you just untie me, I'll go home and not mention this to anyone and if anyone asks I'll tell them it was you who rescued me and you'll be a real hero."

Dualta could tell the form behind the bright light, which was really annoying now, was getting very fidgety and uneasy and evidently scared, Dualta could feel the fear but he knew he hadn't much time left to break him down before the others arrived back.

"This wasn't my idea, I don't want to be here! They just made me do it, I don't even know you" Bingo, he had broken.

"I know, I know" calmed Dualta, "This has nothing to do with you, just untie me and I'll explain everything, you'll be fine, you can just go home, how does that sound?"

The form was panicking now, "I don't know, they'll be cross, Kyle will hurt me"

Dualta thought quickly, "Kyle? Is that what he's called? He doesn't care about you, he only cares about himself, just let me go and I'll sort everything out, you could actually come with me and I'll tell them you had nothing to do with it and Kyle made you. Is that ok? Does that sound good?"

The form was broken. Dualta knew it and when he came from behind the light Dualta recognised him from the party house. He just kept thinking, "Keep him calm and he'll let me go."

"Good lad, you know you're doing the sensible thing. What's your name, Ruairi, oh that's a cool name, now Ruairi just untie me and it'll all be over."

Ruairi shakily started to undo the binding ropes on Dualta's wrists and he was almost done when the unmistakable sound of a speeding car came to a stop outside.

"Quickly" said Dualta, trying not to spook him and finally he was free from the shackles but realised Kyle and his older friend were about to burst through the front door.

"What will I do now?" Whimpered Ruairi

"Fuck off out the back door and go home you wee dick"

Dualta hurriedly looked through the kitchen for a weapon and came up pretty well with a large kitchen knife, "good result" he thought until Kyle and what he realise now was his dad were framed in the doorway and Kyle had a huge shotgun in his hands. The unexpected standoff was a surprise to both parties. Dualta standing with his kitchen knife and Kyle pointing his shotgun was a seemingly unfair fight so Dualta was going to have to use all his guile and wits to get out of this one.

Dualta spoke first, "Look Kyle, just put the gun down and I'll just walk away and we'll forget about it all."

"I'm not stupid" screamed Kyle, "The RA will kill us."

"Calm down Kyle" said his dad, "Let's think about this, don't do anything stupid"

"No, you always tell me I'm stupid, I'm not good enough, I'm inadequate, not like you were, not a real man, well I am now, I swear I'll shoot you" said Kyle but his voice betrayed his fear and anxiety. Despite his Dads pleas, Kyle was wild eyed and frenzied now.

Now was a time for one of those "decisions" Dualta had been contemplating earlier and they weren't going to come much more difficult than his current predicament.

Dualta would call his bluff, "Oh bollix"

"Look Kyle, I'm gonna walk through that door so if you want to stop me, you are going to have to shoot me." Said Dualta resolutely, and he meant it.

Kyle was freaking out, "Don't move, don't fucking move."

But Dualta threw the knife down and walked slowly towards the door.

Kyle was screaming "Stop, I mean it, stop." And he raised the gun and took aim.

"Stop son, seriously this has gone far enough, don't."

The neighbours reported hearing several loud gunshots on that Sunday evening. Dualta's lifeless mutilated and blood stained body was unceremoniously shoved into the back of an unmarked white transit van and driven to nearby peat moss and basically dumped, like an average person would throw out an eaten chicken carcass. A remarkable and shining light, snuffed out.

CHAPTER 90

DOMINIC'S DESPAIR

DOM HADN'T NOTICED DUALTA was gone as he was caught up in the euphoria of the moment and the sheer exuberance of the occasion. He'd looked up a few times towards the bar but he couldn't see his best friend. Eventually the MC called for the team to take to the stage for a round of applause and Dom could see Dualta still wasn't there. Instinctively he knew something was wrong! Dualta wouldn't miss this, something was wrong. He felt himself start to breathe deeply and his heart rate doubled. Outwardly he was smiling but he couldn't enjoy this moment without his other half. Where was he? What was going on?

He made it through the obligatory champions sing song and as soon as it was over he made his way to the door and surveyed the room. No one had seen Dualta for a couple of hours so now the panic was becoming real and he could just feel something was very wrong. He literally sprinted down the road to their house but it was obvious Dualta hadn't been home so he sprinted back up the road towards the social club not really knowing why or where he would end up, until he saw a young child among a group of young children carrying a huge club football hold all like it was a bouncy castle.

"Where'd you get that?" Dominic snapped, the child started to cry so Dom tried to calm down.

"I'm sorry, can you please tell me where you found that big bag?"

The children were terrified but pointed up towards the corner of the town square before they ran away. Dom held the kit bag closely as he sprinted to the corner only to find some tyre skid marks and what could possibly be a few splashes of blood.

Dom was petrified, "What now?"

"Oh my God, please! No, no, don't let anything have happened to him!"

Dom fell to his knees and cried. He knew deep down that this was not going to end well and he had no idea what had happened or how to go about helping his friend. He immediately knew who had taken him and he also knew it was his fault as it was him they were really after. He began to think more rationally again and formulated a plan.

So, they are going to hold him and wait until they contact me and then I'll sort it. This gave him a little comfort cause he knew they were ultimately after him and they wouldn't hurt his friend as he was just a bargaining tool until they got Dom.

Obviously he called his traitorous former commander but the phone line had been disconnected.

Not much now to do but wait. And wait he did, right beside the phone for the next 24 hours. The cops had been informed but he knew they didn't really give a shit about Dualta but still Dom sat by the phone and waited and waited. By now the rumours were spreading throughout the town about Dualta's disappearance and it was open season on small town speculation. The general consensus was he'd disappeared before so he'd do it again and therefore it wasn't a big surprise and others had heard he was going back to Canada where he'd been living and he'd obviously just gone back there.

As the night turned into day and day turned into night, there was no information or leads on what had happened. Dom knew that "no news wasn't good news" and he felt sicker and sicker by the minute.

The town was still on the up because of the championship victory but Dom couldn't play anymore part in that and he didn't want to even think about it. He had been awake for 36 hours when he decided to take a quick shower and leave his station beside the phone. Moving upstairs he turned the radio on to top volume expecting but scarcely believing what he was hearing.

And the radio said, "There's another shot dead"

From his position in the shower, Dominic heard the news that was delivered almost on a daily basis in his community but he knew deep down within himself that this was his best friend. Call it intuition or sixth sense, he knew. He just knew.

What the radio didn't say was this was someone's son, leaving a heartbroken mother. This was someone's brother and uncle, leaving a family torn apart. This was someone's best friend, leaving a man empty and alone. This was someone's love and soul mate leaving a loving heart crushed and dead.

No, the radio didn't say any of that because they just say another death in a parade of endless deaths and no one really, really cared until it touched your own heart and arrived on your own doorstep.

Dominic didn't cry. He'd been around death long enough to accept it for what it was. He'd caused it and now he was reaping what he had sowed.

He didn't cry for his best friend, his other half, but exactly at that moment a huge part of him died as well. He could almost feel it churning and spewing out of him and he knew that he would never be the same again.

Then he made a phone call that he wouldn't wish on anyone to ever have to make.

"Hi, is that Sofia?"

"Yeah, who's this?"

"Sofia, you don't know me my names Dominic, I'm a friend of Dualta's"

"OMG, of course I know you Dom, Dualta never stopped talking about you, you're going to come over and visit us. I can't wait to meet you Dom"

"Sofia, I'm so sorry, I've got to tell you, some bad news...."
And for the one and only time Dominic broke down.

During the wake he didn't cry, but he never left the coffin, resplendently sitting in Dualta's sister's front room adorned in beautiful flowers and cards and wreaths. Neither did he look many people in the face or hold their hand too long.

He knew Dualta's death was his fault and that was his only thought throughout the strange event that is an Irish wake. The conundrum of welcoming the most people and putting on the biggest catering occasion you will ever have in your whole life to celebrate the guest of honour who unfortunately due to their present "death" can't be totally present.

The walk to the graveyard takes on a community feel where everyone rallies around to help carry the remains of the deceased to their eternal resting place and this is a very comforting feeling.

The problem and the emptiness comes after the funeral when everyone has gone home and the family is left alone. Dominic stayed with Dualta's family and helped comfort them as best he could. His heart had been torn in shreds earlier at the grave side when Jude had asked him "Is uncle Dualta in the big box in the hole daddy?"

And he held his son tightly but tonight he wouldn't be taking him home to his warm and loving home, he'd asked Jude's mum to take him with her after the funeral was over.

Jude objected, "Please daddy, please take me home, I want to go to your house tonight, please I'm sad"

"No son, I'm sorry but you've got to go with mummy tonight. Daddy loves you more than anything but you can't stay tonight, daddy has to go to work."

THE END!!!

Lightning Source UK Ltd.
Milton Keynes UK
UKHW020634121021
392080UK00013B/979